Lost in Lavender

A BENNETT SISTERS MYSTERY

LISE MCCLENDON

THALIA

THE BENNETT SISTERS MYS

by Lise McClendon

Blackbird Fly

The Girl in the Empty Dress

Give Him the Ooh-la-la

The Things We Said Today

The Frenchman

Odette and the Great Fear

Blame it on Paris

A Bolt from the Blue

DEAD FLAT

1: Bottle of Lies

2: Outside the Bubble

3: Uncorked

Lost in Lavender

plus

The Bennett Sisters French Cookbook

featuring recipes from the books

Lost in Lavender

For my mother, Betty, who planted the travel seed in me very early and showed me how to enjoy the fruits and flowers of the world

MAP OF SOUTHERN FRANCE

SOUTHERN
FRANCE

Bordeaux

Malcouziac
DORDOGNE

PROVENCE

Château Grand Lac

Bellemont

Avignon

Refuge de la Lavande
Aix-en-Provence

Toulouse

Montpellier

Ari's house

Carcassonne

Marseille

Saint-Tropez

Mediterranean Sea

Most places—cities, towns, and villages—portrayed in the book are as accurate as possible. However, the villages of Malcouziac and Bellemont, in the Dordogne and Provence respectively, are fictional, as is Chateau Grand Lac and Le Refuge de Lavande. The villages are based on real places but do not exist. *Tant pis.*

CHAPTER ONE

*T*he moment the road rose over the lip of the plateau, as if they would fly off into the blue Provençal sky like birds, Merle Bennett felt gravity release them. It was such a small moment, a split second where the tires lifted them up and over the hump of the asphalt road. She felt her heart lift. Was it just the action of the car? Or was it the sight of the fields beyond?

Elise, sitting next to her, grabbed the dashboard. "Oh my."

Oh my, indeed.

The lavender fields were in full bloom, stretching in endless, bumpy rows toward the horizon. The purple was so vivid, as alive as blood in veins, the blossoms shivering in the wind. Merle hit the brakes and pulled to the side of the road. She shut off the car and the sisters sat in silence, looking at this impossible scene, the beauty of nature structured by man.

Merle rolled down her window. The scent rushed in on the breeze. This was Provence after all, where the wind blew all the time. This particular wind was coming from the peaks to the east, the Hautes Alpes de Provence, where the chilly *mistral* wind was born. But it was July and the breeze was warm now, full of the aroma of lavender, rich and soothing.

Elise opened her car door. She crossed the asphalt and knelt at the edge of the field, next to a fence that warned off the curious and the flower pickers. Merle joined her, leaning over the fence to get the full effect of the lavender plant just inside, its purple spikes open.

"Is this your farm stay?" Merle asked.

"Could be. It's close to here," Elise said, standing.

"I hope this is it. Maybe they're all this amazing though." Merle glanced at her youngest sister. Elise's dark hair was loose and curly, swirling around her pale face. There were dark circles under her blue eyes. That was worrisome. Maybe related to travel? She looked fit for a change, having started jogging last year and lost some weight. As the shortest of the five sisters, she had always struggled a bit with that. It was good to see her looking healthy.

Ten years separated them, and sometimes it felt like a lifetime. Merle didn't feel she really knew Elise, not like she knew some of her other sisters. As the middle one, Merle often felt like the playground director, trying to manage the sisters, set up games, keep everyone happy. She called herself the tent-pole the four other sisters revolved around. But Elise had been seven when Merle went to college, in second grade. Now in her early forties, she too was a lawyer like all her sisters. And like the rest of them, especially Merle who lived here now, Elise had developed a fondness for France. Elise had visited a few times but this was her first solo adventure, deep in the Luberon at a lavender farm. It had surprised the sisters that Elise had chosen a vacation that involved physical labor. She wasn't seen as particularly energetic. But people change. Or at least want to change.

At any rate, a farm stay in Provence was more for the experience than actual farm work. To see how a real French family lives and works, to immerse oneself in the classic fragrance of the south of France. That Elise had apparently not brushed up on her French beforehand would make things interesting. Merle had tried to encourage that but as far as she could tell, Elise had ignored the advice. Elise ignored most of the advice from her older sisters. Well, it was her prerogative. And her vacation, after all.

"Let's find the farm," Elise said, heading back to the car. "And some lunch."

They had driven from the Dordogne, leaving Malcouziac early that morning. Elise had come down from Paris on the train three days before and they'd spent some quiet days together. Pascal, who lived with Merle when he wasn't working in Bordeaux for the wine fraud division of a government agency, had been gone. He'd traveled to Paris for meetings, then back to Bordeaux to his new office in the Cité du Vin, a combination museum and futuristic office tower celebrating French wine.

Elise had not been very talkative on the drive, or back in Malcouziac. Merle tried to get her to share what was happening with her life but she hadn't offered much. She didn't like her law firm, that was obvious. Beyond that, nothing. Merle didn't want to pry but was a little concerned. Elise said she was looking forward to the change of pace of the lavender farm. Who wouldn't, Merle thought as they drove past field after field of delectable purple. It was enough to bliss you out, as their oldest sister Annie would say.

They reached the village of Bellemont in time to catch the end of the lunch service at a café perched overlooking the patchwork of lavender and gold fields below. The café was a popular spot and you could see why. Despite a rustling breeze that moved napkins and hats, the view was to die for.

Merle ordered her usual, the *salade de campagne*, which was different depending on which "campagne"—countryside—you were in. This one featured goat cheese and anchovy, plus the hardboiled eggs and boiled potatoes. Elise ordered gazpacho and ate a lot of the baguette. Their conversation was minimal. The silence began to wear on Merle as they ended the meal with a coffee.

"So. What are you expecting at the farm stay?" she asked, trying to be nonspecific.

"Farming, I guess. Right?"

"The lavender looks like it's in full bloom. I guess it's ready to be harvested?"

Elise nodded. "That's what they told me."

"Anything else?" Merle was unwilling to let this conversation die.

"Sleep a lot?" Elise shrugged. "Eat good food?"

"Bien sûr." Merle squinted at her sister. "How long are you there, did you say?"

"Ten days. You're picking me up, right?"

Merle pulled out her phone and checked the calendar. Once upon a time, she hadn't needed to write things down. Her mind had been a steel trap of times and dates. Her late husband had called her 'Calendar Girl' for her memory for dates. But in France that had evaporated like the morning mist on the river. "What day?"

"Thursday. Midday, I guess? Unless I get a better offer."

"Got it." Merle set down her phone. "Ten days should be an amazing adventure. I can't wait to hear all about it. Maybe Tristan would like to do it sometime."

Elise looked out at the view, disinterested in the conversation. "We'll see."

"Is—" Merle hesitated. She wanted to know what was going on inside Elise, why she seemed so shut down, so quiet. But Merle hated it when people pried into *her* feelings, *her* life. Even her sisters, sometimes. Okay, especially her sisters.

Elise looked at her. "Is what?"

"Is everything okay at home? With Jack and Bernie." Their parents were in their 80s now but still traveling and golfing and all the things retired people did.

"Yeah, all good. I saw them right before I left. I told you."

"So you did." Merle dabbed her lips with her napkin. "Ready to check out your farm?"

THE BUILDINGS of the farm came into sight as soon as they turned off the road, following the sign that read 'Le Refuge de la Lavande.' The arrow pointed in the only available direction, straight at a collection of farm buildings. The main house was two stories, made of stone and partially stuccoed in ocher with gray shutters. The other buildings, barns, workshops and sheds, were stone and wood,. The main house had huge pots of lavender on the front steps and was shaded from the intense sun by a large weeping willow.

Merle parked her beat-up Peugeot in the shade. She loved her little car. She was still proud that she'd finally bought a car on her own after all these years. Despite the dents and scratches, it ran well and it was hers. She'd finally junked her old minivan back in the US, donating it to a charity.

Elise grabbed her canvas bag from the back seat and waited while Merle popped the trunk. With black roller bag in tow, they approached the ornate old door of the manse. The paint was a faded blue but still very pretty, with a brass lion head knocker and a fan light above.

A teenage girl opened the door at their knock with a flourish and a smile. *"Bonjour! Entrez, s'il vous plaît!"*

The girl, a slender blonde wearing tight white capris and a red halter top, was tanned and perky. She said her name was Natacha and that she was fifteen. In what seemed to be a canned but animated speech she must give every new guest, she said her brother was seventeen and his name was Lucas. Her mother was Vivianne and liked to be called that instead of 'madame.' She asked Elise her name as she opened a black notebook in the entry hall.

"Your name," Merle whispered.

"Ah. Je m'appelle Elise Bennett." Elise had a strong American accent but Natacha didn't seem to have any trouble with it. She brightened, looked at a list of names and checked Elise off. She said she would show Elise her room and headed for the stairs. A grand staircase wound up to the second floor. Elise lugged her bags up one flight then Merle took the lighter one. They went up another stair, a smaller one, to the third floor. The servant quarters in the old days, of course. The hallway was drab, an indeterminate gray, and poorly lit. Natacha stopped in front of door number eight and pulled the key from the lock.

"Here you are," Natacha said, opening the door.

She talked very fast. Merle could understand her explanation of the times for dinner and breakfast, about the bathroom down the hall, the towels on the cot, the window that didn't open, and the small fan in the drawer, but Elise looked stunned. When Natacha finished, Merle said, *"Elle a seulement un peu de français."* She nodded toward Elise. *"Parlez-vous anglais?"*

Natacha laughed. "Ooh, *oui*, yes. All of us have some English." She patted Elise on the arm. "It can be okay." She looked at Merle. "But you tell her about the times, yes? Because I must go." And she ran out the door.

"Whew," Merle said, setting the canvas tote bag on the bed. "She's a whirlwind."

"What was all that about?"

Merle repeated the information, dinner at 8, breakfast at 6. "It sounds like everyone speaks English. So, don't worry."

"I wasn't."

As it was now past four in the afternoon, Merle decided she would find a hotel in the village for the evening. She had spotted several possibilities at lunch. She worked her phone, looking through the available places, while perched on the bed. Elise unpacked her suitcase into the three-drawer bureau and set her toiletries on the top. She grabbed the towel and said she was going to check out the bath. In a moment she was back.

"Bad?" Merle asked.

"Not awful. I'll survive." Elise gave a brave smile.

"It's an adventure."

"It is. I should take a nap before dinner. I'm still jet-lagged. What are you going to do?"

"I just booked myself a room at a little hotel in Bellemont. I guess I'll go poke around there, maybe buy some lavender oil or something. Find a little dinner. Then I'll come back in the morning. That's when you get the big tour, right? I want to see everything."

"Early, according to the literature. Be back by eight."

Merle stood up and hugged Elise. "I promise."

WHEN MERLE RETURNED to the lavender farm the next morning at quarter to eight a small group was standing outside the big stone barn, next to a tractor. She parked under the tree again and skipped over to

Elise. Standing near the back, head down, Elise startled when Merle bumped her elbow in greeting. The dark circles under her eyes seemed even darker in the harsh morning light.

A strapping middle-aged man in a straw hat stood on the hub of huge tractor tire, gesticulating while he spoke. He was giving a lecture about the farm, how many acres were in production, how many pounds of lavender blossoms they cut, what type of lavender plant they grew, how many liters of lavender oil they produced. Merle found it fascinating but a glance at Elise confirmed her fear that her sister was getting nothing out of it. The man's French had a strong regional accent. Merle had to concentrate to get several of his phrases. She tried to memorize it all so she could repeat it to Elise.

"*Allons-y, mes amis*." The man, apparently the owner or manager, waved them around the tractor into the barn. Ahead of Merle and Elise two young men, college students perhaps, spoke in yet another language, something Slavic. They too looked confused.

Merle pulled out a small notebook and began scribbling notes from the farmer's tour. She jotted down the numbers he'd told them about the farm's production. He showed them where the lavender was stored after cutting, where it was baled, how it was baled, how the distillery worked— enough for a quick study but nothing else— where to avoid, where danger lay. He drew them out the back door into the fields where far in the distance another tractor was cutting the lavender.

"And so it begins," he said, extending both arms in a grand manner. "The sacred harvest of our precious essence, the heart and soul of this land, this Provence, this heavenly flower. This lavender! Any questions?"

CHAPTER TWO

"*W*as that the owner?" Merle asked Elise as they walked on the side of a field of so-called 'heavenly flowers.' Perhaps the adjective 'flowery' had come from a speech like that, she thought, stepping over a pile of rocks in the ditch.

Elise threw back her arms like the man had, lowering her voice an octave: "*Oui, madame et mes amis!*"

Merle smiled. "Did you understand all that?"

"What do you think?" Her voice had returned to snarky-ness. "I didn't take those French lessons you told me about. I'm screwed, aren't I?"

Merle stopped abruptly, causing Elise to bump into her. She pulled her notebook from her pocket and turned to her sister. "Look, I made notes." Merle began to rip the pages from the notebook but stopped. "Here, take it. I wrote down everything I could remember. It should get you started."

Elise leafed through the pages. "You're always so organized. Unlike some people." She rolled her eyes. "I forgot a bunch of stuff."

"I can get them for you."

"No, I'm fine. It'll do me good to improvise."

"Nothing vital then, like toothpaste." They walked back toward the manse. It looked smaller from the back, less imposing. There, under the eaves, was Elise's nonfunctional window. "Did the fan work last night?"

"It rattles. But who cares, right? I'll be here amongst all this beauty."

Merle snuck a glance at her. Was she being sarcastic? Trying to put a good face on— whatever she was feeling? "I forgot to ask, how's that guy you're seeing? What's his name? I know I met him at Christmas."

"Scott? Oh, he's fine."

Merle waited for more but nothing more came. "He's what? An accountant?"

"Right. Numbers, figures, columns. He's a whiz."

Again, a hint of sarcasm. "Successful, is he?"

"Partner at his firm. And not yet forty."

"What's he think about this farm stay then? Did he want to come with you?"

Elise laughed. "A CPA on a farm? Can you imagine?"

Actually, Merle could imagine. Most of the guests here had the pallor of inside work. That was the point, wasn't it? Get a tan, get your hands dirty?

"You didn't ask him then."

Elise sighed. "I wanted to come on my own. Use my muscles instead of my brain. Learn some French— okay, just a little. Experience a different way of life. I didn't want to have my boyfriend watching me, buffering me from everyone, criticizing me."

Merle frowned. "Does he— criticize?"

"Maybe I'm just sensitive. But whatever. I wanted to come alone. Is that so hard to believe?"

"Of course not. It's a great idea." They had reached the gravel drive in front of the main house. Merle's car waited there, under the willow. She still had questions. *How was the food at dinner? How early did they go into the fields? Who were the others, where were they from? Why did you really come here alone?* But Elise backed away. She was done talking, about herself, about the trip, and definitely about Scott.

"So, I'll see you in ten days." Merle opened her car door. Something about Elise's expression, her stubborn chin, her dark eyebrows furrowed together, her tight mouth: it made Merle sad. What was going on with her?

"Sure. Okay," Elise said.

"Have fun. And call me if anything comes up. I can be down here in a flash."

"Like if I break my leg or something? Haha." There was no humor in her fake laugh. "Bye, Merle."

A shiver of melancholy ran through Merle as she drove away, down the farm lane to the road, the dust kicking up behind the car. Elise was visible in the rearview mirror, standing alone outside the barn. Would she be all right there? She was hardly a child, Merle reminded herself. She had a phone, she had people around her. If she didn't like farm work, she could quit. Who was going to stop her? She wasn't going to be vital to the operation of the lavender farm. And she had promised to call if she needed anything.

Merle sighed and turned right toward Avignon, heading across the edge of the plateau where the world's best lavender was grown, where the beauty stretched on and on. She was glad she had seen it, at the right time, just before harvest. Glad Elise had asked her to drive her here, glad she'd taken a few photographs. Next week, these fields would be stubble. Like most things in life, timing is everything.

Time. Calendars. *Tick Tock.* Life.

Merle looked at her wristwatch. It was ten o'clock. She could make it back to Malcouziac easily today but maybe not Bordeaux where Pascal was working. She missed him but had become accustomed to long distances between them.

He was still living in a hotel that the department had rented for him but that deal ran out soon. He had asked her to find him an apartment in Bordeaux, a place where they could more easily spend time together, and she had accepted the challenge. On her last visit, she'd looked at a couple places near the center of the city but nothing had been acceptable. She might have to lower her standards. She didn't think they were all that high, not after opening her late husband's childhood home after fifty years of neglect. But maybe she'd gotten soft. Too used to household conveniences like sinks and refrigerators. She was over fifty now. Luckily, nothing seemed to be falling apart yet.

"Knock on wood," she muttered, tapping her head.

She stopped for lunch in Carcassonne, under the grand walled city that had inspired Cinderella's castle at Disneyland, or so the story went. The *Cité* was medieval in parts, having survived the Cathars and near starvation during a siege, but had undergone beautification in the 19th Century by Eugène Viollet-le-Duc, the famous architect, who had added the conical turrets. Merle had been through the old *Cité* with her sisters so settled for a view of it, on a sunny terrace.

Salade terminé, coffee in hand, she called her sister Francie. She was closest in age to Elise and they lived near each other back in the States. Merle hoped Francie would have some insight into Elise. But the call went unanswered. What time was it back in New York? Still early. She left a message instead.

Back in the car, Merle headed north through Toulouse and onward to the Dordogne. The sun was hot, glinting off the passing cars and the tops of distant peaks. The traffic thinned as she entered the middle of France, off the highways, onto the narrow roads that followed old cart paths. Her phone rang but she couldn't answer while concentrating on these rural byways.

Her phone rang again as she pulled into the city parking lot outside the walls of Malcouziac. She parked quickly and and answered.

"Hey, it's me," Francie said. "What's up?"

Merle told her to hang on as she locked her car and got her overnight bag from the trunk. As she slung it over her shoulder and walked into the village, she told Francie about delivering Elise at her farm stay and how beautiful the Luberon was.

"Super," Francie said flatly. "You're killing me with the France travelogue, Merle. I wish I was there but I have to get to work—"

"I just wanted to get your reaction," Merle said. "About Elise. She seems withdrawn. Is she okay?"

"Withdrawn? Like not talkative?"

"She moped around my house, making snarky comments. I thought it was jet lag but she never really got over it. I got exhausted in the car, trying to draw out a conversation. Plus, she didn't flirt with a single Frenchman."

Francie laughed. "That is odd. Seriously, I haven't spent much time with her for the last month. I saw her just before she left, at lunch with Jack and Bernie."

"And she was fine, normal?"

"Yeah. I guess."

"And she's still dating that accountant?"

"She didn't mention him. Maybe not."

"Maybe that's why she's depressed. Do you think she broke up with him?"

"Hey, listen, Merle. She's a grown woman. She's single, she can hook up with anybody she wants, within reason. She can take care of herself. Don't worry about her."

"It's just—remember when she ran off with that Bruno character in Scotland? That was bad. Maybe she has bad judgment in men." It was one thing all the sisters agreed on, that Elise had terrible taste in the male department.

"Oh, come on. She's not alone in that. She's got to figure that out for herself, Merle. You can't play matchmaker for her. You know that, right? I'll call you later. Have to run."

Merle pocketed her phone. It was annoying that Francie suggested that some of the other sisters had poor taste in men. Was she talking about Merle's marriage? That *had* turned out rather badly, but Harry was dead and buried by the time she discovered it all. She wouldn't obsess about Elise. Obviously, nothing was really wrong. Maybe she just needed some alone time. That was perfectly natural. A farm stay amongst the heavenly flowers of Provence would be a health cure for anyone.

So, forget about it, Merdle.

She switched her bag to her other shoulder as she turned onto Rue de Poitiers and caught a glimpse of her cottage at the end of the street, where the cobblestones ended at the broken wall. Beyond, on the hillsides, the grasses were turning gold in the summer heat, the sky was hopelessly blue and cloudless, and the grapes were ripening on the vines. In a pasture a white horse stood by himself, posing with his tail waving in the breeze. A lace curtain billowed from a neighbor's window. A rose bush that grew at the bottom of a downspout in front of Ninon's cottage held fat pink blossoms on thorny branches. Merle stopped to smell one, as she knew she should. The delicate smell was sweet and pure and alive.

It was good to be home.

CHAPTER THREE

$\mathcal{E}$lise slipped into an empty seat on the long bench by the communal kitchen table. She was late for breakfast, by about fifteen minutes. Her alarm had failed to go off, or at least that was the story if anyone asked. But no one spoke to her. They were busy drinking hot chocolate and eating yogurt, oranges, and hardboiled eggs. At the end of the table the daughter of the farmer, Natacha, picked up a slice of honeydew melon and popped it in her mouth, all the while staring accusingly. Elise straightened and raised her head, determined to ignore the nonverbal jabs.

The kitchen sat in the back of the house, nearly the entire width. Dry bouquets of lavender hung from the rafters. Dominating the space was a large black range. Vivianne, the farmer's wife who had met everyone at dinner the night before, stood in front of it, watching pots and fixing coffees.

Opposite Elise sat one of the college students she hadn't met yet. He stared at her with icy blue eyes. She wasn't even sure what nationality he was. Yesterday had been busy, learning so many things around the farm, that she hadn't talked to anyone but the guy who ran the tractor. And he chattered away in incomprehensible French.

The student half-rose from his seat and stuck out his hand to her, while chewing on a croissant. He was red-haired and pale. "Angus," he said, smiling. "From Perth. The one in Scotland."

She shook his hand. "Elise. From Connecticut. USA."

"Pleased to meet you." Angus sat down and the young man next to him, much shorter and darker, gave him an elbow in the ribs. "Oh, right. *Enchanté, mademoiselle.* We're supposed to speak French all the time."

"Are we?" Elise looked around the table. "Are you all in a class or something?"

A girl down the row with brown braids and a white hippie shirt embroidered with green leaves leaned forward. "*Nous sommes étudiants dans un programme d'échange de l'Université de Strasbourg. Moi, je m'appelle Heidi. Je viens d'Allemagne. Plus précisément, Munich.*"

Her hard accent and slowness of speech was enough that Elise could understand her. They were students from Strasbourg. She was Heidi from Munich.

"*Bonjour*, Heidi. *Je m'appelle* Elise." The women nodded to each other, then silence fell over the table again.

Elise looked at each of them, squinting a little as she was near-sighted but refused to wear glasses. Down the row, mostly men. They were all twenty years younger than her. They must all be college students in this exchange program, learning French. The boys barely had facial hair. Heidi from Germany and the one other girl looked fresh-faced. Their hair was thick and luxurious and natural. Elise had been coloring her hair for ages. She had *gray hair*. She felt like a dinosaur.

She had been proud of herself for getting into shape. Now she wondered why she bothered when everyone else here was so slender and nubile. She ate a spoonful of plain, tasteless yogurt. What had she been thinking? That there would be other middle-aged lawyers to hang around with? That she would make cool, new, adventurous friends? She glanced at the farmer's wife, Vivianne, sipping her espresso. Vivianne was tanned with strong arms and a pleasant, unlined face, her light brown hair pulled back under a yellow scarf. Elise realized with an

unpleasant shock that she was about the same age as Vivianne. Or—
merde—older.

Elise sipped the hot chocolate on the table in front of her. It was
too hot outside for cocoa but there would be little to eat for quite a
while. She was a farm worker now. Besides, it had been ages since she'd
let cocoa pass her lips.

Ten quiet minutes passed. The students picked at yogurt and eggs
and pastries. Another young man came into the kitchen and spoke to
Vivianne. Elise had seen him the day before. He was Lucas, the
brother of Natacha. He turned to the table and gave a quick order.
The students rose as one, throwing their napkins on the table and
stuffing a last bite of croissant into their mouths. Elise blinked, the last
to get up. By the time she had disentangled herself from the bench,
everyone was out the door.

She stood for a moment in the threshold, looking out into the
sunny fields then back at the kitchen. Vivianne gave her a smile of
encouragement and waved a hand to shoo her out. Elise stepped into
the sunshine.

Here we go, Provence. Here goes nothing.

AT SIX O'CLOCK THAT EVENING, Elise slipped a little lower in the bath
water so she couldn't hear the person banging on the door, shouting in
French. She didn't care about the others. She wanted to savor her bath.
She was sweaty and filthy.

The morning had begun with a forced march around the fields as
Monsieur Vernay explained whatever it was he was explaining. Something about the names and types of lavender— maybe. It was lost on
her. She did enjoy being out in the purple rows, dragging her hand
along the scented stems (until she was told to stop), and getting a light
sunburn under the towering mountains.

She touched her nose. It was sore and red as she'd forgotten her hat
this morning. Everyone else wore one. She looked like a total rube out
there, hatless. The temperature rose to at least 95 degrees. Hot, hot,

hot. At least it was, as they say, a dry heat and a light breeze kept it from getting too awful. That and a big picnic lunch on a wagon pulled by a tractor.

After lunch she'd been assigned to work in the barn where the big distillery vats cooked the lavender, distilling the essence through steam so it could be added to oil. There was a model of the process in the shop where the farm sold oil, soap, lotions, and bouquets. Elise had taken a detour there to look around. Natacha worked in there, looking cool and confident. She had no dirt under her nails. No hay in her hair. The little minx.

After throwing bundles of dry lavender from the previous year into the cooker, the scent of lavender had become less pungent, more background odor. She could still smell it but it no longer had the power to transport her, to make her swoon. She'd hoped to float on a cloud of perfume for ten days. This was a terrible development for Day One. She hated that too.

The guy who drove the tractor wasn't one of the students. At least she thought he wasn't. He was older, for one thing. He drove her back to the barn after lunch. She was grateful for the cool air inside the tractor cab. She didn't catch his name. He had rugged good looks that in other situations might have perked her up. But this situation? Ugh. He went on and on in French and she just kept nodding and frowning and nodding some more. Then he left her in the barn with some grizzled old guy who wielded a pitchfork and scowled like he wanted to poke her with it. At least he didn't speak to her; he just grunted now and then.

The knocking on the bathroom door stopped. Elise poured water over her head. Would she have to wash her hair every night? Her hair was not exactly her crowning glory. It didn't respond well to over-shampooing. It wasn't red like Francie's, or blond like Stasia's, or wild and thick like Annie's. It was more like Merle's— dark brown, wispy, and shapeless. She should have had a haircut before she left home but she couldn't really be bothered. Who would care in France? But she would have to figure out how to wear it better while she was here. Did she bring hair ties? She had forgotten so many things. She wasn't as organized as her older sisters but she usually packed her bags adequately.

"*Allo? Mademoiselle?*"

A tentative knock, as if she might be asleep. Well, she had to give the bathroom to someone and this person sounded nicer than the last one.

"*Un moment, s'il vous plaît!*"

She stepped out of the old tub and pulled the plug, letting the brown water go down the drain.

When she stepped into the hall, wrapped in her robe, the blond college girl from Sweden stood there with her towel, looking sweaty, dirty, and tired. "Sorry," Elise muttered. "I mean—*excusez-moi depuis longtemps dans le salle de bain.*" The girl just blinked at her and disappeared inside, locking the door behind her. Elise knew just how she felt.

Back in her stuffy room, Elise tried for the twentieth time to open the window. Still stuck. She turned on the rattly fan and stood in front of it, bending to dry her hair. She flung off her robe and relished the cooling air on her bare skin. Oh, the simple pleasures. Well, hadn't she come to the lavender farm stay just for these things?

Lying back on her bed, stark naked in the breeze of the fan, Elise felt some of her energy come back. How many days could she be first in the bath though? That angry person who knocked for such a long time would make her pay tomorrow. She closed her eyes. Tomorrow. Another day in paradise. Or hell. Or whatever this was.

The only thing she was sure of was that this definitely wasn't Webster, Lake & Osborne, Attorneys at Law. She let herself smile. If she never saw the inside of that wretched office again...well, 'never' was a long time. And right now, she was in Provence. At a lavender farm. Wouldn't that stuck-up Heather Osborne be jealous now? It was Heather who had given Elise the idea to do this, at a cocktail party in the spring. Elise had never heard of farm stays before, and certainly had never thought about working on a farm. Heather surely hadn't either, not with her delicate cheek bones, manicured nails, and four-inch heels. Her husband, the newest partner, had almost spit out his martini, presumably at the mental image of his wife in overalls at a farming vacation. Heather reddened, sticking out her ample and quite expensive chest, indignant, saying it had always been her dream to work on a lavender farm in Provence. *Well, Heather, I'm living your dream.*

The fan wheezed, clanked, and died.

Perhaps this wasn't exactly what Heather had in mind.

CHAPTER FOUR

*D*inner that night was a feast, more food than Elise had seen in one place for a long time. The smells coming from the kitchen sent an aroma of bacon, garlic, and herbs throughout the house, whetting their appetites. The long table was set outside, under two gnarled olive trees. Elise was glad she had decided against a sundress. She had to high-step it over the picnic bench in full view of eight young men on the opposite side. As it was, they ogled her bare shoulders in her tank top as they sat, waiting for the dishes to be passed down.

She adjusted her top self-consciously as she realized the tractor guy was sitting next to her. He nodded and went back to his water glass. Elise scanned the long table. The Swedish girl hadn't arrived, no doubt late because *someone* used the bath too long. The evening was warm with a glow on the hills beyond the fields. Her hair was still damp and a breeze tickled her scalp.

The lamb stew was amazing. Elise began quietly humming as it melted in her mouth. The white sauce held delicate secrets, herbs of some sort. She wasn't a cook, of course, being a single person with a life. Her knowledge of herbs was confined to lavender. She bent over her bowl, trying not to slurp it down too fast.

"*Delicieux*," the tractor guy said to her.

"*Oui*," she muttered and tore off a hunk of baguette to wipe out the bowl. "So good."

"Hard work builds up an appetite," he continued, glancing at her bowl and smiling.

What was the point of that comment, she wondered, then sat back. "Aren't you supposed to be speaking French?"

"Do you want me to speak French? I rather thought—" He paused, raising his eyebrows.

"You're right. My French is miserable. And your English is perfect." She examined his face again in the evening twilight. "You're not French, are you?"

"Half. My mother grew up here. My father is Welsh."

"Oh. Then you're not in the college group, I assume."

"Correct."

He offered no more personal details. His reddish-brown hair was wavy and long, hanging over his collar and damp like hers. He hadn't shaved in a few days. He had broad shoulders and was more muscular than the skinny college boys, with big, strong hands. Now that she'd settled in a little, she realized the situation wasn't impossible. This farm stay thing would be fine. She could still meet some people, make some friends like Merle had in her small town. It would be a kick to go home with real friends in France. What would Scott think about that? She banished the thought of her boyfriend. He was the last person she wanted to think about right now.

"This must have been a fabulous place to grow up," she said, happy to be able to converse in English.

"Mum's stories make it seem like a paradise."

Elise glanced at him. "But you don't see it that way?"

He shrugged. "It's a farm. Farms are work. Day in and day out. There is always another chore."

"I can see that." She drank a sip of cool white wine in the sweating goblet. She wondered how much wine was appropriate to drink at a French dinner. The college students had gulped theirs down quickly. It was so cold and tasty she wanted to do the same. But she took her time, savoring the moment and the wine.

"So, you're American," he said. She still didn't know his name. "Where do you live?"

"Connecticut. The part that's a suburb of New York City. Sprawling, town after town."

"It's pleasant?"

"Pleasant is a good word."

"And you work there?"

"Lawyer. Thrilling stuff." She pursed her lips.

"You don't like it?"

"Kinda dull. Office work, you know."

"So that's why you came here, for a change of pace?"

"Ding-ding-ding! How did you guess?" She squinted playfully at him. He didn't seem offended by her sarcasm.

"We get a lot of that here. Usually there are quite a few Americans but we got all these college students this time."

Elise looked down the table. "They seem nice."

He snorted. "No comment."

Elise glanced up to see if any of the students had heard that. "What?" She grinned at him and lowered her voice conspiratorially. "That snort was a comment, you know."

He held up his hands. "Sorry about the snort then."

Dinner wound down. Homemade ice cream was followed by a short cheese course, only three choices. Francie, Elise's closest sister in age, would have been incensed to have such a meager cheese course. She was obsessed with cheese. But dinner was over. The students got up in twos to go off and do whatever college students do in France.

Elise felt wiped suddenly. Every muscle in her back was screaming. She could only think about sleeping. Then she remembered her stuffy little room.

Before the tractor guy could run off, she turned to him. "Do you think you could repair my fan? It broke before dinner. My window doesn't open and it's pretty hot in there without it."

He frowned. She wondered if she'd made a wrong assumption that he was handy with equipment. Then he nodded. "Let's take a look at it."

He followed her up the two flights of stairs to the third floor and down the hallway to her room. Unlocking her door, she saw Heidi and the Swedish girl staring at her openly. "*Bonne nuit*," she called cheerfully. Their envy was hilarious.

The room was as hot and awful as she'd described. A wall of heat slammed into their faces. She led the way inside then swayed the door back and forth madly. Her savior made for the window, pulling a pocketknife out.

"First things first," he said. He did have a charming accent, not full-on posh British but maybe a little Welsh in there. She'd never met anyone from Wales before so she had no way of knowing. But those Scots at Annie's wedding in the Highlands had a similar but slightly different lilt.

He stuck the blade into the window frame, muscling out the paint in the crack. He worked quickly and silently, like a real pro. Elise stepped back into the hall to stay cool. She could hardly wait for the window to be open. Heidi had moved closer, as if her curiosity was unbearable. Elise smiled at her.

"Trying to get my window open. It's so hot in my room," she explained.

Heidi craned her neck to see inside. "Oh, *mon Dieu*, yes. Mine too," she whispered.

"Is your window painted shut?"

"*Oui*."

They both turned toward the window as the guy began to bang on the sash. After several whacks with the heels of both hands, the window popped and released its grip. He kept hitting it until the window was open four inches. He closed his pocketknife and turned toward the women. "*Voilà*. Now where is this bad fan?"

"Oh, forget that. Fresh air! It's amazing. Thank you." Elise stuck her hand through the gap and felt a breeze as the hot air in her room rushed out. "You should help Heidi. She's got a stuck window too."

"This way, monsieur, if you please." Heidi gave him a big, happy smile as she turned to walk back toward her room. "How can I thank you? And you too, madame!"

Elise just waved them on. She didn't like being called 'madame' by the whippersnappers. She made a sour face then turned back to her room, newly released from its prison of heat. It was a small miracle. She dashed out again into the bathroom and threw cold water all over her arms and legs and face. It felt delicious.

She could do this! She was resourceful! She would figure out a way to thank the tractor guy.

Maybe by learning his name.

ELISE FELL ASLEEP ALMOST INSTANTLY. The breeze through the window was light but it was a breeze and a cool one at that. The night sky hung its purple curtain to the west, holding on to the summer day. Tomorrow she would look at the stars coming out but tonight she was completely exhausted.

The fluttering was light, almost imperceptible, like the old fan. Had it come to life? She reminded herself the fan was indeed kaput as she came up from a deep sleep. What was happening?

She opened her eyes. Her room was in shadow, only the faint glow of the night sky radiated from outside. She craned her neck to look out the window. Maybe she would move her bed so it was right under the window. That would be nice, especially for the evening breezes.

There it was again, a movement in the dark. Had a bird flown in? The window was open and had no screen. Maybe it was just a big insect, but what? A dragonfly? A butterfly? A large moth?

She sat up. She didn't like bugs. She had a slight phobia about insects, if she had to admit it. Bugs and spiders: *ick*. She didn't really even like birds, up close. She listened in the dark. Should she turn on the light? Whatever it was would no doubt fly right back out if she stayed quiet.

She lay down again, her eyes wide open. Dammit, she wasn't going to be able to sleep. She lay tense and rigid under the thin sheet, straining for the sound of fluttering.

Then she felt it, right by her head: a flapping of wings, air movement. It passed by her and, before she could react, it came around again. She sat up in a panic and felt the light touch of something hit her shoulder and glance away.

With a shriek she was up, jumping toward the lamp. She snapped it on. The low wattage bulb flared. The shadows stretched across the room, from her feet to the wall, up to—

Was that a bat? Oh, holy hell.

It launched itself from the ceiling beam and did another circle around the room, bumping into a wall in the process. That brown, furry thing with the little mouse ears and leathery wings and little clawed feet was no dragonfly.

No siree.

CHAPTER FIVE

*T*he screaming brought out two women and eight men, heads poked into the hallway. The overhead lights came on. Heidi and the Swedish girl stepped out completely. All male eyes turned to them. They had already gotten a good look at Elise in her underwear and tank top. The Swedish girl wore nothing at all but red panties. Her skin glowed white. She had the dazed look of sleep in her eyes. She stood rubbing them and saying something incomprehensible. A college boy went back to his room then came out to hand her a shirt.

Heidi rushed toward Elise who was jumping around, waving her arms like a maniac. "What is it?"

Elise pointed to her open door. "It's a bat! In my room."

Heidi's eyes widened but she stayed calm. "We must close the door, Elise." She stepped up and yanked the door shut. "It will fly out, sooner or later."

"Sooner or later?! How long do—" Elise came to her senses and realized Heidi was speaking English. "Thank you, Heidi. Have you dealt with bats?"

The sound of footsteps on the wooden stairs made them turn. Two heads poked up then there was the guy who drove the tractor and the farmer at the end of the hallway, barefoot, wearing t-shirts and boxer shorts. "*Que se passe-t-il ici?* What is happening here? I hear screaming," the farmer asked gruffly, looking up and down at Elise and Heidi in their not-much.

"Are you hurt?" The tractor guy suggested.

Elise tugged self-consciously at her tank top. Did she look injured? Had she scratched or bloodied herself? She looked down. No blood to be seen, just a lot of bare skin. Her nipples were clearly visible through the thin white tank top. Heidi had the good sense to wear a black one. At least they'd worn *something*, unlike Miss Sweden.

"Um," Elise began, then recovering herself, putting an arm across her breasts. "It's a bat. In my room."

"Is it still in there?" the younger man asked.

"I closed the door," Heidi said. "Maybe it flies out?"

"We didn't check," Elise said.

The farmer groaned, clearly annoyed and rocking some serious bed-head, straw-colored hair sticking out in every direction. "Back to bed, all of you."

Heidi hung back as the others shuffled into their rooms. The farmer squinted at her. "You too, *petite*. The excitement is over. Tomorrow is another day."

The three of them watched Heidi's bottom as it bounced down the hall and disappeared. Elise turned back to the men, realizing they'd all shared that moment, and smiled.

"What now?" she asked.

The farmer muttered something. Discussing bat strategy, she assumed. The tractor guy gave the farmer some side-eye and a look of *seriously?* He sighed then pulled his green t-shirt over his head and balled it up in his hands. The farmer barked at him, grabbing it, and held it by the shoulders.

"*Comme ça,* Conor." He said something derisive, Elise figured, because the tractor guy—who must be named Conor—winced at the comment. He took the shirt back, holding it as instructed, and slipped into her room.

"He catches it," the farmer told Elise in heavily-accented English. "It is common. You open your window?"

"Yes. Sorry, it was so hot. I didn't know about the bats."

"They are harmless and eat the insects for us, the mosquitoes and moths. Do not be alarmed. You have no bats in America?"

"Oh, sure. Just—not in my neighborhood."

"Why you didn't use the fan? We provide a fan for every room. You should not open the windows at night. I am sure Natacha told you. You can see what trouble it causes. Do not do this again please."

Elise was about to protest about the heat and the broken fan when they heard a thump in her room followed by a curse. Conor fell out the doorway. "It— it's gone. Out the window." He straightened, regaining his dignity despite now being bare-chested in his green boxer shorts which were patterned, on closer examination, with little white and brown Corgi dogs.

"Did you close the window?" the farmer demanded.

Conor's shoulders sagged. He turned back to the door, took a breath, and opened the door again. In a moment he returned. "Closed up." He glanced at Elise as if to apologize.

"*D'accord.* Go to bed. *Allons-y*, Conor."

Elise watched the farmer and—yes, mostly—Conor who had a lean, muscular back like a body builder, as they walked away. Conor glanced back at her as he grabbed the bannister. She gave him a little wave of thanks and turned the doorknob to face the now-short, stuffy night ahead.

The rescue was almost worth the bat scare.

ELISE WAS up with her alarm, feeling oddly peppy after the weird nighttime adventures and lack of sleep. She entered the kitchen to find only Vivianne and two male students in attendance so far. Vivianne handed her a soft-boiled egg in one of those English breakfast cups. Elise sat down across from the boys. They had sly grins on their faces, no doubt remembering her in her underwear.

"*Bonjour*," she said, nodding. "*Madame? Café crème? C'est possible?*"

"*Bien sûr*," Vivianne said, turning to the espresso machine. None of the college kids drank coffee, only cocoa, or else they were too nervous to ask for it. Well, adults need coffee. Elise drew back her shoulders with pride and whacked the egg with the side of her knife.

"*Vous avez eu un peu d'excitation dans la nuit, madame?*" Vivianne inquired as she set the coffee with cream in front of Elise.

"A bat in my room, *dans ma chambre*. What is French for 'bat'?"

"Bat?" Vivianne frowned.

"*Une chauve-souris.*" One of the college boys, a pimply English kid, piped up. "I looked it up."

Vivianne shuddered, whispering something about terrible bats. The rest of the students trickled in. Heidi and the Swedish girl crept into the room, eyes down. Had they already heard teasing about last night? The thought of it raised Elise's hackles. They sat next to her in welcome solidarity, mumbling '*bonjours*'.

"*Pardon*," Elise began, turning to the Swedish girl. "*Comment t'appelles-tu?*"

The girl blinked, her blond hair uncombed and hanging in her face. She was very reserved, Elise thought, shy and soft-spoken. Or just mortified by her public nakedness. Elise raised her eyebrows at her encouragingly. She needed to know the girl's name. *Come on, child.*

Heidi poked her with an elbow. The Swedish girl whispered: "*Je m'appelle Britta.*"

"Britta. What a beautiful name. Nice to meet you, Britta. *Je m'appelle Elise.*"

"*Bonjour*, Elise," called red-haired Angus from Perth from down the table. He waved at her, smiling. "*Un peu d'excitation?*"

"*Oui*, Angus. *Mais seulement un peu.*" She held up her finger and thumb an inch apart. *Only a little excitement, you prat.* "*Dommage.*"

Angus whispered something out of the corner of his mouth to the student next to him; they both glanced at her and chortled. The laughter rippled down the male students, one expelling a loud guffaw, another hunching over, giggling.

Elise rolled her eyes as the chuckling continued. She could see the middle of the night's entertainment was a subject of interest, and would be for a while. The bat was forgotten for more lurid thoughts. Poor Britta. They would no doubt tease her mercilessly about her bare breasts. Heidi's bouncing bottom and her own nipples would also be hot topics.

This was, what—day three? This was unacceptable.

Elise took a sip of her *café crème* and set it down hard on the table.

"All right, everybody. Listen up." They looked at her, wide-eyed. "I don't have to speak French like you so I'm going to say this in English. Try to keep up. I'm only going to say it once."

A hush fell over the table. Spoons froze in mid-air. Conor and the farmer's son, Lucas, had stepped into the room and moved back against the sink, out of range. Vivianne turned from her stove. Elise swallowed and stared at each of the students.

"You guys had your little jollies last night, at our expense. Congratulations. You caught us in a state of undress. It's the first time you saw lady parts, am I right? Exciting for you. Well, there is no changing what happened, no wiping those images from your little brains. But here's the thing—there are only three of us women here, compared to —what—twelve of you? So your jokes will now end. No teasing, no snide looks, no giggling behind our backs. No comments to us or each other or anybody, from here forward. No pranks. No mash notes. No sending photos of your prowess, for godssake. No sending anything. Are you listening? We do not—categorically—*do not* want to hear from you on this subject."

Elise paused to make sure they were listening. Whether they understood English was another question. Most were looking at their plates but Conor and Lucas stared at her, slack-jawed. Heidi and Britta were wide-eyed.

Now that she had their attention she went in for the kill. "I shouldn't have to say this but I don't know you or where you're from, what your culture permits. Here's the rule: no grabbing or touching of any kind. No pressure, no innuendo. My culture does not permit catcalls, lewd comments, or the unwanted touching of women. So, let's go with my culture here, okay?

"Heidi and Britta and I were caught in an uncomfortable situation last night. You were witnesses. But now, it's over. It will not be mentioned again."

She pressed her lips together, knowing she looked like a schoolteacher, or a librarian, or, hell, a cranky, middle-aged lawyer. She was angry. Why did this need to be said? But it did, obviously. There were way too many hormones in this room, on this farm. There was nothing she could do about what they thought about her. She didn't even care. Still, she tried not to meet anyone's eye. She cleared her throat.

"Have I made myself clear?"

CHAPTER SIX

*E*lise stepped outside, jamming her hat and sunglasses on her head. She'd tried to exit before all the students. She didn't want to run that gauntlet. Already she was wondering if she'd just doomed this farm stay with her harsh lecture. Well, it was done, and it had had to be done. It wasn't fair to Heidi and Britta to have the boys teasing them, whispering about their bodies, pinching their asses.

It. Would. Not. Do.

She rolled up the sleeves on her cotton work shirt and pulled the leather gloves from her back pocket. At least she'd remembered the more important things like gloves. How long would it be until she got into town to buy sunscreen, lip balm, shampoo, and moisturizer? She hadn't wanted to tell Merle how many things she'd forgotten. This morning she had smeared petroleum jelly on her lips and nose. Why had she even brought that? What a dunce.

The weather was fair again, the sky pale blue with the promise of heat. Perfect for the harvest, she supposed, but hard on humans. She walked to the barn, the gathering place where the orders for the day were handed down. Which nincompoop would she have to work with today? It didn't take long to find out.

"Bennett," Monsieur Vernay called out. She was the second alphabetically so at least she didn't have to wait. "Jiri. Ivan. *Vous aussi. Conor vous emmènera au côté nord.*"

What did that mean? Elise glanced around the group. Nobody was moving. Who was Jiri or Ivan? The only male she knew was Angus, and of course, Conor.

Then she spotted the two guys she thought might be Jiri and Ivan. Someone had said they were Czech. They were quiet ones, sullen in the Slavic style. They wore all-black: slacks, t-shirts, and hats, like a couple of ninjas. They squinted at her then peeled off the group and headed for the tractor. There was Conor, already up in the cab. She fought her way out of the students and reached the tractor as the two guys swung themselves up on the back. That left her the seat next to Conor again.

She paused. She'd found Conor's bat-catching t-shirt under the window that morning. Suddenly the vision of him walking to the stairs in his boxers popped into her head. She'd been trying to forget it.

Conor fiddled with the instrument panel of the tractor. It was a fancy machine with an enclosed cab, air conditioning and a radio. It must be nice driving the tractor, a perk for relatives. She hauled herself up into the cab with a grunt. Conor reached across her and shut her door, then put the tractor into gear.

"So, what's on the agenda today?" she asked as they puttered along a dirt track.

"Going to *le côté nord.*" Conor gave her a look. "That means the north side."

"I knew that," Elise said unconvincingly. "But to do what?"

Conor didn't answer and she settled back to see what forced labor the day would bring. The north side was a good distance from the farm buildings. About twenty minutes passed as they chugged by lavender field after lavender field, then some wheat fields, and more lavender fields, some already shorn, some waiting to be harvested. As the time ticked by, Elise felt the awkwardness grow. Finally, she had to speak.

"I just wanted to say thank you. For catching the bat and all."

Conor nodded silently.

"And I have your t-shirt. I can leave it somewhere for you."

No reply.

"What room are you in? I'll leave it on the doorknob if you're not there."

"I'll get it sometime."

He didn't want her knowing where he was staying. That seemed unfair since he'd already seen in her in her underwear, and vice versa. Why was he being such a pill?

"Was it difficult—catching the bat?"

"No."

And another conversation dies. He seemed friendly last night, glancing back and all. But again—what was she expecting here? Romance? Pen pals? No one liked her and then she had given that speech at breakfast, pissing off anyone who hadn't made up their minds. Was that it? She glanced at Conor again, his jaw muscles tight.

"Sorry about that rant just now. I freaked out that the guys were hassling Britta. I don't know if she was naked when you got up to our floor but, well, she was naked. On the top, you know."

He looked at her waving her hands around her breasts. She added, "I guess I should apologize to all the guys. And Heidi and Britta too. They didn't ask me to say all that. Sometimes I just can't help myself. Up on my high horse I go."

He turned his cool blue eyes on her. "It's not a problem. Everyone is on notice now and no one will tease me about being undressed. So, thank you for clarifying."

Elise frowned. What was that? Was he being sarcastic?

He jerked the tractor to a stop next to a line of fence. Jiri and Ivan hopped off the back so Elise opened her door and climbed down. She slammed her door without another word. She'd already said enough 'sorrys' this morning.

The old man from the distilling shed stood next a pile of coiled barbed wire. He was handing the boys some kind of tools. She walked around the tractor to join them. Conor backed up, turned around, and headed back toward the barn. She watched the dust behind the tractor for a moment then took out her gloves and put them on.

The two Czech students weren't big talkers, that was obvious. Jiri introduced himself; he had a super long last name with a lot of 'z's in it. Same with Ivan, except he scowled like a scary Russian bear. The old man was speaking to them in French but none of them understood what he was saying. She couldn't speak to the guys, if they were conversationalists in any language, which seemed doubtful. The instruction ended up being pantomimed. Pull the wire, stretch it, nail it.

"Got it," Elise said, giving the old man a thumbs up. Then she handed her tool back to him. "I'll be the puller."

The work was harder than Elise had thought it would be and the lunch break was seriously welcome. As the sun rose high in the sky, beating down on her shoulders and back as she leaned to pull wire, she dreamed about something delicious for lunch, a cool soup perhaps. Shrimp on ice. But when noon came, instead of joining the others for lunch Lucas arrived on a bicycle with sandwiches and bottled water. There was no shade so they sat in the blazing sun and ate silently.

"This is like the gulag," Elise muttered. Was she being punished for her lecture this morning, or for being such a ninny about the bat? Everyone had to work of course. Jiri and Ivan weren't complaining. They just stared at her, chewing their sandwiches. "The gulag? *Connaissez-vous 'gulag'?*"

Jiri, the smaller of the two, grinned. "Gulag," he repeated then pulled the back of his shirt up and made a choking face as if he was being hanged. Ivan laughed. Great. The gulag, place of great mirth.

"Okay, not that bad. *Pas si mal. Le travail*, huh." She squinted at them. "What do you guys do back in the Czech Republic? That's where you're from, right? You—" She pointed at Jiri. "You work at home? Are you students? *Vous travaillez? Ou êtes-vous étudiants?*"

Jiri glanced at Ivan who shrugged his massive shoulders. Neither answered. Elise gave up, drank the rest of her water, pulled her hat over face, and lay back in the grass. It was too hot to nap so she gave herself a little lecture about trying to make friends here. Then she tried to accept her own advice. She was completely inadequate in the self-advice space.

No one wants to get to know you, Elise. No one cares about your bad French and nonexistent farmer skills. Nobody is here to make friends. Suck it up. We're here to work and learn a little French. That's the beginning and the end of it.

Get over yourself.

WHEN SHE GOT BACK to her room that evening a small blue fan sat on the floor by her door. It looked new but it was tiny, even smaller than the one that had crapped out. Still someone had taken pity on her and brought her a fan. She looked up and down the hall. It was deserted. She took the fan into her room, set the broken one in the hall, and plugged in the new one. Better than nothing.

Struggling with the window she got it open a couple inches, enough to let out the accumulated heat from the day. She pointed the fan toward the window, sighed, and lay back on her bed in the weak breeze. She would let someone else take the bathroom first.

Her hands had multiple wounds from today's fencing chore. What devil had invented barbed wire? Puncture marks, scratches, a bruised knuckle. The leather gloves hadn't helped much. At least the guys had done most of the work. Jiri got a bloody calf from falling against the pile of barbed wire. Ivan squealed like a girl when he poked his thumb. They'd been abandoned by the old man at mid-morning and no one picked them up at quitting time. They trudged silently back to the *maison,* Elise trailing the two Czechs all the way.

In her room the minutes ticked by. She closed her eyes. She'd heard no one in the hall since her return so she skipped into the bathroom and ran herself a cool bath. She washed quickly this time, hoping to be finished before anyone else showed up.

When she emerged into the yard in her blue and white sundress, refreshed, Elise realized she was late. Again. The western sky was purple and stars had popped out all over. The summer night sky was velvety soft. The string of lights between the trees that lit the long table cast small puddles of yellow onto the plates and glasses. It was enchanting. Everyone was halfway through their meal.

And by the looks on their faces, they had been hoping she wouldn't show up at all.

CHAPTER SEVEN

BORDEAUX

*M*erle spun around in the office chair, feeling like a giddy child. Here in Pascal's small office in the Cité du Vin in Bordeaux, the view was amazing, from the rooftops to the river. She drank in the sunshine for a moment then returned to her task, searching for an apartment.

The hunt was not going well, necessitating a continuing relationship with an 'immobilier,' a property agent. The woman intimidated Merle. Opaline Marc was extremely serious, tall and broad-shouldered with a perfect Catherine Deneuve French twist in her platinum hair and dazzling red lipstick that never smeared. She spoke perfect English but often made little comments in French that Merle missed. She wanted to get all the snide remarks about the places they looked at, but then she could see the defects for herself. A sorry lack of bathroom fixtures was number one. It was appalling.

Merle checked her watch. She had an hour before she met with Opaline. She'd worn a dress today for the occasion, a green one that had a white collar and bands on the short sleeves. It felt like a uniform but it would give her confidence. Opaline wasn't happy that she hadn't found any of the apartments satisfactory. They were either wrecks or too expensive. Opaline accused Merle of being a 'Goldilocks' during their last outing. Everything was either too this or too that, nothing was just right.

She refreshed her search on her iPad. To her surprise something new popped up, a townhouse just outside the *Vieux Ville*, the old part of the city. She clicked on it, her eyes watering at the proposed rent. But maybe Opaline could work her magic. Merle forwarded the information to her with a note that she'd like to see it. Moments later Opaline replied, telling her to meet at the location. She would get them in to see the property.

Pascal was visiting vineyards today, south into the Sauternes region. His job had changed, now that he was a supervisor of other agents in the field, but he still liked to get out and talk to the wine makers and feel the dirt in his hands. He would make a good vintner himself, Merle had come to believe. Would he ever do that—mix and bottle his own creation? Probably not, but she had also come to believe that life made liars of us all. Here she was, living in France with a Frenchman. She never could have imagined this life.

As she drove toward the townhouse, checking the directions on her phone, Merle thought about the phone call she'd had the night before with Stasia. The second oldest, Stasia worked as an in-house counsel for a fashion magazine. They were discussing Elise. The sisters all had an opinion on what was going on with the youngest Bennett but nobody knew for sure.

Except, of course, Stasia, who was positive it had to do with her job at the law firm.

"Not because of Scott then," Merle asked. She thought it had to be a romantic problem that had made Elise go on such a so-called vacation to a French lavender farm.

"No," Stasia said. "Look, she only became a lawyer because basically she felt pressured into it. She took three years off after college, working at that ski resort in Montana, waiting tables."

"I know, but I don't remember any of us forcing her to go to law school. She doesn't like it, is that what you're saying? Because she wouldn't be alone in that."

"True. I hated working at a law firm." Stasia often complained about her fashion magazine lawyering in New York City, saying contracts were just as dull there as anywhere. But it was a job the other sisters envied for its access to designer clothes.

"She told you she hated it?"

"We were together on Mother's Day. She wouldn't answer any questions about what she was working on, even though several of us asked. In fact, she shut down Daddy so hard he was hurt. She had to apologize to him. He told me all about it the next day."

"She does seem cranky. She wouldn't talk to me at all."

"What does Francie say? She was in Paris so we didn't see her at Mother's Day."

"She didn't know. She said she hadn't seen Elise much."

"She's keeping her distance. Annie tried to organize a sisters' night and I was the only one who could go. Francie had something, Elise just said 'no.'"

Merle sighed. "I hate this."

They decided to keep emailing and calling Elise, showing her they cared even if she didn't. Merle had sent her three emails and four texts since she'd been at her farm stay but Elise hadn't answered any of them.

"Oh, did Willow write to you about her visit?" Stasia asked.

"Yes. She's going to Paris first? I can't wait to see her," Merle said. Stasia's daughter had just graduated from college.

"Thanks again for hosting her. I know we spoil her. But she needs one break before law school starts."

Another one bites the dust. The law school curse carries on.

Merle turned the corner. This was the street, Boulevard Alienor. She double-checked then sucked in a breath at the sight. The cobblestone street had leafy trees and shade and flower boxes and rose bushes. The houses were lovely, with brightly painted doors and wrought-iron balconies. She felt a rush of anticipation. *Please be decent and not over-priced*. She'd been disappointed so many times.

Opaline waited on the sidewalk, thumbing through her phone and tapping a patent leather pump impatiently. She wore a stunning turquoise dress, elegantly wrapped around her figure. Merle parked and quickly walked toward her.

"*Bonjour*, Opaline." They air-kissed then Merle looked up at the townhouse. "This is it?" She couldn't believe it. The stone was washed and repointed, the shutters gleamed in burgundy paint. The three steps up to the door were clean, leading to hopes that the inside would be too.

"*Oui.* The owner is meeting us here." She led the way to the door then turned quickly to Merle. "He is someone I know, an official on the Aquitaine Regional Council. He—" She broke off as the glossy black door creaked open. A portly gentleman of about seventy-five years, his head wreathed in white hair, smiled broadly at Opaline. "*Bonjour, Henri.*" Her voice went up an octave as she rattled away in French with her friend. Finally, she introduced Merle. Henri beckoned them inside.

The two-story building was long and narrow. A steep stair rose from the front hallway. The bannister and old, worn treads were dark wood. Henri opened the white double doors to the parlor, chattering away in French. Merle couldn't follow him so just looked around in wonder.

The townhouse was furnished. It was amazing. She would have to ask if the furniture stayed. It was worn and smelled a bit musty but she didn't care. She knew Pascal would love it. He despised hard modern furniture. These worn velvet chairs showed the indentations of decades of use. The windows facing the street were big and bright, letting in summer sun. As a townhouse there were no windows on the sides where it abutted other houses. But in the back, the kitchen was also bright, facing a tiny yard where weeds had taken over.

Henri came to stand next to Merle, looking into the garden. He apologized, saying he loved to grow vegetables but his back wouldn't allow that anymore. The kitchen itself was basic but not too small, with a center dining area complete with a round table and two bistro chairs.

He let them go upstairs on their own, patting his knees. In one bedroom there was a double bed, in another two twin beds. A small bathroom with actual fixtures like a sink, toilet, and bathtub sat between the bedrooms. It had a tiny window that looked over the neighbor's roof.

"He says he can't do the stairs anymore," Opaline explained. "He's moved in with his brother and it is time to rent this place."

They headed back down the stairs. Merle whispered, "Is the price negotiable? And the furniture stays?"

Opaline's nostrils flared. "Everything is negotiable, *mon amie*."

Back in the hallway with Henri, Merle complimented him on his home. "*Très agréable*." The French were suspicious of gushing so she took a breath and said no more.

Opaline walked Henri back into the parlor where they sat next to each other on the sofa. Merle perched nearby on a needlepoint armchair. Opaline went into her pitch, a saccharine attempt at renting the place for the lowest price she could. She fawned over the old man, asked him how long he'd had the place, talked about the classic furniture and made sure it stayed in the house. He seemed to enjoy the attention. She took his hand, patting it with her other one.

"Henri. It is time, *n'est-ce pas*? You have been lucky today because Merle and Pascal are the first to see your house and they adore it." Opaline told him that Merle was a careful, fastidious woman, despite being an American, and an excellent housekeeper. Her partner was a French policeman. "He is doing the state's work as only the best patriots like yourself can do," she said, laying it on thick. "But he does not make the kind of money that affords these delightful comforts. You understand?"

He nodded. "Having a policeman in the house would make me very comfortable." He glanced at Merle. "And you too, *madame*. You will take care of my furnishings? Keep the dust at bay? Fill the house with the good smells of your cuisine?"

Merle felt his pain on losing his home. She put a hand over her heart and said solemnly, "*Bien sûr, monsieur. Ce serait mon honneur.* It would be my honor."

Opaline nodded to Merle: *well done*. To the old man she added: "It would be worth a consideration on the rent to know your beautiful things are safe and well cared for, *oui*?"

He agreed. She proposed a number. He thought about it for twenty seconds then he was in. He wanted it done. He would remove his personal items by the end of the month and then it was theirs. Opaline promised to drop the lease agreement by his office.

Out on the sidewalk Merle grasped Opaline by the shoulders and gave her three quick, enthusiastic cheek kisses. Opaline squirmed away, making Merle laugh.

"Oh, *merci*. A thousand thank-you's."

Opaline raised one eyebrow to show her disdain for the show of emotion. She straightened her shoulders and leveled a glare at Merle. "Being a Goldilocks pays off sometimes. Congratulations. Next week, the place is yours."

Merle raised a fist to the sky and called out an enthusiastic 'Yes!' That only made Opaline more horrified. She trotted back to her car.

Merle took out her phone, took a photo of the front of the adorable townhouse and sent it to Pascal with a caption that read: "*Un peu* over budget but completely furnished and ready to move in! A full kitchen and real *salle de bain*! Our new *maison de ville*!!!"

CHAPTER EIGHT

PROVENCE

$\mathcal{T}$he hillside offered an expansive, incredible view, there was no debate about that. Even in the late evening, the rolling landscape down the plateau to the rivers and towns in the distance was stunning. Heidi and Britta had dragged Elise away from the cheese at dinner, claiming that tonight was the night for their hike. Elise wasn't feeling like anything but a good night's sleep—as usual—but the cool breeze floating down along the rows of lavender made the outing worthwhile.

This area of the farm, closest to the house and barn, was the last to be harvested. Monsieur Vernay, the farmer, had explained the strategy but the only thing Elise could remember was that they kept the view of the lavender from the house for as long as possible. She leaned down and plucked a stalk, its flower-head dry. In the distance lay the remains of wheat fields, already shorn to stubble.

Heidi and Britta had started speaking in English around her, which only made Elise more grateful for them. Heidi was enthusiastic about everything, quite extroverted, and she brought out Britta from her shy, withdrawn state. Britta had a big smile on her face right now, framing the view of the valley lights with her hands. "Magical," she whispered. "Am I correct?"

"You are," Elise agreed.

They kept to the road, winding up along the hillside, through an olive grove, past sunflowers and more lavender fields, terraced into the mountain. Where were they taking her? Elise paused, feeling the ache in her back from bending over in the fields today. Oh, to have a twenty-year-old back.

"Enough?" She called to them. "It's getting late, girls."

Heidi and Britta had their heads together, whispering. Britta grinned. Heidi gave a yip, and they turned back, linking arms with Elise as they ran down the hill. They arrived, breathless and giddy. They were such *girls*. So young. It made you smile to be around them. Elise said good night as they ran up the stairs. She headed to the kitchen for a glass of water, or wine if she could find it.

As she reached the door to the kitchen, she heard voices. She paused in the dark hallway to listen. It was a man, berating someone by the tenor of his voice. Elise backed away. She didn't need to involve herself in any more drama.

She had reached the outside door and stepped back into the yard as the footsteps came toward her. Suddenly, Monsieur Vernay stepped out, followed closely by another man who was yelling at him. Elise ducked her head and stepped to one side, up against the shadows of the stone house. The farmer turned and shouted at the man. For a moment it looked like he was going to spit on him. Then they were gone, around the corner of the house.

What was that? Elise took a breath. A car engine revved in the stillness and faded away. Monsieur didn't come back but she heard a door slam somewhere.

Now she definitely needed wine. She tiptoed back to the kitchen and pushed open the door carefully. The light was still shining over the farmhouse table and all the pots and pans drying on tea towels there. She crept up to the table and picked up a jelly jar from the mound of dishes. That was when she heard the sobbing from a dark corner of the room.

Elise stepped closer. "Vivianne?" The farmer's wife was curled in on herself, crying into her hands.

"Are you all right? *Ça va?*" She whispered. Vivianne looked up and nodded, biting her lip. She wiped the tears on her cheeks with the back of her hand.

"I'm sorry to intrude. Is it all right if I get some wine? Um, *un petit peu du vin?*"

Vivianne gestured toward a sideboard where two jugs of wine sat surrounded by half-empty bottles of cordials and *eau de vie*. "It's okay?" Elise asked. Vivianne waved again.

Elise picked the rosé even though it was lukewarm, pouring herself a good slug. "Would you like some? I can get you a little? *Un peu pour vous?* You look like you could use a little something," she asked Vivianne who shook her head sadly. "Okay. Good night, madame. *Bonsoir.*"

In her room, Elise sipped her warm wine in the breeze of the fan and wondered. What were they yelling about? Why was Vivianne so upset? Was her husband mad at her? Had she done something with that other man, whoever he was? She hadn't got a good look at him. He was shorter than Monsieur Vernay—Guy—that's about all she could tell in the moment as they passed her. She couldn't understand a word they said.

Maybe Conor knew what it was about. But she hardly saw him these days. He was up in the tractor and she was relegated to some menial task. One day she'd been asked to help fill bottles of lavender oil and paste on labels. She'd made a mess of it, spilling oil all over the new labels. They'd sent her back out in the fields with the Czechs.

Not everyone is right for shop work, Natacha told her.

BY THE SIXTH day at the lavender farm, Elise had a deep tan, a few blisters, and her nose had burned and peeled. Her muscles hadn't gained definition, she was sad to see, but she felt stronger. Her mind was clearer. She was so tired at the end of each day, physically, in-a-good-way tired, that is, not emotionally drained and angry, that she didn't think about anything but bathe, eat, sleep. It was nice. Very nice.

On Saturday night, the dinner table conversation was all about the village gathering the next day. Everyone got Sunday off, whether church was involved or not. Church was not even mentioned at the table, but dancing and music were. A local band was to play, accordions and trumpets and who knew what else. Elise found a couple of the students looking at her, as if sizing her up as a dance partner. It made her laugh, but she tried to keep it to herself.

Dessert was homemade peach ice cream again, one of Vivianne's favorites. Elise lingered over her bowl in the twilight and tried not to think about the emails she'd been getting from Scott. They had become more frequent, two or three times a day, as if he was obsessed with her. She never replied which only seemed to make him wild. She had told him, in no uncertain terms, that as a couple, they were done. She liked him just fine. They just weren't a good fit. She'd told him that two months before she'd left, yet he still pursued her.

Totally honest was what she'd been. Brutal, maybe, but completely honest. She wasn't going to lie to him. He was about as far from her type as a man could get. Why had she ever gone out with him? She had dated ski racers and investment bankers and even a professional football player for about two minutes.

There was nothing *wrong* with him, she'd made pains to tell him, but she could tell he didn't believe her. Their last evening together, the night before she left for France, had been bad. She was tired of explaining, tired of him. She had hurt him, she knew, but was that a reason not to break up with somebody? Someone you didn't love? Someone you knew, deep in your heart, would never be your soulmate?

She had told Francie this once, the soulmate part, that she wanted to meet her soulmate. Her sister had laughed uproariously. "Soulmate? What the ever loving—?"

"Exactly! 'Ever loving.' Someone you can always love, forever. Thick or thin. Respect, honor, all that."

Francie had shaken her head. "Okay. Well, good luck then. Because I don't believe there is one such person for each of us."

"What about Dylan? You said you'd never gotten over him when you met again in Paris."

"That doesn't mean he's my soulmate. You can't expect—wait, are you that much of a romantic, Elise? The earth moves, then a big fancy wedding? Love, honor, obey, 'til death do you part?"

"Of course not. Ugh. That's so—" Elise had stopped talking then, the mental pictures crowding out her words. She had realized she did want something like that, something beautiful and pure and magic. The love that never dies. Or she'd settle for a hot romance with no obstacles at this point.

"Oh, Elise," Francie had said sadly. "I can see you have ideas about this. You need to work them out. Nobody— and I do mean, nobody— is going to save you and make your life special with their undying love. Love is great but it does not conquer all your troubles. That's a myth. You're still you. You know that, right?"

"Sure. I know that." *What if you wanted to be somebody else?*

Francie had taken her hands. "You know that montage in the movies about two-thirds of the way in, where the love bomb explodes, the girl is swept off her feet, the boy brings her breakfast in bed, the sweet birthday surprises, the big diamond ring, the babies—"

"What? There are never babies."

"Okay, but all the rest. They leave out all the ugly stuff, when the shine is off. The time apart, when he works on the other side of the world and you're lonely. When you're having popcorn and cheese for dinner again in your shitty apartment. The arguments about leaving the toilet seat up and picking up your socks and whose turn it is to cook. The times you're not in the mood and he calls you a cold bitch. All that is relationships, all of that is life."

Elise had stared at her. "Who called you a cold bitch?"

"Tom. Does that surprise you?"

"Well, Tom." Francie's now-deceased ex had been a piece of work. "He was probably drunk."

"Not an excuse."

"No. Definitely not."

Now, as she gazed up at the stars, Elise thought about Scott. Her old boyfriend would never mistreat her like that. He would fawn over her endlessly. She couldn't take that either. It made her nauseous.

Conor appeared at her left shoulder, reaching for her ice cream bowl. She looked up and smiled as she handed it to him. "Thanks."

"No problem."

He was walking away when she asked, "Can I help with the dishes?" He motioned her toward the house with his head.

She hadn't seen Conor much since the bat-catching incident and her subsequent rant at breakfast. Everyone tiptoed around her. Heidi and Britta had forgiven her and held a seat for her at meals but the male students were definitely aloof. It was fine. Better than the reverse. She doubted any of them would be brave enough to ask her to dance tomorrow. Did she want to be asked? She had to admit that a twirl around the town square wouldn't be the worst part of this vacation.

Natacha and Vivianne were into the suds up to their elbows, washing and rinsing a tower of plates and bowls and glassware. Conor set the bowls down next to Vivianne then held out a hand. "Give me the sponge. I will take over."

Vivianne looked surprised and pleased as she passed him a scrubber and dried her hands on a towel. Elise stepped up next to Natacha. "I'll rinse."

Natacha backed away from the double sinks, hands aloft in retreat, smiling broadly. *"C'est une bonne idée!"*

The two women dashed outside. Elise laughed. "I guess they thought we might change our minds."

"It is a big pile," Conor said. "But they already did most of it." The entire kitchen table was covered with pots, pans, plates, and silverware.

They worked in silence, Conor scrubbing, Elise running plates under the faucet and stacking them on the table. Nobody dried the dishes apparently as they would be in use again shortly.

"So, tell me about this party tomorrow. Is it every Sunday?" Elise asked.

"Oh, no. But there does seem to be an uncommon number of *fêtes.*

This is for the lavender harvest, a special one. The lavender farms sell products, bunches of lavender, oils, all that."

"Oh, so it's like a regular market?"

"No, not really. It's more like a *fête*. A festival."

"Which entails what?"

"Music, food, wine, dancing. Small children running around. Old men kicking up their heels. General merriment."

It sounded fun and they had all been working hard. They deserved a day off and a party. "So, I never gave you back your shirt. Sorry. I'll try to remember it tomorrow. I'll bring it to the fête."

He looked at the sudsy water for a moment. "I won't be there. I have a tournament in Avignon."

"A tournament?" She raised her eyebrows and glanced at him. "Like—jousting? Don't tell me! You're a Knights Templar re-enactor."

He smiled. "Golf."

She frowned. "Oh, you're a golfer. I didn't know."

He gave her a strange look. "Seriously?"

She shrugged. "Should I have known? Wait, are you famous?"

He tried to suppress a grin. "A little."

Elise took a bowl from him and rinsed it. "What do you mean? Are you kidding me? You're a professional golfer?"

"Is that so strange?"

"But you're a farmer."

He laughed. "This is my cousin's farm, *ma cousine* Vivianne. Her mother and my mother grew up here."

"But you work here. You live here."

"For a couple weeks in the summer, that's all. To help with the harvest. It's my way to stay connected to the family land, to France."

"Wait—where did you grow up?"

"London."

Elise didn't know what to say. She had so pegged him as a French farmer that to see him in another way was difficult. She struggled to picture him in a swanky suit in London, or in plaid golf pants. Her stubborn brain refused. He wore dirty coveralls and boots caked with mud. His neck was filthy. He wore corgi boxer shorts. He was afraid of bats.

What was wrong with her, that she could be so wrong about a person? Finally, she blurted out: "I'm sorry. I wish someone had told me."

Conor stopped washing dishes. "Why? Does it matter?"

"No. Of course not." But obviously, it did, and he could tell.

"Okay." He felt around in the suds. "We're done."

BACK IN HER room that night Elise saw she had yet another email from Scott. In this one he sounded desperate, or tipsy maybe. "I just want to see you again, darling. Can I still call you 'darling?' It sounds so old-fashioned, doesn't it? Well, I am old-fashioned. I want a family, with you, Elise. I won't make demands on you, honestly! We can adopt. I will raise the kids myself—"

Ugh. She couldn't read anymore. He was making a fool of himself. It made her sad that he was so crushed by their break-up that he had no self-respect. She should have found a better way to break up with him. They had dated for not quite a year but it seemed much longer to her. She had been wanting out for months.

She leaned back in bed, trying to get the little fan to blow on her face. She thought about Conor's revelation that he was in fact not a tractor driver but was a professional golfer. Was he serious? Maybe it was a prank he was pulling on her.

She entered his first name—she never had learned his last name—and "golf" into the search engine. And bingo, there he was: Conor Albion, British junior champion for two years then on the pro tour. In Australia, in the US, in Scotland. There he was at some horse-racing shindig, caught grinning with his mates, then there he was with his girlfriend, some slut named Sarah. Oh, she wasn't a slut, she was the daughter of a duke or something. La-dee-dah.

Elise slammed her iPad shut, mad at herself. Why did it matter who his girlfriend was? It wasn't as if she liked him or anything. Still, he had given her that look as he headed down the stairs in his boxers. Such a fine body, she had to admit. A body a princess could love.

Oh, stop it, Elise. You've still got a Hollywood film plot in your head. No love bomb will be exploding. This is life, silly girl. Just life.

CHAPTER NINE

*P*ascal d'Onscon waited to get out of his car, parked in the shade of a spreading evergreen near the winery thirty miles south of Bordeaux. He had seen Merle's text earlier but re-read it, feeling her joy and letting himself smile in it.

The last months had been difficult, living out of a hotel room. It was easier if Merle wasn't there but he hated that too. The room was so small it nearly suffocated them. They were constantly on top of each other, picking around clothes and books and *everything*. Eating out every meal had become ruinously expensive. Now, with this town-house, they could live like real citizens, real lovers, again. He clicked on the photograph, enlarging it. The place looked amazing. He knew the street, vaguely, and approved. Bordeaux had some dangerous neighbor-hoods but this was not one of them. This avenue was perfect.

Merle had sent the lease agreement as soon as she'd received it from the property agent. The owner hadn't signed it yet, he saw, but that gave him time to read it thoroughly. He glanced at his watch. 'Thoroughly' would have to wait. He scanned it, saw the agent had penned in some extras to be included: furniture, beds, bedding, refrig-erator, range, rugs. The paintings did not stay, oh well. It seemed they would need to only bring a plate and spoon and a few rock-and-roll posters. It would be like college again.

He went back to the beginning of the agreement and read the owner's name. Henri St-Jean Delcroix. A name you didn't forget. Merle said he was in the government. Pascal copied his name into the search browser and found that he was currently vice-chair of the regional council, a man with a significant amount of power. Apparently, he was old now, past seventy-five, and had moved in with his brother because of the stairs.

It all seemed quite plausible but something made Pascal's neck hair tingle. He finally registered the amount of the rent they'd agreed on. The number was low for a large townhouse in a prestigious neighborhood, and a furnished one at that. He had to squint to make sure the decimal point wasn't misplaced. Merle said it was because he was a policeman that they'd gotten a discount. That was a pretty big police discount. What would come along with that, he wondered. What would this Delcroix want from him in return?

He took a breath and tried not to be suspicious. It was the nature of the police. Everyone had an angle; he'd learned that much about life. Whether it was benevolent or not was another matter.

The black Range Rover pulled into the drive ahead of him, pointing toward the squared-off tower of the old winery. Pascal sent Merle a quick text, saying it all looked fine on the lease agreement. And it did, of course. Until, perhaps, it didn't.

He stepped outside into the dry summer heat, smelling the bitter tang of the soil as the gravel absorbed the sunlight, straightening his sore back, locking his car. He brought his sunglasses down from his hair, jamming them into place on his nose then cursing with the over-eager gesture. His nose had taken so much abuse over the years.

And then it was time to work, to interview a *vigneron*. To suss out the guilty, lean on the innocent, separate the wheat from the chaff.

The secrets of Henri's townhouse would have to wait.

CHAPTER TEN

*T*he village square was strung with triangular purple flags, as were the three roads that led into the center of Bellemont. When the guests at Le Refuge de la Lavande arrived, shuttled into town in shifts in the Vernay family car, the market was well underway. Stalls lined three sides of the *place*, full of everything lavender: soaps, sachets, bouquets, garlands, oils, and more. Dozens of people, tourists and locals alike, strolled the cordoned off streets and relaxed in the center of the village. Folding chairs filled that area, next to tables covered in white paper and decorated with vases of lavender and tied with purple ribbon.

Elise climbed out of the car with Heidi and Britta, the three of them inseparable outside of fieldwork by this point. Safety in numbers, Elise told them. So much older than them (Britta was only nineteen, she'd discovered), Elise felt like a mother hen, especially after her breakfast rant. That speech had never been mentioned, just as she had instructed, but the consequence of it, a tense standoffishness from the male students, was obvious.

Standing in the afternoon sunshine, Elise looked curiously at the crowd. Lots of ladies with fair English complexions, men of a certain age. Young families, dragging children along. She was looking for

Conor, she admitted to herself. At least he was close to her age and talked to her. Then she remembered: he wasn't coming. Oh, well. She'd worn an off-the-shoulder blouse she'd bought especially for this trip, in a pale lavender color. With tight white jeans and wedge espadrilles, she thought it was the perfect south of France outfit. Britta and Heidi wore cut-off jean shorts and midriff tops. They looked casual and cute and teenaged.

As the three of them walked into the market, heads turned. Elise may have overplayed her outfit, looking too shiny and obvious with lots of shoulder showing. The younger girls got lots of looks but didn't pay any attention, chattering about what they would buy, sampling the lotions, sniffing the sachets in paisley cotton. Elise straightened her sun hat and put her bare shoulders back, trying to look nonchalant as she wandered to an earthenware booth with Provençal dishes in every color, decorated with cicadas.

Slipping her sunglasses down her nose, she checked the price on a set of adorable mugs. She squinted at the label, realizing she was going to need reading glasses soon. She moved her hand farther away until the writing came into focus.

"Nothing so cheap here, is there," a man said, very close to her. Her head popped up. Dark eyes under darker eyebrows twinkled as the man looked at her, up and down. She stepped back and assumed a startled look.

"I beg your pardon. Were you speaking to me?"

He was a handsome devil, she saw immediately, and doing what devils do, trying to pick up random women. His black hair was slicked back but coming loose, held by sunglasses on top of his head. He had very white teeth and a wide, sensual mouth, twisted into a smirk. "I was, madame. Is that allowed?"

She shrugged her bare shoulders and went back to the mug, feeling his stare. "This says seven euros. Is that right?"

"Let me look." He reached out for the mug, taking his time brushing her hands with his large, warm ones. He wore a short-sleeved blue shirt and baggy white linen trousers with soft black loafers, no socks. Was he a tourist, she wondered? Doubtful but he didn't look like a farmer either.

"Definitely seven." He handed her the mug. "How many do you want? Perhaps I could get you a price."

"Really? I do like a bargain." Elise glanced at the man minding the booth, a grouchy sort in dusty working clothes and a straw hat with a broken brim, chewing on a piece of straw. "I never haggle very well."

"Haggle?" His eyebrows pinched together.

"Bargain for a better price." She leaned toward her new friend, suddenly conspiratorial. "Would you? I want four green ones."

"Only mugs? Not full sets of dishes for your beautiful home?"

She smiled at his obvious fishing. "Just mugs."

He nodded, taking back the mug and stepping up to the vendor. He rattled on in a soft, friendly way. It made absolutely no impression on the vendor. He shook his head several times and finally said, "*Sept euros, monsieur. Sept. C'est définitif.*"

Her new friend turned to her and shrugged. "He says final but it never is." He turned back to the man and whispered in a low voice. Whatever he said must have been menacing as the vendor's face froze for a second and he mumbled his answer. Her friend turned back again.

"He will give you one euro off each mug. Twenty-four euros for four, okay?"

As Elise dug out her money she wondered if the two men were working together, reeling in young, naïve Americans. Oh, well, she got her four mugs anyway. The vendor wrapped them in newsprint and handed them to her. "No sacks," he said, shoving them across the table.

"You have a market basket? They outlawed plastic bags here years ago," her new friend said.

"No, but it's okay." She swung her backpack around and placed the mugs in it, then hoisted it back on her shoulder. "There. Thank you, monsieur." She nodded to them both as she turned to go.

Linen Trousers caught up with her, as she expected he would. "*Attendez, madame.*" He put a hand on her wrist. "We must introduce ourselves, yes?"

His name, he said, was Arsène. She told him only her first name as well. It felt a bit coy and out of character to her, but who was this guy? His English was good, with a delicious French accent. As they walked through the stalls, he stayed with her, telling her about this cheese, or that herb mill, or his own small *mas*.

"What exactly is a *mas* anyway? I've never understood that term," Elise said, picking up a pretty bunch of lavender tied with raffia and burlap. Twenty euros? She set it down. She had plenty of lavender at her disposal.

"Ah, come sit with me, have a glass of wine and I will explain," Arsène said, waving toward the tables. "There, in the shade. Madame?"

His manners were quite nice, she had to admit. In some ways he reminded her of Bruno, the rogue who had lured her out of Scotland. She had wiped that incident from her mind, she was happy to discover. It no longer came back in the middle of the night, or any time. She had put it behind her. Except for that French accent.

Arsène had the dark good looks of Pascal, she thought, settling into a hard chair under a plane tree. Not as tall as Pascal, he had a strong chin and a dark tan. She set down her backpack carefully. Maybe she would buy a market basket while she was here. Oh, and sunscreen and all those things she'd forgotten. She glanced around for a shop and saw the green cross of the pharmacy. But it was Sunday, and the day of a *fête*. No shops were open.

He returned, trousers flapping, with two glasses of icy rosé. She took hers gingerly, trying not to appear too eager. But rosé, in Provence, in the summer, at a lavender *fête*, with a dashing Frenchman? A pleasant frisson of satisfaction descended on her. She blinked to make sure she wasn't dreaming.

"Is good?" He asked, urging her to sip. She obliged and nodded.

"*Exquis*," she said, proud of her new French word for delicious and delightful. Heidi had taught her the word.

"Your accent is adorable." He smiled warmly at her. "And mine? Terrible, am I right?"

"No, not terrible. Quite good. Where did you learn English?"

"At school. Then I travel a bit."

Elise watched the people and sipped again. "You were going to explain what a *mas* is," she said.

He leaned forward, eager. "Ah, yes. A *mas* is a farmhouse, nothing more. No fancy château, no palace. Just an old stone farmhouse with a garden for vegetables and some ancient rose bushes."

"A farmhouse in the Luberon. Sounds nice."

"Oh, it is. I would love for you to see it."

She peeked over her sunglasses. "Whoa there." She bit off saying, *Big boy.*

He gave an abashed, crooked smile and leaned back. "I'm sorry. People always tell me I scare them by going too fast. I know I drive too fast."

"You didn't scare me, Arsène."

"I am glad. I get so—how do you say—enthusiastic."

"I can see that." She looked him over, took off her sun hat, and set it on her backpack. "I like decisiveness in a man."

He preened a bit at that. Elise chastised herself: *Dear god, what are you doing?* But she was on a roll. She was single and in France and what were rules anyway? She decided right then and there that she would see where this roll went.

"So, tell me, what type of car do you drive too fast?"

THE CONVERSATION, a blatant flirtation from both sides, went on for about an hour, as the crowd grew in the *place* and the afternoon faded into evening. People sat near them at the table, making a chat less private. It was time to end this. Elise saw Heidi and Britta watching her, whispering. Finally, she put her hat back on, picked up her backpack, and stood up.

"Well, monsieur, it's been a pleasure. Thank you for the wine. *Au revoir.*" She turned to walk around the chairs, brushing her head on the drooping leaves of the plane tree.

Arsène jumped up, nearly knocking over his chair. "But surely, you do not leave, Elise. We will have a dance later, when the band starts to play?"

She looked back over her shoulder and shrugged. "If I see you."

His face drooped. She kept walking toward the girls, a little laugh of triumph bursting out of her. She was finally getting the hang of this French *femme fatale* business.

Heidi and Britta peppered her with questions about the handsome man she had been talking to for so long. Their eyes glowed, looking over her shoulder at him. "He is so sad, Elise. His head hangs low," Heidi laughed.

"Oh, well," Elise said breezily. "There are plenty of men here. Who have you met?"

They walked together around the plaza, pointing out items they would like to buy, things they thought were quite ugly, and gossiping about all the old men who leered at them.

"I think this is a matchmaker's market," Britta said. "I feel like a chicken at the grocery."

"Well, chickie, you could have worn a little more clothing," Elise said. "Although with these men it wouldn't matter. They just enjoy looking. I think they're harmless."

"And toothless!" Heidi exclaimed.

The food stalls were almost open, pushing away the lavender booths for delights of supper. They walked by vats of *coq au vin*, chicken swimming in red wine and onions, sausages and ribs in sauerkraut, beef kabobs, crêpes of all flavors, *tartiflette*, a cheesy soufflé, and even tiny slices of foie gras for an exorbitant price. Heidi chose the *choucroute*, the ribs and sauerkraut, as it was obviously German. Britta sprung for a slice of foie gras and bought a small baguette to gnaw on. Elise bought a crêpe with cheese and ham. They snagged chairs and set down their paper plates.

"I'll get the wine," Elise announced. She glanced at the girls. "You want wine?"

"*Oui, madame*," they said in unison and laughed.

Elise stood in line for wine for ten minutes and finally snagged three glasses of rosé and a bottle of Perrier. When she returned to the table, Arsène sat in her chair, talking to the girls. When he saw her, he jumped up and held the chair. "Let me," he said, taking the bottle of water from the crook of her arm. "Oh, you need glasses. One moment." He dashed away to find them.

Heidi wiggled her eyebrows. "He's a charmer."

"Smooth operator, you mean? Yes, obviously. Here you go." Elise handed them the wine and sat down. "Is my crêpe cold?"

"Not very likely," Britta said. "It is so hot here. I am not used to weather like this; sometimes I feel faint in the fields."

"You did faint, right?" Heidi said.

"Almost. I had to sit in the tractor and cool off for long minutes."

"Conor helped her," Heidi told Elise. "He was very worried."

Britta blushed as only the very blonde can blush. She hung her head self-consciously. Elise said, "Oh, was he? Did he turn on the air conditioning for you?" Britta nodded. Elise smiled at Heidi.

"Where is Conor anyway?" Heidi asked. Britta's head popped up and she looked around.

"He's not here. He has a golf tournament in Avignon." Elise leaned toward them conspiratorially, lowering her voice. "Did you know he is a professional golfer?"

"What?" said Heidi. "He's not the farmer's nephew or something?"

"He's Vivianne's cousin. And a golfer."

Britta frowned. "But he—he runs the tractor."

"I don't think it's his tractor," Elise said. "It belongs to the farm. He lives in the UK, in London or somewhere."

"But his French is so perfect," Heidi said. "At least to me it is."

"His mother is French. She grew up on the farm with Vivianne's mother."

"Ah." Britta let this new information roll around in her head. "He is not a farmer."

"Nope." Elise washed down a bite with wine.

"He told me he was twice my age," Britta said. "Too old for me."

"He's at least forty, I bet," Heidi said.

Elise said, "Hey, have you guys heard about any trouble on the farm, like some financial problems or something like that?"

They shook their heads, mouths full.

"I overheard an argument. It was in French so I couldn't follow what they were saying but it was heated, you know? Then I found Vivianne crying in the kitchen. I sneaked in to get a glass of wine and there she was, tears on her cheeks."

"Crying?" Britta asked. "A grown woman? I didn't think adults cried. In Sweden, never."

"Not much in Germany either," Heidi said. "But down south here, passions, you know. The Latin blood. But why was she crying?"

"She didn't say. But something upset her. Her husband and another man left the kitchen. I think they were arguing."

"Maybe the French argue and cry about any little thing," Heidi suggested. "She seems fine today."

They turned to see the Vernay family—Vivianne, Guy, Natacha, and Lucas—choosing their supper from the various booths. They had definitely made an effort today, everyone's hair washed and combed, clothes pressed, not a muddy boot or a kerchief in sight. Vivianne had done something fancy with her hair that Elise fixated on: how do French women do it? They look so healthy and happy and *fine*. Was it all the outdoor work, the family working and striving together? The four of them chatted and laughed with their neighbors, giving cheek kisses to all.

"They clean up well," Elise said. Heidi gave her a look. "I mean it, they look amazing."

Britta nodded. "He is always so kind to me. And she is such a fabulous cook. A perfect family. That is what I wish for, one girl and one boy, and a handsome husband."

Elise smiled at her. She really was very young. "Aren't you going to finish college first?"

"Of course. But someday, you know? That is what I want."

"What are you studying?"

"I am deciding between computers and nursing." She eyed Heidi's eyebrows. "What?"

"Nothing." Heidi tilted her head and asked Elise: "Do you have a husband and children back home?"

"Oh, no." Elise scoffed. "Never been married."

"Never?" Britta asked. "Not even a—how do you say it? A live-in? A boyfriend?"

"Oh, sure. Lots."

Heidi leaned in and whispered saucily: "Girlfriends?"

"Not that kind. But thanks for thinking of me."

"But why? Why did you never marry?" Britta demanded. "You have been finished university for how long? And law school too, right? How old are you?"

Heidi swatted her. "Britta, do you ask that in Sweden?"

"Sure. Why not?" the nineteen-year-old cried. Heidi rolled her eyes.

Elise sipped her wine. "I'm forty-two. I may never get married."

"Forty-two. Probably not," Britta agreed. Heidi swatted her again.

Elise almost told them about Scott. He wanted to get married so badly. Was that a reason for a woman to say 'yes'? She didn't think so. That image of the fancy white wedding that Francie's comment had brought to mind faded in a sugary mist. She didn't care about that, not really. She wanted something else. But what exactly? Some excitement, an adventure perhaps. Something that made you feel alive. In a way that idea, that promise, felt freeing, all the glorious possibilities—but it also felt crushing. How would she know when the right thing came along? Was it a man or a job or something else? She didn't want whatever she had right now. Maybe she'd know it when she saw it, like pornography. One thing she knew was that Scott was behind her now, in the rearview, not completely gone but disappearing into the distance.

"Look. You made her sad, Britta," Heidi scolded. "Sorry, Elise."

"Nothing to be sorry about. You haven't made me sad," Elise said, straightening her face. "But you have made me thirsty. I'll get another bottle of Perrier."

"But Ari said he was coming back with glasses," Britta said.

"Who?"

"Your new boyfriend," Heidi said.

"Him? He told me his name was Arsène."

"He told us to call him Ari. He looks like an Ari, doesn't he? Maybe he is from Israel," Britta mused. "I love Hebrew names. I will name my boy Noah. Or maybe Joshua."

Amazing how a little wine loosened a girl's tongue. Elise was turning away to get back in line at the beverage booth and there he was. Ari, holding four plastic cups and another bottle of Perrier and a fresh, uncorked bottle of Provence rosé. He beamed sheepishly.

"I am taking so much time, so sorry. Everyone talk and talk and talk."

Heidi moved over one chair so there was an empty one next to Elise's. "Come, sit down, Ari. Talk to us!"

BY THE TIME the dancing started Elise was in a very happy mood, along with everyone else. A breeze like liquid sunshine, delicious food, cool wine, lavender everywhere, male admirers—it was a wonderful *fête*. She turned down Ari's request to dance and sent him out on the dance floor with Britta, then Heidi. He danced quite well, much better than the girls who had no idea what they were doing, all arms and legs. Ari was wiry and flexible, unlike some of the clumsy, muscled farmers. The gypsy music the band played was enjoyed by the oldest and youngest, as grandfathers danced with toddlers, mothers with small boys, grandmothers with strapping lads. The farm stay crew mostly watched although a couple of the enthusiastic English boys found girls somewhere and spun them awkwardly around the makeshift dance floor.

Around ten, Elise began to wonder how and when they would get back to the farm. She should have thought about this earlier. Where was Monsieur Vernay? He had driven them into town. Heidi and Britta were dancing with the Czech boys now. That was a sight. She glanced around for Vivianne or Guy. Shadows encroached, making anyone beyond the lights strung between the trees difficult to see. She stood up to look around, hoping they hadn't left already.

And there was Ari, his hand outstretched. "Madame? If I may?"

CHAPTER ELEVEN

$\mathcal{A}$rsène—Ari—had an incredibly light touch. Just a twitch from his fingertips set Elise spinning, then back into his arms to do it again. She couldn't believe how he made her look like she could actually dance. None of her male acquaintances at home knew how to dance like this, so effortlessly, so smoothly, light on their feet, making it all seem so easy.

The music helped. The band had transitioned into some Spanish ballads more suitable for ballroom dancing than your basic gyrating. The night sky was dark purple, velvety and soft. Ari was damp with sweat. He must have danced every dance. Elise felt privileged, somehow, to be on the dance floor with him.

A twirl and a dip and she was back on her feet, breathless. The tune finished. The band set down their instruments.

"Is it over?" Elise said, dabbing her cheeks with the backs of her hands.

"I'm afraid so," Ari said with a smile. "But there is always another *fête*."

They walked back to the table where Elise picked up her backpack. Heidi and Britta were nowhere to be found. "Have you seen the girls? The ones who were with me?"

Ari looked around the thinning crowd. "Where could they be? Did they leave?"

"I better go look for them."

"I will come with you." He stuck out a gallant elbow. "This way, we will find them."

They circled the tables, the empty food booths, the men folding up the chairs. No sign of the girls. "Maybe they went home already," Elise said. "I'm just surprised they didn't find me to go with them."

"Ah, they probably thought you were finally having a great swing around the dance floor and didn't want to interrupt."

She smiled. "Well, that was true. You are a fabulous dancer, Arsène."

He shook his head but didn't disagree. She took her hand off his arm and repositioned the heavy backpack. "I should go. It was great meeting you."

They were at the edge of the lighted area, near the bandstand. Elise took a step and caught her shoe on the lip of the wooden dance floor, pitching herself forward. She gave a gasp then Ari caught her arm, pulling her upright and holding her close.

He smelled like lemon oil and sweat and wine. She put a hand on his blue shirt and felt his warm body. "I can take you home, Elise," he said in a low purr.

She took a step back. "No. I mean, it's not necessary. I just need to find—"

Ari was looking over her shoulder, his face darkening. She turned and saw Conor, standing at the edge of the *place*. He took a step closer, into the light. "I'm leaving, Elise. Heidi sent me to find you. I have the car."

"Oh, I—" She frowned, looking between the two men. "I thought you were at your tournament."

"I was." He paused. "Are you coming?"

"I am giving her a ride home," Ari said. "You can go on your way."

Elise winced. His tone was so dismissive. Was there something going on between them? Before she could make up her mind Conor disappeared into the darkness. The crunch of his shoes on the gravel faded into the night.

"No. Wait! Conor!" She walked quickly in the direction he'd gone. There was no sign of him, or the girls, or the car. She turned back to Ari. "Well. That's that, then."

DESPITE THE USUAL niggling fears of the single woman, of being squeezed into some compromising position, Elise found that Ari acted the perfect gentleman on the drive back to the farm. His car was, just as he'd told her, a BMW. It looked like an ordinary blue sedan to her, like Pascal's old green one but newer. The fact that he had a BMW like Pascal was reassuring. Not only did he have black curly hair like Pascal, they drove the same car. Was he a cop too? It seemed unlikely.

Ari drove carefully out of the village, toward the farm. He knew the place, he said, she didn't need to give him directions. Elise leaned back in the leather seat, suddenly very tired. He turned at the big sign and in a moment, they were parked in front of the house. He put the car in park.

"*Bonsoir, madame.* It was lovely." He smiled at her. She set her backpack in her lap and took the door handle. Before she could say goodbye, he asked, "Could I call you perhaps? Do you go back to the US soon?"

She looked at him, considering. What could it hurt? "Not too soon. Give me your phone."

He handed over a large black cellphone. She tapped in her name and number and handed it back. "It will be international rates."

He smiled. "I can handle it."

She got out. "Thanks for the ride. Good night."

He put the car in gear, pressed the accelerator, and shot gravel as the tires skidded down the driveway.

MORNING CAME VERY EARLY. Elise rolled over in bed and opened one eye at the alarm clock. She jammed her palm against the buzzer. Monday morning: always a delight.

Hastily dressed, she made her way down to the kitchen, eager for a strong cup of coffee. She wasn't quite awake until she had her coffee.

But she noticed the silence that fell over the room as she entered. The students all stopped talking, looked at her then glanced away. Of all the body language, she knew that one. They had been talking about her.

Elise stood near Vivianne as she made her *café crème*. The farmer's wife looked tired today too, with her pinched mouth and puffy eyes. Had she been crying again? Or just a long night at the *fête*? Vivianne handed over her coffee without a word and Elise perched at the end of the long bench.

No one spoke to her. Their conversations between each other were low, almost whispers. There was a strange tension, an animosity, as if she'd betrayed someone or done something horrendous. She drank her coffee, grateful for that pleasure, and ate a stale pastry. The ache in her stomach, the one that came when she felt lonely and low, was back. All the pleasure of the day before was gone, evaporated.

Elise squinted at each of the students, trying to eke out what had happened, what she'd done. Why were they being so mean? Was it the rant? Wouldn't one of them tell her?

Heidi and Britta kept their shoulders hunched, eyes averted. They hadn't saved her a seat this morning as they usually did. It was like middle school all over again, the juvenile squabbles, the backbiting, the popularity slams. Elise told herself she was above all this. She was an adult. She wasn't going to let a snub, or whatever this was, ruin her day. She wasn't in seventh grade anymore.

Then Conor entered the kitchen.

He got a cup of coffee from the urn by the stove, the weak 'American' stuff that most of the Europeans hated. Elise hated it too and was confused by Conor's liking it. Wasn't he half-French? He rarely sat down with the students at breakfast. He looked tired today too although on him it still looked pretty good. She blinked away the thought, concentrating on her yogurt. When she glanced up, he was staring at her in a cross way and she felt her spirits sink again.

No. They did not have power over her to make her feel bad. She raised her head and put her shoulders back. She would not let them affect her. What had she done? Talk to Arsène? Get a ride home with him? Was that it? She was her own woman. They couldn't tell her what to do with her life.

On the other hand, it was the longest meal of her life. Only thirty minutes, but an eternity just the same. She took her dishes to the sink. As she passed Conor, she couldn't help a pleading look but he wasn't looking at her. Outside the kitchen door, she paused to put on her sunglasses and hat. Angus and another British student came through the door behind her. The room burst with talking, laughing, arguing, now that she was gone.

She looked at the pale blue sky and sighed. How many days did she have left here? Four? She couldn't take the silent treatment. She wasn't built for that level of humiliation.

The workday began, in the same tedious manner that every day on every farm in the world began. Chores were assigned, the crews spread out. Elise was assigned to clean the distillery, a job no one wanted. She didn't want it either. She set her jaw and congratulated herself on not whining.

She was washing glass jars after lunch when Ari called. Her hands were soapy so she let it go to voicemail. No point in looking too eager, although the thought of someone who liked her and talked to her and was an adult was a definite draw. Her morning companion had been the old man again. All he did was grunt and point. She didn't even know his name.

Drying her hands, she stepped out of the distillery into the sunshine. Across the yard Conor drove the tractor from one field to another, cutting the stems of the lavender. Dusty puffs rose behind the tractor. In the distance she saw two groups of students, working in the fields, bundling sheaves of lavender. She punched the button and listened to her voicemail.

"Bonjour, Elise, it is me, Ari. I have an idea we go to dinner tonight in a village nearby. There is a restaurant that is open on the Monday so I always try to go on that day. What do you say? I pick you up at seven? Call me. Ciao."

The door to the retail shop in the front of the barn creaked open. Natacha poked her blonde head out. She saw Elise and quickly went back inside. Elise sighed. She texted Ari that she would be delighted to go to dinner and that she would be ready at seven.

"With bells on," she muttered as she put her phone back in her pocket.

ELISE QUIT early to get into the bathroom before the others. The hallway was quiet at five as she gathered up her washing-up supplies—a tiny borrowed bottle of shampoo, almost gone, a sliver of somebody's soap, a not-too-clean washcloth, and her towel. It was almost relaxing to plunge into the soapy depths of the tub. But not as nice as it had been at the start of this adventure. She didn't linger.

As she lay in her bed in her underwear and bra, the fan doing its best to cool her, Elise listened to the students arrive from the fields. She heard Heidi and Britta chatter in German, another language that the Swede was fluent in. Elise couldn't understand a word and felt, stupidly, they were discussing her. Then three of the boys clomped by, slamming their doors at the end of the hall. Heidi and Britta faded away and the hallway was silent again. Elise closed her eyes and took a ten-minute nap.

At 6:45 she made her way down the two flights of stairs, walking carefully in her wedge sandals. The day before at the *fête* had been the first time she'd worn them, and now she realized how uncomfortable they were, squeezing her toes and causing wobbly ankles. How had she managed to dance in them at the festival?

In the large front hall, paved with colorful tiles, she smoothed her dress. She'd only brought two on this trip, thinking correctly that dressing up would be infrequent. This one was her favorite, a faded rose color with a nipped-in waist that fit her perfectly. She may have lost a pound or two working the lavender fields. How delightful.

Would Ari be on time? He drove fast, so maybe. She checked the time on her wristwatch then on the big grandfather clock. Wait here or outside in the heat: those were the choices. Before she could make up her mind, the door to the back hall, under the stairs, opened and Conor stepped out. It took him a beat to look up.

He didn't look happy to see her, frowning like at breakfast. She tried to smile. "*Bonsoir,* Conor."

He slowed, looking her up and down in a way that made her self-conscious. What was he going to say about her dress? Was the neckline too revealing? The hem too short?

He passed her silently. At the big front door, he turned back. His voice was almost accusing. "Going somewhere?"

She put her shoulders back bravely. "Out to dinner." He squinted at her. "With a friend," she added.

"You've paid for dinner here."

"Well." She shrugged.

He paused again then asked, "Did you have a good time at the *fête*?"

"It was all right. The food was pretty good. The kids liked the dancing."

"But not you? You didn't dance?"

She looked hard at him, his eyes blue and piercing, as if he was trying to say something with them. Had he seen her dancing with Ari? She swallowed hard. "If you had been there, I would have danced with you."

He dropped his gaze to his feet.

"I wish—" she began. He looked up. His face made her change tack. "Did you play well at the tournament? Was it a good day?"

"Third. Not as good as I wanted."

"But still quite good," she said, smiling. "Congratulations."

He hitched a shoulder. "Who are you going to dinner with?"

She bristled at his tone. "Not that it's any of your business. Ari. Arsène."

He blinked hard, his jaw clenched. "Arsène Delcroix?"

Elise realized she hadn't known Ari's last name. She raised her chin defiantly, knowing it made her look like a petulant child but unable to stop herself. "What's it to you?"

Conor's chest heaved, as if fighting rage. His face reddened. "Do you know who he is? What he's done—"

"What's he done? Tell me." They stared at each other, Conor's lips twitching and Elise's eyes wide with simulated fury. They stood so close she could feel his angry breath on her face.

The sound of tires on gravel came through the door. Elise felt the moment ease. Still, Conor had his hand on the doorknob and stood between her and the yard. She felt almost frightened for a moment, as if he would bar her from leaving, yell at her like she was a naughty child, ruin a perfectly good evening. Make her cry.

"May I—may I go, please," she stuttered, blinking hard.

He opened the door. With a look of disgust, he waved her through it. She paused next to him. "What the hell did I ever do to you?"

CHAPTER TWELVE

$\mathcal{E}$lise tried to be flirty and chatty on the way to the nearby village even though her heart wasn't in it. Ari wore full Provençal garb, tan linen pants and a white silk shirt he had unbuttoned to his sternum to reveal a full chest of dark hair. That made her look away nervously. Then she chastised herself. What was she afraid of? He was just a man, a nice man who was taking her to dinner, who was proud—in a Mediterranean way—of his hairy chest.

She watched the landscape go by. The conversation with Conor hung over her, dampening her spirits. Luckily, Ari had to concentrate on his driving on these narrow country lanes and had little time to talk. Crazy drivers, little vans careening toward home, right down the middle, he explained. He had lost four side mirrors in the last few years from such drivers. Even one on this beloved blue BMW.

He did talk about his car a lot. He told her that the color matched her eyes. Her laughter sounded false but he didn't seem to notice. Maybe she could just laugh like a maniac all evening. What a plan.

The restaurant was called Le Couteau. Ari demonstrated the meaning with a stabbing motion and a laugh. "The Knife. Many good cuts of beef there. Do you like beef?"

"Oh, sure. I love a good steak." She had given up red meat the year before and didn't miss it a bit. But she was no vegetarian. If all they had was beef, she would manage, somehow. "I'm not terribly hungry," she mentioned, trying to get ahead of that.

"I am ravenous." He glanced away from the road for a second. "That is the word? Ravenous?"

"Your English is very good, Ari." She'd already told him this but men, she'd observed, liked compliments even more than women did.

The village was smaller than the one near the farm, just a cluster of old stone buildings at a crossroads. Most of the storefronts looked closed or abandoned. It was strange to find places in this beautiful countryside where people simply gave up on their assets. Real estate contracts were a big part of her law practice. If she even had a practice anymore.

Le Couteau sat at the end of one of a cross streets, where the pavement ended and the farm road began. They sat in the middle of the large dining room, some thirty tables of tourists and locals alike. It was a busy restaurant but not too formal. She wasn't going to have to worry about which fork to use. No white tablecloths here, just the Provençal designs, paisleys and bright colors to set off the deep blue plates and chunky glassware. Elise was glad it wasn't a snooty, oh-so-French place. It relaxed her.

That, and the wine. Ari ordered them a pitcher of rosé. "Just to start us off right," he said with a wink. She watched the people, one of her favorite pastimes anywhere, but always fascinating while traveling. She vacillated between feeling inferior to these chic French women and simply trying to not be too vulgar and American. Sometimes the fitting in was exhausting.

"How was your day today, Elise?" Ari asked her after a long silence between them. Then he laughed at himself. "Oh, that is what my wife would say. Bless her soul."

Elise startled. "Your wife?"

Ari nodded, looking sad. "My late wife. Gone these three years."

"I'm so sorry." She was focused now. "She must have been—" *So young.* "Was she ill?"

He shrugged. "I can't talk about it. It's hard."

"I'm sure. I'm sorry." She sipped the chilled rosé and waited. "You must miss her very much."

"I try—I try not to think about the loss. The void, you know?"

"Of course. I can't even imagine."

He waved a hand. "It's fine to remember. We must remember. Otherwise—" He set his wine glass down on the table. "She was unhappy. How do you say? *Triste. Mélancolique.*"

"Melancholy? Like depressed?" He nodded sadly. "Did she—? Um, harm herself?" Elise whispered. Why had she said that? *Oh god.* She bit her lip, embarrassed.

But he was fine. Nodding more. "In the garage. The car was running. Not this car, not the BMW," he hastened to say. "Her own *voiture*. A silly little Deux Chevaux."

"Your wife drove a Deux Chevaux?" Elise remembered Merle's friend, Father Albert, with his little rattletrap Citröen, the 2CV. It was adorable.

"Oh, *mais oui!* It was her pride and joy. She had it painted purple. That was the silly part."

How had they moved on from suicide to cars? Elise blinked at him, his chest hair blaring out from the white shirt like a siren call. He would talk about cars. He loved them. She looked away, at the next table, where two women were staring at Ari and whispering, heads together.

Without a prelude, Ari grasped her hand across the table, prying it from her wine glass. "You look very beautiful tonight, Elise. Did I say that yet? You do."

She smiled awkwardly. "Oh, aren't you sweet." She pulled her hand away, suddenly feeling the weight of the strangers' whispers, the students' snubbing, Conor's disgust, the ostracizing at the farm, all the troubles back home at Webster, Lake & Osborne. What had happened? Why was everyone turning against her? What had she done?

She had never felt so lost, so sorry for herself, to commit suicide. Never. She had four sisters and lots of nieces and nephews who loved her. And her parents! But she had a little empathy for those who felt the weight of the world on their shoulders.

She felt her eyes fill and reached for her napkin to dab them.

Get a grip, girl.

The waiter appeared. Elise found a chicken something-or-other that sounded good and ordered the chocolate soufflé in advance. Ari ordered a steak and poured her more rosé.

He was quiet. She could feel his eyes on her face, her hands, her décolletage which was much too much for this casual place. Yet other women were dressed similarly. She wasn't being too slutty. Maybe it was him, the way he eyed women in his white silk against his tan and chest hair. It was outrageous. She had the odd desire to touch it, to pet it like it was a small dog, see if it was real.

He leaned forward, closer. "What is it, *chérie?* Why are you sad?"

She shook her head. "It's nothing. I'm sad about your wife, that's all."

"But no. Do not feel sad. You didn't know her."

She shrugged and drank more wine.

"Tell me, Elise. You can tell me anything. It is good to unburden the soul. Who will I tell your most intimate secrets? No one!"

She looked at his earnest face. He wasn't as handsome as she first thought, with those sunken cheeks and heavy eyebrows. He would never be a potential boyfriend. Her comparisons of him to Merle's Pascal were laughable. But here was someone who wanted to hear her troubles. Someone she would never see again. Who knew none of her friends and family. He looked so sympathetic.

She sighed. "It's the farm, Ari. I shouldn't have come alone to that farm. I don't know what I was thinking. All those *children.* Like the girls you met, Heidi and Britta, maybe twenty at the most. I have nothing in common with them and now it appears they've all taken against me."

He frowned. "Taken against you?"

She didn't want to say it was because of him but it appeared to be. But that wasn't all of it. "They don't speak to me, they give me the worst chores. It's not all fun and games at the lavender farm, I can tell you that. It's work, work, work."

"Why do you stay then?"

That was a good question. "I've committed to the full ten days. I have three left."

"Admirable, of course. But if it is making you miserable—"

She shrugged. "There are other things. My job, my boyfriend. . ."

His eyebrows jumped. "Your boyfriend?"

"Ex-boyfriend. We broke up."

"Ah, that does make a person sad."

"I wanted it to work but he just wasn't the right person. Do you know what I mean?"

"*Bien sûr, petite.* We are not all matched perfectly."

"And I—" She hadn't told anyone this. "I quit my job at the law firm. Soon, I mean. I'm a lawyer, you know. But I hate the law. I never want to go back to that place."

"You are a lawyer—an *avocat?*" He looked shocked. "How commendable. And you, so young a person. I did not know."

"Well, we only just met." She smiled, already feeling better with the disclosures. And his expression of awe at her profession was gratifying. It was almost the only thing about the law that was.

Their dinners arrived. Ari was right, the food was amazing here. All around them people were ooh-ing and ah-ing and washing down food with wine. The noise level in the restaurant went up a few decibels. The chicken dish had a mustard sauce that was divine.

Over the shared chocolate soufflé, he studied her again. She felt his gaze but the wine and the food made her mellow, relaxed again. She didn't care anymore. He cleared his throat.

"I have a little proposal. What if, dear Elise, you come back to my house in Aix-en-Provence with me? No need to stay in that awful farm where the work is so demeaning and everyone is so cruel to you. If you stay with me, you won't lose any money that you've already paid, correct? I mean, no hotel rooms, no restaurant meals. Except with me of course and I would pay. I can pay. I always pay." He looked abashed. "*Pardon.* For your meals, I mean."

She smiled. "I thought you lived in a farmhouse around here. A *mas,* you said."

"Yes, when I am in the country. But in town I live near Aix. Have you been to Aix?"

"No."

"It is the most beautiful city. So many trees. And the mountains surrounding. You know Cézanne painted them, many times. He lived in Aix-en-Provence."

"I remember that."

"There are boulevards and universities and bistros. You will love the shopping! It is without equal."

Leaving the farm sounded so good. She felt a rush of recklessness come over her. Should she tamp it down? Should she be the 'good girl' everyone wanted her to be? Why not see how the real French live, not the farmers who used students as slave labor? What did she have to lose except three more days of misery?

Honestly. It was tempting.

"What holds you here?" he continued. "I will give you your freedom. It is not like a man-woman thing. I know all women think that when they look at me. But, it's not. I am not like that. I have the highest regard for women. It is summer, the beautiful season. There are parties, I believe. All the Parisians come down. My housekeeper will make you welcome. She will be there so you won't feel uncomfortable. Come stay with me, your own suite, the pool, enjoy yourself. That is the real France: enjoying life."

A vision of running off with Bruno came to mind. Bruno, the bastard who had seduced her in Scotland at Annie's wedding. She squinted at Ari, trying to determine if he had that same meanness in him. Between Bruno and Scott, she didn't have a lot of faith in her judgment concerning men.

He smiled a lopsided smile and raised his eyebrows encouragingly.

She sipped her wine. "I ran off with a Frenchman once. It didn't end well."

"I'm sorry," he said sadly. "Did he break your heart? All of us are not nice, are we?"

"All American women aren't angels either."

"Now that I do not believe. You are obviously an angel! But you have my solemn word. I will not let any harm come to you. You can come and go as you please, swim in the pool, drink from my cellar. We will go into the city for shopping. Whatever you wish."

She twisted her spoon. Grownup adventures is what that sounded like. The most enticing kind. But could she trust him? She wondered.

"No pressure to do anything? No pressure at all? I don't really know you, Ari. I am very independent. You must promise no midnight ambush."

He laid a hand over his heart. "You have my solemn word. Do anything you wish. I may not even be there! I just hate to see you so unhappy."

She sat back in the chair and crossed her arms. "When are you going to Aix?"

He threw up his hands, grinning. "Tomorrow, *chérie!* Tomorrow!"

The next morning, just before six, as the students dragged out of bed and shuffled down to the bathroom and down the stairs to breakfast, Elise stood brushing her hair, her door wide open. She paid no attention to the kids but made sure they saw her just the same. She'd been up for an hour-and-a-half, getting everything ready. She waited five minutes after she heard the last footfall on the stairs, then she made her move.

AT SEVEN O'CLOCK Heidi climbed the stairs. She hadn't seen Elise at breakfast and wondered if she was sick. No one missed breakfast, even if they were late. Heidi felt bad about the day before when she and Britta hadn't saved her a seat. It seemed petty now. Today they had saved her one but there was no sign of her.

At Elise's door she knocked gently, then a little harder. "Elise? Are you in there? Are you okay?" No answer. "Playing sick today? I know the feeling. Working so hard is not fun, is it?"

Nothing.

She tried the knob. The door swung in and the breeze from the open window swooshed into the hall. The room was empty. No suitcase, no toiletry bag. Not even a bat.

She glanced at the faded purple bedspread pulled tight across the mattress and saw the paper. Ripped from a small notebook it was

folded in half. "M & Mme Vernay," it read on the outside. Heidi hesitated. She listened to the empty hall then opened the note.

She closed it again and walked down the stairs slowly. As she
reached the front hall and turned to go into the kitchen, Conor came
through the door under the stairs. He stopped, looking quizzically at
Heidi then at the paper in her hands.

"What is it?"

"Elise." She handed him the note and watched as he scanned it, his
jaw muscles tight. He thrust it back in her hands.

"Good," he said as he stomped out the front door.

Vivianne was scrubbing pots from breakfast, sweat beading on her
forehead. She looked at Heidi and said, "*Oui?*"

"*Une lettre pour vous.*"

"*Ça dit quoi? Lisez-la moi.*" She waved her soapy hands to indicate she
couldn't take the note and Heidi should read it out loud.

"*Madame et Monsieur.* Pardon me for leaving without saying goodbye. I have had an emergency come up and must go. It was lovely
spending time at the farm. Elise Bennett."

"*Quoi?*"

Heidi translated the letter into rough French. Vivianne shrugged,
frowning, then waved it away. "*Tant pis pour elle. Au revoir, Elise.*"

CHAPTER THIRTEEN

*E*lise woke late, the sun streaming through the east-facing window of the bedroom. It took her a moment to remember where she was. She'd had such a solid night's sleep for once. She stretched and felt luxurious under the silky sheets.

It was nearly nine o'clock. She sat up, wondering if her host, the polite and generous Ari, had looked for her already. He had been good to his word yesterday and treated her with respect. Maybe he was waiting for her to join him for breakfast. She slipped out of bed and got in the shower. A real shower, with hot water and loads of good smelling lavender shampoo and body wash. It was heaven.

They had arrived yesterday, about midday, in time for lunch by the pool. Ari's house was not a palace but still it was large and full of marble floors and counters, fancy crystal chandeliers, expensive furniture, and luxuriant fabrics. Clean and tidy too, thanks to a housekeeper who met them when they arrived and laid out the lunch on the terrace. She was a tall, big-boned young woman whose name Elise didn't catch. They called each other 'madame.'

Elise stood in her towel, staring at her open suitcase on the luggage rack by the closet. She had no clean clothes. She scrounged through the pile for a decent pair of underwear and a wrinkled sundress. She put them on then gathered her dirty clothes into her arms and backed out of the room.

The living room was deserted. She padded barefoot into the kitchen. Also deserted. She kept going, hoping to find a laundry room somewhere. After a few wrong turns into pantries and wine cellars she found it, tucked into a corner of the house. She loaded her clothes, poured in some detergent, and punched a few buttons at random. Miraculously water started filling the washer and the cycle began.

Back in the kitchen, she looked for coffee. Where was Ari? She called his name but there was no answer. Where was the housekeeper? A fancy espresso machine stood by, waiting to be put into service. She looked at the levers and buttons and decided it was too complicated. Instead she stepped through the French doors to the terrace bathed in sunshine. The pool shimmered. Tiny yellow birds flitted through flower beds. No Ari though.

They'd had a quick dinner the night before. Cold chicken, salad, melon, baguette. And wine of course. Then Ari had driven off somewhere, waving as he went through the door.

A discreet search of the house proceeded. No Ari, no housekeeper, no anybody. She was alone. Although Ari had told her he lived in Aix-en-Provence, the house was situated in the countryside between Aix and Marseille, close to a small village but nearly 15 miles south of Aix-en-Provence.

She stood outside the front door, looking for Ari's fancy car. The narrow lane was empty, as was the curving driveway. She could see the village in the distance, about a mile away, at the top of a hill. She could walk there, she thought, and get coffee and sustenance.

She worked on her hair for a while then transferred her clothes to the dryer. She pulled on her tennis shoes, grabbed her hat and purse, and set out for the village. The sun felt warm on her bare arms. She would swim. She hadn't brought a suit but there was must be one somewhere in the house. Or she'd swim naked. Why not? Ari was nowhere to be found. She couldn't remember where he had said he was going. She had been so tired, she'd gone to bed early.

Being left alone didn't make her anxious. She luxuriated in it, after the forced togetherness with all the students and farm workers. She certainly didn't need Ari around to entertain her. His absence was almost a relief. She would eat alone, at her own pace, and with absolutely no chores on her agenda. A real vacation.

The hill was steep. By the time Elise made her way to the ancient village at the top she was damp with sweat. She found an outdoor café and sat down under an umbrella. Taking off her hat, she fanned herself with it, pulled out her cellphone, and settled in for a long, leisurely breakfast the way Provençals intended.

CHAPTER FOURTEEN

BORDEAUX

*M*erle struggled with the tote bags she'd filled at the antiques market in the market town east of Bordeaux. It had been a good haul and she was pleased with herself. She'd gotten up at the crack of dawn to be there early and was rewarded with stacks of white plates with an intricate floral pattern around the edges. Also, a full set of silverware that cost a little too much but was perfect, plus a pile of white linen napkins that needed a good bleaching. The flatware in particular was very heavy, a sign of quality, she was sure. Still, as she set it down on the sidewalk for a minute to rest, she wished she had parked closer to the townhouse.

They had moved in, such as it was—toothbrush, hairbrush, clothes, shoes—on Sunday and reveled in the novelty of all the space. Pascal had gone right out and bought new pots and pans, the heavy enameled cast iron ones so loved in France. It made Merle smile, that being his first purchase. He was a fabulous cook and she had only a meager collection of battered pots in Malcouziac. They went to the grocery two blocks away and stocked up on spices and mustards and pickles, and he had cooked their first dinner in the new place that very night. Unfortunately, they'd had to eat on paper plates because the owner had cleaned out the kitchen cupboards, leaving them nothing but dusty shelves.

It was his prerogative, of course. He had left most of the furniture, taking only the two sagging velvet chairs in the parlor. Merle didn't mind, they had smelled a little. Pascal had marveled at their luck in renting the townhouse so cheaply. He sounded suspicious of the low rate but Merle waved off his concerns. Don't look a gift horse in the mouth, she said, confusing him.

Merle set down one tote bag on the front steps, unlocked the door, and went inside. She came back for the second bag and sighed, heaving it onto the table in the kitchen. Setting up house with Pascal was like a dream to her. Of course, he lived with her in Malcouziac but that was different. She had lived there alone, or with her visiting sisters or her son Tristan, first. And it was such a poky, old stone cottage. This, now, was a shared experience. A housewarming. Together they would make a home.

Running hot water in the big old sink, squirting in dish soap, she carefully washed each plate, bowl, spoon, fork, and knife. She dried each piece and put them away in the drawers she'd lined with printed blue shelf paper. Then, like a good housewife, she walked to the grocery to buy something for dinner.

Grocery shopping had helped her French over the years. She now almost felt comfortable asking for something. After she returned home, she filled the sink again, added a glug of bleach, and threw in the linen napkins. Some had decorative embroidery, some were plain. Some had holes. She swirled them around with a wooden spoon and left them to soak.

At three o'clock she stepped into the back garden. It was overgrown and weedy but she'd spotted a few garden plants in the tall grass and would attempt to rescue them. But now she sat on the steps, enjoying the afternoon sun. She closed her eyes, tipping her face up to the sky. She was in that same position five minutes later, happily thinking of nothing, when her phone beeped. Stasia checking in.

"Willow should be there in the morning! Please send proof of life pix. And thanks again for having her."

Merle sighed. She should have said 'no' or at least 'how long will you be visiting' when Willow asked to stay at her cottage in the Dordogne. She was supposed to pick up the girl, now nearly 23, at the Bordeaux train station and drive her to Malcouziac where she would be left to her own devices. Merle didn't have the energy nor, honestly, the time to play tour director for her niece. She'd been told Willow just wanted a few days away before law school started. She'd been in Paris for almost a week. Now she would decompress in the Dordogne.

As far as Merle knew, her sister didn't expect her to entertain Willow. The girl was resourceful, and cheerful. She would be fine on her own. Still Merle felt a little guilty just dumping her there.

She texted back to Stasia that she couldn't wait to see Willow. Then Stasia replied:

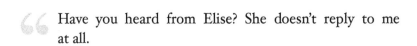 Have you heard from Elise? She doesn't reply to me at all.

I'm picking her up in Provence on Thursday so I can't stay long with Willow. I'll tell her to call you.

The timing had worked out fine. One night in Malcouziac then on to Provence.

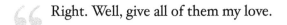 Right. Well, give all of them my love.

PASCAL GOT HOME LATE, as usual in the summer when he liked to do a drop-in at a winery to check in with the *vignerons*. Tonight, he needed a shower before dinner. His hair was damp when he entered the kitchen, rubbing his hands together. "I smell something delicious," he announced. He opened a pot simmering on the stove. "Is it—no. *Blanquette de veau? Vraiment?*"

"Truly. Just for you."

In France Merle had discovered what so many before her knew—
that food is love. That to make something special, to labor over a hot
stove, to fix something deeply satisfying and full of flavor, was to show
you care. She cringed, thinking of all the take-out pizza she served in
the US, or nondescript casseroles, or dry pot roasts, *something* to get
calories into her family. She had never given it a thought. Here, food
was a religion, the growing of it, the picking of it, the selection of a
recipe, then at last, the preparation and the eating of it, slowly,
reverently.

Finished at last, wiping a piece of bread around the bowl to soak up
the last of the sauce, Pascal tipped the rest of the Pinot Noir in his
glass into his mouth. "To what do I owe this amazing meal, with these
fabulous new-to-us bowls and spoons?"

"The antique market in St-Émilion. Isn't it all great? And so
reasonable."

"It is lovely, blackbird."

"Then there is the fact that I must leave tomorrow. Willow, Stasia's
daughter—remember her? She's arriving in the morning and I am
commanded to drive her to Malcouziac where she can commune with
the flowers in the back garden."

He nodded. "I remember. Then what? Elise is done with her farm?"

"Right, the day after next."

"I wonder what she thinks about all that farm work? Have you
heard from her?"

"It seems nobody has. Everyone is in the dark whether she's having
a good time or hates it."

"I vote for Door Number 2."

"That might be why she's not answering. Believe it or not, she
doesn't like to complain to her sisters. She told me once it made her
feel like a whiny brat."

Pascal shrugged. "Well." They laughed.

"She's my sister and I try to help her."

"Ten years younger?"

Merle nodded. "I don't feel like I know her that well. I thought I
did, I started to, then I moved to France and haven't seen her very

much. Remember when we got hit by the paint bomber outside my house?" He raised his eyebrows. "She got pretty worked up about that. But rightly so; her dress was ruined."

"Her dress."

"Seems petty, I guess. But I was mad too."

"Never be angry about a dress, *chérie*. There are so many other things more worthy of your wrath."

They did the dishes together, washing up quickly and putting away the leftovers for Pascal to eat while she was gone. "Oh, I almost forgot," Merle said, hanging up the dish towel. "Our landlord stopped by early this morning. I was on my way to the car. He said he wanted to see how we were doing. He wants to meet you. I told him to come back tomorrow evening. You'll be around?"

"Maybe. I don't think I can plan my schedule around an old man's drop-in."

"No. But don't be surprised. He seemed lonely. Give him a glass of wine."

"*Bien sûr*, blackbird. What am I, a savage?"

THE NEXT MORNING Merle found a parking spot on the street across from the train station. She was early for Willow's train so she sat in her car for fifteen minutes, reading the US news and her email on her cellphone. She read a note from Francie, also about Elise. It seemed no one had heard from her in almost two weeks. Merle assumed the work was harder than expected and Elise was exhausted. Merle wrote back to Francie that she'd report on Thursday, after picking up Elise.

Her sisters sounded worried. Merle had felt that way initially, after delivering Elise to her farm stay, but she'd been too busy with the new townhouse to fixate on it. Plus, this was the new Merle. She was trying to give up worrying. It was a worthless habit that did little to better the world. Action was an improvement on worry, even if the action was minor and inconsequential. Worry was the source of her old 'Calendar Girl' mentality, the obsessive keeper of dates in her head, a walking, talking parlor game, as her late husband called her. A ridiculous habit.

She would not go back to that. She would be active, go forward, plan wisely but not obsess. It was the only way.

Still, as she waited for the light to signal it was safe to cross the boulevard, her sisters' worry seeped into her head. Why was Elise not answering anyone? Was she mad at them? She hadn't mentioned any incidents back in the US that would be the source of anger. You never knew what set people off though. Merle went over the three days she and Elise were together, sifting for odd moments, for telling remarks, and found none.

She found the platform where the Paris Express would arrive and heard her phone beep. *Not another worried sister*. But it was Scott Orr, of all people. Elise's special friend, Scott, who she currently mentioned to no one.

His text was not a new topic: "Have you heard from Elise? I've been emailing and calling and texting but nada."

"No, sorry," she replied. It was odd that she wasn't even communicating with her boyfriend. Or maybe, as suspected, they had broken up.

"You're picking her up on Thursday, right? I would love to be there but...what's your address in Dordogne?"

An odd segue. Maybe he wanted to mail Elise a letter or something. Merle typed in her address in Malcouziac as the train approached the station. She threw her phone in her purse, excited now to see her niece.

As the train screeched to a stop, travelers poured from every car, dragging suitcases and small dogs and children. A dark-haired toddler passed by her and stared. Her heart clanged at his challenging stare— he was so like Tristan when he was small. Then the crowd parted and there she was: beautiful, long-legged, blonde Willow. She saw Merle and ran into her arms, squealing.

"Oh, Aunt Merle, I had the most wonderful time in Paris. I can't tell you how fabulous it was to be there on my own, no pushy mother telling me what to see and where to go and what to eat!" Willow laughed merrily as they walked back to Merle's car. "It was so different from that time when you first came to France, remember? When

Tristan toured Paris with us? He was so sulky, I thought my mother would blow a gasket. How is Tristan, anyway?"

"He's good. He'll be in France tomorrow." Merle unlocked the car and put Willow's bag in the trunk. "You know he's coming to the cottage, right?"

"What?" Willow stared over the roof of the car, eyes wide. "No way!"

"Didn't your mother tell you? He'll be here by the weekend. Saturday or Sunday. He's taking the train to Bergerac then renting a car."

"Oooh." Willow flopped into the passenger seat and put on her seat belt. "Well, that'll be great. And a car, that's awesome. We can roam around."

"You'll still be there on the weekend?"

"Oh, sure."

"Stasia didn't mention Tristan was coming to France?"

"Nope." Willow slouched into her seat. "I am so tired. That train leaves at zero-dark-thirty." She closed her eyes, set her head back on the seat, and went to sleep.

Everyone, it appeared, wanted to come to southwest France this summer. The roads were clogged with cars and trucks. Merle concentrated on getting out of the city, onto the toll road, and beyond, into the countryside. Even though she had driven this route many times now since Pascal had taken his new job, she was glad she didn't have to talk to Willow. She needed to concentrate.

She couldn't wait to see her son. His second year of college had come and gone and they had only been together at Christmas. Had she told Tristan that Willow would be at the cottage? Probably not. Just like Stasia didn't tell Willow. Oh, well, they got along fine. It would be fine.

There were, however, going to be a lot of relatives at her cottage. Merle counted with her fingers against the steering wheel. Tristan, Willow, Elise, herself, maybe Pascal—where were they all going to sleep?

CHAPTER FIFTEEN

THE DORDOGNE to PROVENCE

*M*alcouziac never changed, as far as Merle could see. The last time a new business had appeared, a tiny jewelry shop off the main square, was three years ago and it closed after one season. The walled *bastide* town, dating from the time of the Hundred Years War between the French and the English, sat atop a hill, a few of its gates intact but some of its wall crumbling. The golden stone of the intact portion swept gracefully up, incorporated into buildings and gardens. One such portion formed the north wall of Merle's cottage and garden, giving it the feeling of safety and permanence.

Willow had seen pictures of the cottage but this was her first visit. "It's so quaint and adorable," she exclaimed as they unloaded their bags from the trunk of Merle's Peugeot.

"Small, you mean. Yes, it is. I did some research. It belonged to a winemaker from Toulouse for a while, then a prosperous farmer from the region, then, of course, your Uncle Harry's family."

Willow hugged her duffle bag and stared up at the facade of the house. "Oh, right. Mom told me about that." She glanced at Merle. "Is all that legal stuff finished?"

"Done and dusted." Merle unlocked the door shutters, then the front door behind them.

"No ghosts or bad spirits?"

Merle laughed. "Nothing like that. Maybe a stray mouse, that's all."

The inside of the cottage definitely looked more like a home since Pascal had moved in, bringing with him some paintings he'd inherited, colorful fruit and floral still lifes, plus a hat tree full of coats, and a comfortable armchair, upholstered in blue velvet. The major improvement of the last year was a wood stove in the fireplace that kept them toasty over the winter.

"Oh, this is so sweet," Willow said, throwing her bags at the bottom of the staircase and poking her head into the kitchen, the other major room on the first floor. "I love it. And thank you so much for letting me stay here, Aunt Merle. It's just what I need before starting law school."

"You will be busy once that gets going," Merle said. She squinted at Willow. "Are you sure about law school? You're not doing it just because of—"

"Family pressure?" Willow blurted. "Oh, no. Why would that make me do something I didn't want to do?"

Merle frowned. "Are you being sarcastic?"

Willow spun to face her aunt, eyes wide. "Sorry. No. I mean, of course that was a factor in making my decision. Maybe I'll hate it. Maybe I won't make it past the first year. But it was my decision."

"Keep your options open, Willow." Merle set a hand on her arm. "But if you're going, you should commit yourself. Don't go in half-baked."

The girl rolled her eyes. "Thanks for the advice."

Merle crossed her arms. "So, your mother said the same thing."

"Of course, she did. You know her, full of a million opinions. Now, where am I to sleep?"

Merle showed Willow one of the twin beds in the loft and left her to get settled in. It was just as well, she thought, that she wasn't staying long. Willow seemed less the sweet girl she used to be. Merle wondered if Stasia had sprung for this "last adventure" before law school as a plum for doing her mother's bidding and following the family tradition. There could be no worse reason in Merle's mind. But it wasn't her decision, or her daughter.

Merle drove her car to the city lot outside the walls and walked back, picking up a few things at the tiny grocery along the way—cream, coffee, a couple croissants. The next day was market day and Willow could do her own shopping then. Whether Willow would enjoy herself in the Dordogne was an open question.

They went out to dinner at Les Saveurs, Merle's favorite restaurant, and the conversation was stilted. Willow seemed angry with Merle—or somebody—which didn't exactly endear her to her niece. But she took a photo of her and texted it to Stasia as requested. Willow was squinting into the sun, hand shading her eyes, frowning.

Merle left early the next morning. She left a note for Willow on the dining table, instructing her how to make coffee, to go to the market for goat cheese, vegetables, and sausages, and that she'd be back on Friday or Saturday with Elise. She left the extra set of keys and told her to always lock the house. As she walked to her car in the dawn, she saw her neighbor, Madame Suchet, was out on her stoop, sweeping.

"*Bonjour, Merle,*" she called.

It was a major coup to Merle that she was finally on a first name basis with more than one neighbor. Albert, who lived across the alley, was the exception. They had taken to each other as fast friends since the beginning.

"*Bonjour, Paulette.*" She walked across the cobblestones to greet her. "I'm off to Provence again, to pick up my sister from her lavender farm. Is there anything I bring you from there?"

"*Ah, la belle Provence.*" Paulette's blue eyes shined. She wore a red headband in her gray bob today, looking very girlish for her seventy-plus years. "*Un petit sachet de lavande, peut-être?*"

"But of course. Only one?" One lavender sachet was a very small gift.

"*C'est tout.*" Paulette waved a hand. That was all she wanted.

"*Bon. À bientôt.*" Merle said goodbye and relished the cool morning air as she walked through the wakening village. In the plaza, *la place,* the market was going up, the tables and old wood wagons in a circle, under the arches of the ancient market stalls, spreading out into the open air. She slowed, spying the goat cheese vendor. She loved exploring markets in France. But she had to go. She'd promised Elise she would be there by midday.

It was almost noon when she reached Narbonne, near the coast of the Mediterranean. The traffic had been painfully slow, with road construction, toll booths, and lots of traffic. She was hungry and tired and decided to make a detour to Narbonne Plage, the beach community over the hills from the old town. Surely, she could find a relaxing lunch there. As soon as she arrived, she knew she'd made a miscalculation. The beach town was jammed with people, tourists and vacation homeowners, all clamoring for a meal at the same time.

Instead of lunch, Merle put gas in her car and dug a granola bar out of the bottom of her purse. She gulped some bottled water and got back on the road. She'd gone almost the entire width of France in the last 24 hours and felt a little annoyed with her relatives. Maybe it was just the lack of food.

At Avignon she exited the highway onto the narrower roads that led to the lavender fields of the Luberon. Almost immediately her mood shifted, cheered by the scenery, the roses, the villages, the slower pace. By now it was after two o'clock and her stomach was growling. She remembered the lovely *salade de campagne* she'd had in Belmont, the village near the lavender farm, and decided she would go there and call Elise.

Lunch service was almost over when Merle arrived, breathless from walking quickly from her car. A harried waiter gave her a table and menu. Before he could leave, she ordered her salad and a glass of rosé. She took a breath, trying to relax after hours on the road, and called Elise.

Her sister didn't pick up. Merle left her a message, saying she was eating in Bellemont and would be at the farm in about 45 minutes to pick her up. She apologized for being late. "I can't wait to see you, Elise, and hear all about your farm stay! See you soon."

Merle felt slightly renewed by the time she turned at the sign for Le Refuge de la Lavande and drove up the winding lane to the house.

She'd found a gift shop on the way back to the car and purchased a sachet for Paulette. She hoped Elise would be packed and ready. Maybe they could go to Isle-sur-la-Sorgue tonight. She'd always wanted to explore that town.

Merle parked her car under the big tree again and stretched. The farm was quiet, just the faint mechanical noise of equipment in the fields. She entered the house without knocking. No one appeared so she went back outside and rounded the barn, looking for Elise.

An old man in filthy pants and a battered straw hat appeared from another outbuilding, carrying a sheaf of lavender tied with string.

"*Bonjour, monsieur.*" He nodded warily but did not stop to talk. "*Excusez-moi. Je cherche ma sœur, Elise. Savez-vous où elle est?*"

The man paused and frowned at her. "*Quoi?*"

Merle repeated her request. She was searching for Elise, did he know where she was?

He shook his head and moved on. Not particularly helpful.

Merle looked around for someone else to ask but there was no one nearby. She walked out into the fields. Was Elise still working? She could see some people in clumps, far off. Was Elise out there? A green tractor was chugging toward her, down the lane between the fields. As it approached, she flagged down the driver. He stopped beside her and opened his door.

Merle repeated her question about Elise. He frowned, shut off his engine, and got down from the cab.

"What's this about?" he said in English. He had a British accent.

"Oh. I'm looking for my sister Elise. I'm supposed to pick her up today."

He stared off at the horizon. "She's not here."

Merle winced. "What?"

"She left. A few days ago."

"Elise Bennett? From the US?"

He nodded and didn't elaborate.

"Where did she go? She didn't call me or ...."

"I don't know. She just said she had an emergency and had to go."

"What kind of emergency?"

"That's all she said. In a note."

Merle squinted at him. Was there more he was holding back? If she kept him engaged would he finally spill whatever it was? "My name is Merle Bennett. I live over in the Dordogne." She stuck out her hand. "And you are—?"

He examined his dirty hands and offered an elbow, in the French style. "Conor Albion."

"Are you doing a farm stay too?"

"This is my family's farm. I help out during harvest."

"Do you have any idea where Elise might have gone?"

Conor glanced up and met her eye. "She didn't say," he repeated. He turned and pulled himself up into the tractor and started back down the lane, leaving Merle in a cloud of dust.

Back at her car she called Elise again. "Elise. I am here at the lavender farm. Where are you? What's going on? They say you left. Please call me. You're making me worry."

CHAPTER SIXTEEN

*B*ack in Bellemont Merle went first to the little hotel where she'd stayed the last time. Luckily, they still had one room available, although it was on the top floor and had no air conditioning. She paid for it and took her small valise up the stairs and sat on the bed. Who should she call about Elise? Her sisters claimed to know nothing.

Instead she called Pascal. He would know what to do. But he didn't answer so she texted him, asking him to call. That Elise was now missing-in-action. He called her back within five minutes.

"What's this?" he demanded.

"Elise isn't at the lavender farm. They said she left a note that she had an emergency and had to go."

"Go where?"

"Nobody knows. Or at least the one guy I talked to didn't know. He's one of the owners of the farm or something. A British guy."

"How long has it been since she left?"

"Several days, I think. None of my sisters have heard from her and now this. Why would she just disappear like this? It's so annoying."

It sounded like he was at his desk, papers shuffling. "I don't know. But maybe she wants to disappear for a while."

"What? Why?"

"Why do people usually want to disappear? Others ask too many questions. Or to hide from responsibilities. The usual things."

"I know she doesn't like her job. Maybe that's it."

"Hiding in France won't help her job problems."

"True. And why won't she just tell us? I hate it when people aren't upfront with me. I certainly don't care where she works, or if she's a lawyer at all."

"I know, blackbird. But everyone isn't you."

"Thank goodness."

"I did as you asked and gave our tiny landlord a glass of wine last night."

"Oh? Did you get along all right?"

"Of course. He is a funny little man though. Very curious about the police. Asked all sorts of questions."

"Maybe that's because he is in government."

"*Peut-être*. He stayed for over an hour, grilling me."

"What about?" Merle asked.

"About wine fraud mostly. But all sorts of other things that I have nothing to do with, like migrant workers and gangs and murder."

"Well, he must be lonely, like I said. I better run, *chéri*. I need to find Elise."

"Call me tonight. Maybe I'll think of something."

Merle stretched out on the bed and flicked on the fan on the night-stand. The room was stuffy with heat. She called Francie next.

"Hey." Francie said, rushing on. "I'm on my way to JFK. I'll be in Paris by evening. Woo hoo!"

"Great. Is Dylan there now?"

"Nope. He's right here, traveling with me. You know how nervous I used to get flying? Not with Dylan."

"Lucky you. Listen, Francie. I can't find Elise. I was supposed to pick her up at the lavender farm and they say she left a few days ago. Did she call you?"

"What? That little squirt. What's she up to?"

"I wish I knew. You haven't heard from her?"

"Not since she left here. Wait. She texted me once from your cottage, before the lavender thing. Hang on." There was a pause. "She wrote: 'So nice to be back in France. Merle's garden is bursting with blooms. I am all about the bloom these days. More later.' But there was no more later."

"So, she ran off with a florist?"

Francie laughed. "Anything is possible. Hey, we're here. Gotta go. Text me later."

Merle sighed and closed her eyes, suddenly tired of all the Elise drama. Maybe she should just let her sister disappear, if that's what she wanted. Everyone deserved their privacy. But to not know where she is, who she's with? Not know if she was safe? It didn't feel right.

She searched on her phone and found a recent photograph of Elise. Maybe she could show it around the village and someone would remember seeing her. Was she still in the area? How would she get out of here? Did she take a bus? Or did someone abduct her like had happened to Francie that time?

Merle put it out of her mind. She wasn't going to go with Worst Case Scenario worries, not this time.

Not yet.

AT SEVEN O'CLOCK Merle drove back out to the lavender farm. There had to be someone here who knew what Elise was up to, where she might have gone. She'd been gone only a few days, they said. She could be anywhere by now. She could have gone to Italy or Switzerland or North Africa or the Greek Islands or...well, this travelogue wasn't helping.

She stepped out of the Peugeot and admired the sky. It was turning orange above the fields, a fiery show against the hillside. It really was stunning landscape, as everyone has said about Provence for ages. The smell of something burning came from the big shed. That was where they distilled the essence, she remembered, so they must be busy doing that. She walked to the shed, the smoky char getting stronger, mixed with the sweetness of the herb.

She pushed open the door, just enough to peek inside. The old man she'd seen earlier stood over the big cooker, poking into it with a long-handled rake. She looked around but he seemed to be alone. No point talking to him again.

Merle turned back to the yard. The farm work must be finished for the day. Soon it would be time for dinner. So the kitchen must be occupied. Where was the kitchen?

Back through the front door of the house, still unlocked, she stood for a moment in the hall next to the stairs. Would she find anything in Elise's room? They must have stripped it by now, getting ready for some new farm stay person. But maybe the other residents knew Elise and knew where she went.

One foot on the stairs Merle heard a clatter of utensils, porcelain, and pans, coming from behind the staircase. She rounded the bannister and saw a door tucked in there. She put her ear to the door and heard voices. Ah ha, *la cuisine.*

She pulled open the small round-top door. The smell of garlic and spices wafted out. She followed the delicious trail into a large kitchen dominated by a long, rough-hewn table and benches. In front of a fabulous old Aga range stood two women, one older, one a teenager. Merle recognized the young one as the girl who had shown Elise her room on the first day. She cleared her throat to get their attention.

"*Pardonez-moi, madame. Mademoiselle.*" They turned, startled to find a stranger in their kitchen. "*Excusez-moi.* I am the sister of Elise Bennett. I was to pick her up today and now I've found she's not here. I'm worried. She doesn't answer her phone."

She tried to say all this in her best French but could see the older woman, who must be the girl's mother, frown as if confused. Merle stepped a little closer. She put out her hand and said, "*Bonsoir, madame. S'il vous plaît, excusez l'interruption.*"

Madame straightened, wiped her hands on her apron, and shook Merle's hand. "*Bonsoir.* Vivianne Vernay."

"Merle Bennett," she replied, smiling. "My sister Elise seems to be missing. Does anyone know where she's gone?"

Vivianne looked at her daughter. "*Elle a disparu?*" The girl, whose name Merle now remembered as Natacha, shrugged.

"*Je sais pas.*" She looked wide-eyed at Merle. "I did not see her. She didn't come to dinner, nor breakfast, then—poof!"

"What day was this?" Merle asked.

Mother and daughter exchanged glances. "*Mardi*—Tuesday," Natacha said. "A note was found that morning."

Vivianne said something sharp to her daughter. Natacha dashed across the room to a sideboard full of half-full bottles of wine and spirits. She pulled open a drawer and rummaged around, extracting a small piece of paper. She handed it to Merle. "The note, madame."

Merle read the note. It wasn't very helpful. "What could this emergency be?"

Natacha shrugged again. "She didn't say."

"Is there anyone here she talked to, a friend she made?"

Vivianne was back at the stove, stirring a big pot of something. She muttered something to her daughter. Natacha said, "We didn't have much contact with her except at meals. She worked in the fields like all the students."

"That's what you call them—students?"

"Oh," Natacha said, catching herself. "I mean the others. They are all students at some university." She spoke rapidly to her mother. "In Strasbourg. A foreign language exchange."

"Did she make any friends with the students?"

Vivianne replied. Natacha again translated. "Maybe Heidi? One of the girls. She is from Germany. Her English is quite good."

"Where is this Heidi from Germany?"

Vivianne tipped her head toward the front hall and said, "*Allez.*" Natacha said she'd see if she could find her and ran through the small arched doorway and clomped up the stairs. Merle smiled at Vivianne who turned silently back to her dinner tasks.

"*Merci, madame. Pour l'aide.*"

"*Bien sûr, madame. Naturellement vous vous inquiétez. Votre sœur.*" Vivianne turned to look at Merle. "*Vous ressemblez à votre sœur.*"

"*Oui, merci.*" Although she didn't really see it people were always telling Merle that she and Elise looked alike, even though she was so much younger. "*Elle est beaucoup plus jeune que moi.*"

Vivianne shook her head amiably. "*Ah, non, madame. Ce n'est pas possible.*"

Footsteps approached down the wood stairs and Natacha entered the kitchen, followed by a young woman in a gauzy blouse, pleated skirt, and braids, who could only be someone named Heidi. Merle turned to her, smiling. "I'm Merle Bennett, Elise's sister."

They shook hands. Merle asked if Heidi knew where Elise had gone.

Heidi answered in perfect English. "I wish I did. She just disappeared that morning. I'm sure I saw her in her room as we were going down to breakfast but she never came down. When I went to find her, to apologize for the day before when we forgot to save her a seat at breakfast, she was gone."

"Did she get a ride somewhere?"

"She must have because it was so early. Before seven o'clock. Or maybe she walked into Bellemont."

"Too far," Natacha said.

"She had her luggage. And backpack. No, I doubt she walked," Heidi said.

"Then someone must have given her a ride. Does anyone here have a car?"

Vivianne had stopped cooking and was listening hard. *"Une voiture? Bien sûr."* She said there were several cars at the farm but no one had taken them out that morning. She was sure of that.

"There's no other way to get away?" Merle asked. "A farm truck or a bus or something?"

Natacha asked her mother in French if any trucks had made deliveries that morning. Elise could have hopped on the back of one. But no. Nothing out of the ordinary had happened that morning. Nothing at all. Except the disappearance of one Bennett sister.

"So, someone picked her up," Merle concluded. Vivianne went back to her steaming pot. "Well, thank you." She fished a small notebook out of her purse and wrote her name and phone number on a sheet and ripped it out. "Will you call me if you hear from her, or anything about her?" Natacha took the paper and nodded. *"Merci beaucoup."*

"Bonne chance," Vivianne called as Merle retreated, out the hallway to the front door. Heidi followed her.

"I wish I could have helped," Heidi said. "I liked Elise. She stood up for us when we got caught in an awkward situation. About the bat, did she tell you about it?"

"A bat?"

"One flew in her window." She smiled, remembering. "It was flying around her room; it was quite a commotion. We all went into the hall to see what was happening. I was just in my knickers and vest and poor Britta sleeps almost naked. All the boys got a good look."

They walked out the front door together. Merle turned to the girl who seemed genuinely concerned about Elise. "Did something else happen? Like, just before she decided to take off?"

"Not really. There was some gossip. I don't know."

"Gossip about Elise?"

"It was just stupid stuff. The students can be cruel, you know."

"Cruel about what? About Elise?"

"I don't know." She hunched over miserably. "She was the only older person working with us at the farm. All the rest of us are college students. Britta is only nineteen."

Merle took out her notebook and wrote down her name and phone number again, handing the sheet to Heidi. "Call me if you remember something. Okay?"

The girl nodded. "We leave tomorrow."

Merle drove back to Bellemont and had a solitary dinner at the hotel dining room, full of rowdy tourists from all over Europe and North America. Merle drank one glass of wine and took a second up to her room where she stretched out and tried to think about a game plan for finding Elise. She fell asleep to the sound of the fan whizzing in her ear.

CHAPTER SEVENTEEN

*H*er cellphone was ringing. And ringing. Was it a dream? Was it Elise? Merle sat up in bed, confused for a moment about her whereabouts, still half asleep. She grabbed her phone on the nightstand, knocking the small fan to the floor where it made a gasping sound and died against the rug.

"Yes?" She hadn't looked at the screen. "Elise?"

"It's me, blackbird." It was Pascal. "You didn't call last night as arranged and I am at the office already."

"Sorry. You woke me. What time is it?"

"Not quite seven. You had a good night?"

"I guess." She rubbed her eyes. "I can't remember. I went back out to the lavender farm but nobody knew where Elise had disappeared to."

"Are you still worried? Have you called all the sisters?"

"Not all of them. I'll do that today."

"Do you want me to come and help you? I came in early to finish up some papers. *Le bureau* never stops. But I could leave this afternoon."

"Oh, you're sweet to offer. Let me wake up and I'll think about it, okay?"

Merle stood under a hot shower and tried to get her mind back in gear. This whole Elise thing was so confusing. She didn't know whether she should be super anxious, worried about her disappearance, or be calm and assume the best.

She felt more alert as she walked down the stairs to the breakfast area. Tables were set outside on the terrace in the morning sunshine. On the edge of the terrace a hedge of pink roses scented the air. Beyond them was a vineyard with plump grapes in clusters, still green but with a tinge of purple. She sat with the sun on her back and took a deep breath as the waitress brought her a *café crème*.

The terrace was almost empty, just one other table of guests, a couple sipping orange juice and tea. The coffee cleared her head. She plucked a pastry from the basket and called Elise again. Still no answer. She put her phone away and concentrated on breakfast.

There seemed to be no other choice than to go back to the lavender farm and keep asking people about Elise. She finished her coffee and pastry and went to the front desk to ask about staying another night.

The clerk at reception was a tall, serious man with slicked black hair and a dour demeanor. He told her '*oui*,' she could have the room another night. Then she remembered Elise's photograph on her phone.

"*Pardon, monsieur. Je cherche ma sœur.*" She asked if he remembered seeing her in the village in the last two weeks. He frowned as if annoyed by the request but leaned closer to Merle's cellphone. Then he took it from her and enlarged the photo.

He spoke in English suddenly. "She is American, yes?"

"As am I," Merle said, hope rising. "Did you—have you seen her?"

"At the *fête*. Yes." He handed back her phone.

"When was that?"

"Sunday last. *La Fête de la Lavande.*"

"What was she doing?"

"Just the usual things. Eating, drinking wine, talking."

"Did you recognize anyone she was with?"

He shook his head. "Some kids. From *Le Refuge*, I believe."

"Men, women...?"

"Both, I believe. Two women. Young." He raised his eyebrows suggestively.

That must be Heidi and the other girl. "Can you describe them?"

He shrugged, his interest waning. An older woman wearing a sun hat was waiting behind Merle. The clerk stepped to the side to call her forward, dismissing Merle. "*Merci, monsieur*," she muttered, wondering what, if anything, he had helped.

Back upstairs she gathered her day things: camera, hat, sunscreen, sweater, and backpack. She added the hotel's bottled water. Lacing up her comfortable walking shoes she tramped back down the stairs and through the small lobby to the street.

It was still early. Eight-thirty by her watch. No stores were open yet. The village had the air of dormancy. Summer in Provence meant long, hot days and the residents weren't quite ready for this one yet. She walked a block to the edge of village *place*, shaded with plane trees and strung with old-fashioned bare bulbs. It would be magical during a *fête*. Maybe there was music and dancing. There usually was.

She found a chair under a tree and sat down, discouraged. Elise had been fine on Sunday, whooping it up at a festival, but what had happened on Monday and Tuesday? Why had she left the lavender farm so abruptly? Merle cursed herself for not getting Heidi's contact information. She obviously had been at the *fête* too. Merle hauled her backpack onto her shoulder and walked toward her car. As she reached the sidewalk, she heard a high-pitched voice behind her, calling: "Yoo hoo! Madame, miss! Yoo hoo!"

Merle turned to see the lady in the sun hat in the hotel lobby trotting toward her, brim flapping as she held her hat on with one hand. In her other hand she clutched a handbag of the old school, pink patent leather. The woman waved breathlessly, smiling as she reached Merle and skidded to a stop.

"Oh, my! I don't make a run for it very often," she gasped, clutching her heaving breast. "Give me—just a—"

Merle waited while she caught her breath. The woman was eighty or so, if she had to guess, with frizzy white hair under her enormous floppy hat, wearing the type of shift that used to be called a house dress for its shapeless frumpiness. Finally, rosy and damp, she straightened and gave Merle a big smile.

"Sorry! Hunky dory now." She stepped closer. "I heard you at the hotel. I'm sorry, I was standing right behind you and couldn't help it."

"It's all right. I'm Merle Bennett." She stuck out her hand again and the woman shook it with bony fingers.

"Estelle Longbottom." She laughed, a girlish sound. "Isn't it a silly name? If only my Darren had had another. Oh, well." She waved a hand. "So, something about your sister?"

"Yes. Elise, my sister. I was to pick her up yesterday from her farm stay but they say she's already gone somewhere. No one seems to know where."

"And the *fête,* she was there?"

"According to the clerk."

"Right. I was there too, with my daughter and her family, all down from England. They love to come for the festival, plan it every year."

"Oh. Did you see Elise?"

"I saw someone—can I see her photograph?"

Merle got her phone out again. She scrolled to the photos and handed it to Estelle. She squinted at it. "Yes, I'm, well, fairly certain. Her hair was done up and she wore a big hat like mine."

"Did you see who she was with?"

"The woman I saw—I apologize, I am really one of those nosy old women."

"Thank goodness," Merle said.

"I saw this woman, your sister, I believe, with the two girls who were wearing the skimpiest of outfits, you really couldn't keep your eyes off them. Legs up to here and midriffs bare."

"Was Elise wearing that?"

"No, no, she wasn't like that. Although she did have on that off-the-shoulder blouse. That did attract attention, I dare say."

"Okay. I talked to one girl at the lavender farm. Dark hair, braids?"

"Yes! That was one of them. But also, there was a man. He sat with them a long time."

"Oh? Do you know who it was?"

"I've seen him around the area. French, I believe, or we would have run into him at some picnic or card game. My Darren had a name for him. I think he recognized him. What was the name?" She held her chin, thinking hard.

A name, Estelle. My kingdom for a name. "Do you know what he looked like?"

"Dark hair, very tan. Another sign of not English. Oh." She brightened. "Darren calls him The Cavalier."

"Is that his name—Cavalier?"

"I don't think so. I think Darren means he's rather cavalier about his actions. You know what that means, Miss Bennett? Cavalier?"

"Careless?"

"I believe so, yes. Boastful, flashy, and careless. A nasty package. Either that or it means he rides for King Charles!" She laughed at her own joke, quite pleased. Merle frowned, not getting the reference. She'd have to look that one up.

"So, Estelle. Can we ask Darren for the name?"

"I don't think Darren knows his real name. He can't be bothered with most Frenchmen. Doesn't have a lick of French."

Well, hell. "Do you and Darren live nearby?"

"Farther north. We come down here for the food. Nothing too great near us. We had a bit of wine last night so we stayed over."

Merle went through the routine of writing out her name and cell number on a tiny sheet of paper. Estelle promised to call if she or Darren had a brain flash. Merle thanked her. Estelle headed back in the direction she'd come. Merle walked south to find her car.

Once again, hopes rise and crash. *Where are you, Elise?*

WHEN MERLE ARRIVED at Le Refuge de la Lavande five black taxis of various sizes were parked in her usual spot, under the willow. She parked on the edge of the driveway, half in the ditch. Heidi had told her she was leaving today. It appeared everyone else was too. It was now or never if she wanted to talk to any of the students.

Merle walked up the drive, through the taxis, all of which stood empty. As she rounded the corner of the house, into the backyard, she found the students circling a huge outdoor table with backpacks lining the benches and white forms of some kind in front of each student. Vivianne was handing out peaches and bananas, giving each student a friendly *bisou* on the cheek, and an *'au revoir.'* Natacha followed along behind her, giving each student a small sachet filled with lavender. The boys took it, sniffed, and laughed. Natacha looked hurt.

Merle waited, watching, as whatever was happening wound down. By the back door to the house stood four men and one woman who must be the taxi drivers, lounging and drinking espresso, joking amongst themselves. Several were smoking.

The farmer was signing the forms and speaking to each student as he went around the table. Merle remembered him from Elise's first day. He appeared to take this very seriously, speaking slowly in French to each of them, making sure they understood and slapping them on the back.

"Madame." Merle turned to find the man in the tractor standing next to her. "Can I help you?"

"I just want to talk to Heidi again. And the other girl, about Elise." She glanced at him, freshly showered now, not looking or smelling like a farmer. "Is that possible? Can you ask them to come over or should I just wait?"

The man—Conor, she recalled—suggested she wait. "They must get their paperwork signed or no course credit. It won't take long."

Ten minutes passed and finally everyone had their fruit and signatures, stuffing it all into their backpacks and chattering. Conor stepped forward and tapped Heidi on the shoulder and pointed to Merle. He said something to the blonde next to Heidi and they both heaved their packs onto their shoulders and came over.

"Hello again," Heidi said. "It's Elise's sister," she told the other girl. "This is Britta," she told Merle.

"We are finished," Britta said brightly. "I can't believe I did it! Time to go home!"

"No heat stroke," Heidi said. "Good work, Britta." She turned back to Merle. "I haven't thought of anything else. Sorry."

Merle nodded. "I got a tip from someone in the village. That Elise was seen talking to a man with dark hair and a deep tan at the lavender festival last Sunday." She looked between them as they glanced at each other. "You were there, I'm told. Do you remember him?"

Britta looked over her shoulder at Conor who hung behind them, eyes down but still obviously listening. "We remember him," she said very quietly.

Heidi shuffled her feet. "She, um, she got a ride home with him after the *fête*."

"She did?" Heidi nodded, glancing at Conor. "Why didn't you tell me that earlier? This man could be connected with her disappearance."

"Oh, we're pretty sure she wanted to go with him. It was obvious," Britta said.

"What was obvious?"

"She liked him." Britta shrugged. "He took her home. It was fine."

"Yes," Heidi said quickly. "It seemed okay. We didn't think anything of it."

"By 'home' you mean he brought her back here?"

"Yes," Heidi said. "I mean, I didn't see her come in but she was here in the morning."

Conor looked up. "She's an adult. We don't have rules for adults here. They come and go as they please."

Merle frowned at him and turned back to the girls. "And did you also talk to him? That's what my source told me."

Britta nodded slowly. Heidi grimaced. "For a minute."

Merle took a breath. This was like pulling teeth. "And what did he say his name was?"

Now Conor walked away scowling, as if he was done with this conversation.

"Ari," Britta said. "He said his name was Ari."

"Last name?"

They shook their heads. "Sorry."

"Anything else, like where he lives or works?"

"No."

The student group was breaking up now, splitting into small pods to go to airports or trains. Heidi and Britta went separate ways with a quick hug when the farmer called Heidi's name from a list. Off she went with a driver and two students.

"Please, Britta, do you remember anything else about this man?" Merle pleaded.

But she didn't, and in a moment her name was called and she moved off, surrounded by other students. Then they were all in the front of the house, talking, laughing, and piling into cabs.

Merle stood alone, stunned. Ari Somebody. Dark hair and a tan. Possibly French. That really narrowed it down.

Oh, Elise, you cow. I will murder you.

CHAPTER EIGHTEEN

*I*t took two days for Elise to realize she'd forgotten her phone charger at the farm. Her phone had been dead for a good portion of the time since she left, she figured, since the last time she could remember using it was to get the early morning text from Ari. He had told her he was parked down the drive at the farm, hiding in his car behind a rosemary hedge.

Well, she wasn't answering her sisters anyway. She *was* bothered by the thought of Merle looking for her at the farm, calling her, but not enough to do anything about it. What could she do anyway? There was an old white telephone at Ari's house but even if she could figure out how to make a call, she couldn't remember anyone's mobile number.

As she lay by the pool, under the big umbrella, with only her newly painted purple toenails catching the sun, Elise tried hard to care. Nothing seemed to matter, not when the sun was shining, the pool was sparkling, and the air smelled like flowers. The only thing that nagged at her was the whereabouts of her host, Ari. He hadn't arrived back from wherever he had gone that first evening. The housekeeper, who was as sweet as she looked, was unconcerned. Hannah, who was Dutch, kept Elise in food and drink, folded her clean clothes, provided beach towels and sunscreen, and anything else she wanted.

"Monsieur, he often go away and do not say when he is to come back," Hannah said in broken English. "What can I do? He pays me to keep the house nice for whenever he returns."

They were in the kitchen, later, eating celery and carrots. "Do you think he went back to his farmhouse?"

"Farmhouse?" Hannah frowned.

"The *mas*. Up in the Luberon."

Hannah shook her head. "I do not know of a *mas*. He has a vast apartment in Marseille overlooking the old port. That I know. Very nice, he says. Different girl works there. She is from Greece, I think. Speaks no French and no English. I am surprised he keeps her on, but not too surprised."

"Wait. He doesn't have a farmhouse? North of here, in the Luberon?"

Hannah shrugged.

"Maybe it belonged to him before he hired you. How long have you worked for him?" Elise bit down hard on some celery and longed for some cream cheese to smear on it.

"Let's see. Five years in the winter. I come down for the weather. It is hot now but most of the time, so nice."

"Five years? Then you knew his wife."

Hannah frowned again. "Wife?"

"Maybe she lived in Marseille. He never mentioned her?"

"No. No wife. Plenty of girls, yes."

"Oh." Elise was beginning to see where this was going. "So, his wife didn't kill herself? Didn't turn on her car in the garage and breathe in the fumes?"

"*Mijn God*," Hannah gasped. "No."

"I see." Elise mentally chucked herself on the forehead. She was so gullible. "I wonder why he would say such a thing."

"He tells you his wife kills herself? And he doesn't even have a wife?" Hannah's blue eyes were huge. She shook her head again, disappointed with her employer. "What a man."

"What's he like?" Elise asked. "I really only went to dinner with him once."

"Oh, very kind to me. Generous. I have my own little room and bath suite. I use the kitchen when I want, just like it was my own. Many days, weeks even, I am here alone. I walk into the village where I have a friend." She smiled coyly.

"Ah. Good for you."

Hannah's age was a question but she was not as old as Elise. Maybe thirty. She had a cap of brownish-blonde hair that she tucked behind her ears. Busty and rosy-cheeked, she only lacked a white apron and wooden shoes to fit the stereotype of a Dutch lass. She leaned closer to Elise. "You have a friend back home? Or is Ari the one?"

Elise smiled. "Ari is *not* the one. He just saved me from a bad situation at this lavender farm where I was doing a farm stay. You know what that is?"

"Stay at a farm on vacation?"

"And work on the farm. Pretty hard work. I don't know why I chose that as my vacation spot. It was a mistake."

Hannah's head bobbed seriously. "Yes. I hear that. Ari wants to buy a lavender farm, he tells me, and I tell him he is crazy. Too much work for a man like him."

"He doesn't seem like the farmer type." They both laughed.

"With those fancy shoes?" Hannah laughed harder, wiping her eyes.

Elise asked: "If he doesn't have a farmhouse up there, where does he stay?"

"With a friend, he says. Her name is Louise. She is very wealthy. She has a huge walled garden. Like a château, he says. Plenty of room."

"Oh. I see."

Hannah peered at Elise. "Are you jealous? You know he has a reputation," she whispered. "You are not in love with him or anything?"

"Oh, no. Definitely not."

"Good. In the village when I say I work for Monsieur Delcroix the girls frown and call him a '*dragueur*,'" she said. "I had to look that up in my little dictionary."

"What does it mean?" Elise asked.

"Like *beau parleur*. The smooth talker. Silver-tongued devil. Flatters the women. Seduces them."

Elise frowned and looked out at the pool. She was really an idiot.

But not so naïve that she didn't realize the kind of man he was from the start.

Hannah patted her arm. "No harm done. He disappears and we are here, as comfy as can be. Are you ready for some cool rosé by the pool?"

Elise smiled. "*Absolument!*"

ARI DIDN'T APPEAR for dinner that night again. Elise asked Hannah to eat with her outside on the terrace. Since the housekeeper had spilled some of Ari's secrets, they had a great time, laughing and talking about men like him. Elise had many stories about past boyfriends and enjoyed Hannah's reaction to the dorks she'd dated.

"This last one, Scott, he was—how can I say this nicely? He was so dull I used to fall asleep in the middle of one of his explanations."

"Explaining what?"

"Taxes or music—"

"Music?! How do you explain music? It is the feeling, yes?" She swayed to an unsung tune, in her chair.

"I have no idea. But he tried." Elise took a sip of wine and felt the relief of being done with Scott wash over her. "I met a guy up on the farm. I kind of liked him but—"

"A farmer? No, no. You need someone worldly, Elise. You are a lawyer and a woman who travels the globe. You need someone your equal."

Elise smiled at Hannah who seemed even nicer when you both had a glass of wine in you. "You're sweet, Hannah. What about this friend of yours in the village? What's he like?"

"He owns the bicycle shop. He has dreams though. He wants to run tours for Americans, like yourself, and the Dutch like me. The Dutch love their bicycles. And so many British here. The bicycle tours are very popular."

"That sounds fun. And a great idea for a business."

Hannah dipped her chin. "He says we can do it together."

Elise gripped Hannah's hand across the table. "I'm so happy for you."

. . .

ELISE LAY in bed that night, moonlight streaming in the window, silver against the white sheets, and stared at the shadows on the ceiling. The heaviness was back inside her. Was she really happy for Hannah? She could act happy, could feel joy for someone as kind as Hannah. But there was something missing in her. Like a hollow spot where her heart should be. Was she jealous of her new friend's love life? She deserved happiness. Hannah and her bicycle man should share whatever love they could in this harsh old world.

Yet. Of course there is a 'yet.' Her own love life was a pathetic mess.

She rolled over on her stomach and closed her eyes. Not just love life. Her law life as well. Five Bennett sisters, all lawyers. Such a family tradition. Ugh. Well, once upon a time they all practiced law. Now Merle was retired, as was Annie. Or semi-retired. Stasia did lawyering for a fancy fashion magazine, which really didn't count. Francie loved law and her hot new/old boyfriend, Dylan.

Her sisters all loved the law and she did not. She really, really did not. What was wrong with her? Why couldn't she just find a niche in law, of which there were many, and concentrate on something small and juicy?

It was a mystery.

Was it because her love life was a mess that she couldn't commit to anything work-wise? Her sisters had all found love although it had taken some of them quite a while. Elise was the youngest, and least lovable apparently. She couldn't help reliving that last moment in the hall with Conor when he looked at her with such loathing, as if she was scum. And the way she had tried to hurt him, putting it all back on him with "What did I ever do to you?" She must have done something to him. Why would he act like that? She was always doing something stupid around men, saying something dumb. No wonder she sucked in court. She couldn't keep her thoughts straight in her head or think on her feet.

But this line of self-abuse had to stop. It never helped to go back and review it all. She knew that. Really, she did.

She put the pillow over her head. Tomorrow she would do something active, a walk, a hike to the village, something. Maybe she could rent a bicycle from Hannah's boyfriend. Ride through the fields of flowers, the wind in her ears. Get all bliss-y.

There. That was a plan.

CHAPTER NINETEEN

Merle packed her car after a quick breakfast on the hotel terrace. She was disappointed in not finding Elise, not knowing if she was safe, but she had called Pascal last night for advice. He promised to file a missing persons report for Elise, since she had not been seen for four days. He would contact the U.S. Embassy. Merle winced at that. But enough was enough. She had to go home and meet Tristan. He arrived in the Dordogne today and it had been months since she'd seen him.

His text last night made everything seem a little brighter. He was in Paris, staying at the home of his one-time French girlfriend, Valerie, the niece of Merle's neighbor, Albert. Valerie wasn't at home, having taken some exotic summer job in South Africa. But her parents were very kind to Tristan and put him up for a night after his arrival. The photograph of the three of them—Tristan and Valerie's mother and father—made her smile. Tristan made friends wherever he went.

Merle put gasoline in her car at a station on the outskirts of Belle-mont. She was still intimidated by French gas stations. Half of them wouldn't take cash and the other half wouldn't take her credit card. Luckily this one liked her card and she headed west again, toward

Avignon, muttering to herself. "Where are you, Elise…where the hell are you?"

The day was bright, almost blinding, with flashes off the chrome of passing vehicles. The scenery failed to inspire her this time. Again, she stopped in Carcassonne for lunch. The cafés were packed with tourists, service was slow, the waiters stressed. She didn't linger.

It was after three when she parked her car in the city lot outside Malcouziac's walls. She stretched for a moment then grabbed her bags. She ran through the narrow lanes, her tote bag bumping on her hip. Would Tristan be here already? His train was due into Bergerac at eleven. It was not a long drive from there.

Turning onto Rue de Poitiers Merle slowed, catching her breath. She loved everything about this short street: the colored shutters, the uneven cobblestones, the roses blooming against the stone walls, the lace curtains fluttering in windows. Geraniums on windowsills next to sleeping cats. Freshly painted doors in all the colors of the rainbow. At the end of the street was a late model sedan, in front of her cottage. It must be Tristan's rental. Wow, he had rented a very nice car.

She detoured around the red sedan and saw that the front door was standing open. Maybe he had just arrived. Maybe she would catch him just unloading his car, just starting to relax. Merle stepped through the door, a big smile on her face. Laughter from the back garden riffled through the house. No one was in the parlor, or the kitchen. A battered duffle bag that looked like Tristan's sat by Pascal's velvet chair.

"Hello? Tris?"

No answer. Merle closed the front door and stepped over the duffle bag. At the open kitchen door, the sunshine hit her in the face. She shaded her eyes and saw Tristan, leaning against the side wall, grinning at Willow and—someone else. A young man.

"Tristan!" She called, moving toward him, slowly, not to overwhelm, but eagerly, arms outstretched. He pushed off the wall and into her arms.

After a long hug she pushed him back and took his shoulders, squeezing them. "Oh, my, rowing has given you some muscles."

He laughed. "It has."

She ruffled his hair. "You need a haircut."

"That's why I came. To get the most expensive haircut ever."

Willow stood up from the low wall in the shade of the acacia tree. "Hi, Aunt Merle. How was your trip?"

"All right. Well, I—" She didn't want to whine about Elise right away. Maybe wait five minutes. In the pause, Willow took the young man's arm and pulled him forward.

"This is Teague, Aunt Merle. He's—he's—" She stuttered, looking stricken.

"Hello, Teague." Merle stuck out a hand and he shook it. He was a tall, good-looking young man with dusty blond hair and pale blue eyes. His grip was firm. His attire, a pink button-down shirt, pin-striped Bermuda shorts, and boat shoes, screamed 'boarding school.' "Did you come with Tristan?" She glanced at her son.

"No, ma'am," Teague said with a slight southern accent. "I came with Willow."

"I see." Merle looked at Willow appraisingly. "You didn't mention Teague."

"I know—I—." She blushed and hugged his arm to her. "I didn't— don't tell my mother, Aunt Merle, please."

"Why not? Doesn't she know about you and Teague?" Was his name really Teague? What an upper crust name, one Stasia would adore in a son-in-law. He looked like material for that role, a solid stance, an open expression, handsome if dull, fair-haired: everything Stasia liked in men.

"Oh, yes, ma'am," Teague said, repeating his favorite Southernism. "We have met."

Merle looked to Willow for clarification. The girl had her head down, lips clamped together. "Willow?"

Merle heard the front door open and close. Was it Pascal already? She turned as the footsteps clicked across the wood floor and a man appeared in the kitchen door.

"Your crusader returns! Wine, spirits, and cheese!" The thin, freckled man said with exaggerated ceremony. He held up two bottles of champagne. "Time to booze it up!"

He took a few steps then saw Merle and froze.

She turned slowly toward him, hands on her hips. "Scott? What are *you* doing here?"

CHAPTER TWENTY

Scott Orr, onetime boyfriend of Elise, lowered his pale arms, laden with bottles of bubbly, and let his smile sag. Merle was still glaring at him, she realized, so she glanced at the others. Tristan's eyes were wide in surprise, or anticipation. Willow and Teague had frozen smiles on their faces, their eyes shifting between Scott and their hostess.

Merle crossed her arms. This week was turning into some kind of a mess. "What is going on, Scott?"

He set the bottles on the metal patio table and shifted his feet nervously. "Um, well. I came to find Elise, to explain, to, you know, plead with her. As embarrassing as that sounds, as pathetic, I know—I want her back."

"So, you broke up?" Merle squinted her eyes at Scott. He shrugged. She glanced at Willow and Teague. "It seems there is a little more to the story."

Willow stepped a little closer but kept the patio table between her aunt and herself. "Scott is Teague's cousin, Aunt Merle. They traveled together."

"I thought you said you came with Willow," Merle said.

"*Because* of Willow. That's what I said," Teague said nervously. "Scott and I have been here, what? Two days?"

"Three," Scott and Willow said in unison.

Teague darkened. Maybe he wasn't used to being wrong, or so openly contradicted. "Okay, right. Three days. Does it matter?"

Willow blinked at her boyfriend, registering his anger, then watched him relax again and take her hand.

Merle looked at Scott. "Second cousin once removed," he said stiffly.

"So, you came because of your distant cousin? Or Elise? You asked me for my address. Was that a ruse?"

"A what?" Scott blanched. "No, of course not. I would never...."

No one said anything for a beat.

"So, what are we boozing it up about, Scott?" Tristan asked, breaking the silence. "Looks like some good champagne."

Scott set his palm on the top of the bottles. "Oh, it is. It's ...." Again he lost his answer.

"What are we celebrating?" Merle also wanted to know. She glanced at the young couple who were holding hands and gazing now into each other's eyes. What was that glinting on Willow's finger? Merle's stomach dropped. Were they engaged? Or—

"Is it a wedding?" Tristan blurted out. "Did you guys get married?"

Everyone froze except Willow, whose eyelashes were going crazy, fluttering.

"Oh, Willow," Merle whispered. "You didn't."

Willow's face hardened and her chin lifted in defiance. She squeezed Teague's hand, making him squirm and extract it from her grip. He put his arm around her waist instead, drawing her hip to his. Now the diamond was visible, and a wedding band.

"What if I—we—" Willow began. It was one of those days when no one could finish their declarations.

Except Teague. "What if we did get married? I love her, Miz Bennett. We love each other."

As if that was the only consideration. Well, maybe when you're 22 and have a fat trust fund, that's all that mattered. Merle looked more critically at Teague, from his hairy shins and delicate ankles to his shock of blonde hair that hung over one eyebrow. Was he really planning on living with Willow 'til death do them part? Did he play tennis or program computers or sell insurance? Who *was* he?

Willow's mother would never forgive her. Poor Stasia. Merle could see her stricken, disbelieving face. Denying her mother the pleasure not only of planning her only daughter's wedding but even the joy of attending it, not seeing her daughter in white with a dreamy guy, a country club shindig, a society affair—it would stab Stasia in the heart. And he probably had parents with exactly the same mindset. It would be a battle royal. Not the best way to begin married life.

"It's v-very romantic, Miss Bennett," Scott stammered. "Don't you think?"

Willow looked at Merle with pleading eyes. "A honeymoon in France—what could be better?"

Merle couldn't think of anything to say to the thoughtless girl. Maybe she was in love, maybe she resented her mother's overbearing nature, maybe she wanted to thumb her nose at her mother and all her plans and expectations. It was only natural. Stasia *was* a drill sergeant sometimes.

Or maybe Willow just wanted to elope, to get it done easily and quickly, without a lot of fuss and fanfare. Save all that money. Not a bad reason, after all.

Whatever her reasons were, Willow was going to break her mother's traditionalist heart.

"Have you told her yet? Your mother?" Merle asked.

"She's going to have a cow," Tristan offered.

Willow shot him a dirty look. "Not yet. Can we keep it that way for a while? Please? Just a few days?"

Scott cleared his throat. "Okay, then. Time to pop the corks?"

MERLE FOUND herself in the parlor, in the dim light, staring at Tristan's duffle bag like it might have some answers. Where was Elise? Why was Willow being so difficult? Who was this Teague person? Who was Willow? She didn't seem like the girl Merle had known since she was a baby. Why was Scott here? She wished for Pascal's steady kindness in times like this. She got out her phone to call him then put it back in her pocket. She needed to think first.

Tristan stepped up behind her and put a long arm around her shoulders. "It'll be all right. Aunt Stasia can't micro-manage everybody forever. She'll get over it."

She nodded. "You're right. It's just—so many things happening at once. Elise is missing, Scott shows up, you show up and you should have your own space and guess what, some guy is sleeping in your bed." She sighed deeply and leaned her head against his broad shoulder.

"Wait, what about Aunt Elise? Wasn't she supposed to come back with you?"

"I don't know where she is. She doesn't answer her phone. She took off to parts unknown after a week at the lavender farm and they have no idea where she went."

"Weird. Well, she must have got tired of farm work."

"Sure. But why not answer emails and texts and calls? Scott says she never answered him—"

"And now we know why. They broke up."

"Okay, but where the hell is she? She didn't break up with me. It's rude." Merle looked up at her son's maturing face, black stubble on his square jaw, his serious eyes and straight black eyebrows. "Don't ever do that to me. Promise."

"I promise, Mom."

Merle hugged her son again and tried to let her anger release. "I know you wouldn't. How are Valerie's parents? I hope you thanked them."

"And gave them a big jar of peanut butter from the US, just like you asked."

She smiled at him. "You're the best, kiddo."

"They sent me in to get glasses for the champagne," he said, glancing up at the cupboard where the glassware sat in rows. "Are you coming back out for some?"

She shook her head. "I'll just take my bags upstairs and get settled in."

He flinched. "I think you'll find there's someone in your bed too."

Merle put a hand to her forehead and rolled her eyes. "I think I will have a glass of champagne. But bring it in here, will you? I've had enough drama for one day."

CHAPTER TWENTY-ONE

*E*lise rolled over on her side on the lounge chair by the pool, feeling the sun bake her feet. The rest of her body was under the shade of the umbrella. She wore her bra and bikini underpants, having failed to find a swimsuit in the house. Hannah didn't even have one.

The two of them were becoming fast friends and it cheered Elise a little. She thought about her friends at home, Tiff and Jude, and what catty things they would say about Hannah. The housekeeper wasn't slender or fashionable or well-educated or cool. She didn't post on Instagram. She was none of the things they admired. But she was so kind to Elise, as if she knew that Elise needed gentle pampering at this delicate stage in her mixed-up life.

She had woken late again. She'd never slept so well in her life. The scent of the lavender fields came through the bedroom window when the wind was right, calming her. If only she'd been able to sleep with her window open at the farm. The vision of the bat returned, hanging on the beam, and made her shiver, despite the heat. Then she closed her eyes and felt a drowsy nap-like state return. No wonder people liked Provence. Something about it made you drop all your worries and really relax.

Unless of course you worked at a lavender farm. Then you were out in the heat and the dust and the wind all day, getting fried by the sun. Thank goodness that was over.

How long could she stay squirreled away in Ari's house? She had a hankering to see those shops in Aix he talked about. Where was he? Not that she really cared any more. He had done his duty and rescued her from the farm. If he wanted to let her know where he was, he would have called. As it was, things were perfectly pleasant here with just Hannah, the wine cellar, and the pool.

Whew, it was hot. She slipped into the water to cool off. After a couple lazy, cooling laps she climbed out, wrapped herself in a towel and went back to her bedroom to change. Maybe she would go into the village for lunch and rent that bicycle. If she wasn't too relaxed.

She was zipping up her one and only skirt, a cute yellow one, when the knock came on her door.

It was Hannah. "Elise? There is a man at the door—asking for you."

She cracked open the bedroom door. "A man?"

Hannah nodded.

"Who is it? Did he say?"

"No. But he knew you were here."

"One of Ari's relatives?"

Hannah frowned. "I don't know."

Elise pulled on a sleeveless black top. She checked herself in the mirror over the dresser and fluffed her hair, nervous suddenly. Was it one of Ari's family members, or a business associate? Were they here to kick her out? Could it be the police? But why would they be after her? She hadn't done anything except disappear without a trace.

She walked barefoot through the parlor. Hannah had shut the front door, leaving whoever it was on the steps. Elise took a breath and swung open the door.

Conor Albion was looking behind him and turned at the sound.

"Oh," Elise said. "It's you."

He stared at her. "Sorry to disappoint." He wore long khaki shorts, a navy blue golf shirt with a neon green crest on the pocket, and hiking shoes. Sweat beaded on his forehead.

"You didn't. I'm sorry. Come in, won't you?" Elise stepped back.

He hesitated, looking over her shoulder into the living room. "I just came to return your charger." He handed her a paper sack. "It took a few days for anyone to find it."

She looked inside the bag at her charger. "Oh, thank you. My phone's been dead for days." She smiled at him. He was still as nice looking as before, his hair curling over his collar, his shoulders broad, even with an uncertain frown on his face. "You came so far. Please come in and have a glass of water. Or something. I insist."

"What about—?"

"Ari? Nowhere to be found." He let her pull him inside.

Hannah stood in the kitchen door, wringing her hands. She looked worriedly at Elise as if trouble was brewing.

"Hannah, this is Conor. He's half French, half—" She paused.

"Welsh," he said.

"He works at the lavender farm where I was doing the farm stay. I mean, your farm. It's partly yours, right?"

"Technically," he muttered.

"He brought me my phone charger so I can make calls again." Hannah nodded silently at him. Elise continued: "It's time for *déjeuner!* What about a little lunch on the terrace, Hannah? You can join us."

She looked aghast at that suggestion but said she would fix something. "And some wine? *Monsieur?*"

"*D'accord. Merci,*" Conor replied. Hannah disappeared into the kitchen. "Nice house."

"It is. Have you been here before? You know Ari, right?"

He walked to look out the patio doors to the pool. "We're acquainted."

Elise remembered the look that had passed between the two men at the *fête.* She wanted to ask Conor about his comment about Ari ("Do you know what he's done?") but she liked him this way better—calm and courteous. It was possible Conor had a temper.

"Do you want to look around? I guess it'd be okay." Elise set the paper bag on an end table. "Not that I'm the hostess."

He turned from the windows. "I don't need a tour."

They watched as Hannah carried out a bucket of ice, a bottle of Provence rosé, and two glasses, setting them up on the metal table under the awning. "Well, look at that," Elise said, aware she sounded weird and nervous but faltering for conversation. What was wrong with her? It was just Conor. "The wine is ready. Come on."

They settled themselves in the shade on the terrace. He let her pour. Somehow Elise found that interesting, in an analytical way. What was he saying? That she held the cards here? She gave him a strong pour and herself a medium one. She held up her glass and he clinked his to it. Nobody said a toast.

After a sip she set down her glass. "Provence is so lovely."

He stared at her, taking his time. "You look—"

She smiled. "What?"

"Relaxed," he said.

"I'm sleeping a lot better over here, I can tell you that. Have you ever slept in those third floor rooms with the windows shut? Well, you remember, you opened mine for me."

"Got in some trouble for that."

"Sorry." She smirked. "Not sorry."

He tried not to smile. "Why, because we all had a meeting in the hallway in our smalls?"

She laughed. Their eyes met and they both looked away quickly. Elise blinked and grabbed her wine glass.

"I never got to thank you properly for rescuing me from the bat."

He shrugged. "You did thank me. In the tractor."

Hannah arrived with small plates of fruit salad, artfully arranged with a sprig of mint. She retreated quickly. Conor watched her go. "So where is Arsie?"

"You mean Ari?"

"Sure. Whatever."

"Nobody knows. He hasn't been home for days. He brought me over here, we had lunch then supper, then he left."

He looked at her skeptically and picked up his fork. "Seriously. I need to know if he's likely to burst in here and rough me up."

"Rough you up?" Elise squinted, popping a slice of papaya in her mouth.

"For taking his place at the table."

"I invited you. I can do as I please. He's not my boyfriend or anything. I only had a dance at the *fête* then dinner. I hardly know him." She eyed him. "You two have a history."

He shook his head. "It's a long story. More to do with my family than me."

"Wait—now I remember. Hannah told me he wanted to buy a lavender farm. Is that it? He wants to buy your farm?"

Conor said nothing but his look confirmed it. Had Ari been the man she'd seen coming arguing with Monsieur Vernay? She'd like to know the whole story but Conor, with his lips pinched together, seemed unlikely to share more.

They ate their fruit silently. Hannah arrived again, this time carrying a plate of small triangular sandwiches. "Tuna, salmon, and ham," she announced.

"Thank you, Hannah. Won't you sit down with us?"

Hannah glanced at Conor. "Oh, no, madame. I have things to do in the kitchen."

Elise made a face as she skittered off into the house. "We were friends there for a moment. Before you arrived."

"Sorry to break up the team."

She waved a hand. "She'll be back. She's my new bestie."

When they finished the food Hannah did return, this time with espresso for both of them. Elise grabbed an ice cube from the bucket and plopped it into her coffee. "It's too hot for coffee, isn't it? I was going to go on a bike ride but I think I waited too long."

Conor nodded. "Morning is best."

"Is it always this hot in Provence?"

"In July and August? Always."

"It's not global warming or something?"

"Happens every summer."

Elise sipped her now lukewarm espresso. "Is the harvest done? Is that why you came today?"

"Mostly, yes. But today is my day off."

"No golf?"

"I practiced early this morning. Cooler then, as you say. On my way down here." He downed his espresso in one gulp like a true Frenchman and stood up. "I should go. Thank you for the lunch, Elise."

Her heart pounded suddenly as she walked him to the door. Hannah hovered, watching from the kitchen. "I guess I'll see you then," she said. "Unless you want to go biking tomorrow?"

"What?" Conor turned back at the door.

"Biking. On a bicycle? Do you ever do that?"

He shook his head. "I don't have a bicycle here."

Hannah cleared her throat. "There are bicycles in the garage. Two or three, maybe some with flat tires but, I don't know. You pump up the tires?"

Conor looked at Elise. She shrugged. "You want to check them out?"

"I can't go cycling. I work tomorrow." He glanced at Hannah then back at Elise. "But if you need the tires pumped, I can do that for you."

"Thank you." She touched his arm. "I appreciate it."

"I meet you outside. I open the big door," Hannah announced. "There is a button in here."

They walked out the front door and waited for Hannah to operate the garage door opener. The big double door glided up smoothly. The heat inside the garage poured out. There were two cars in the garage, to Elise's surprise. One was the blue BMW, the other was a red sports car, an Alfa Romeo. *The BMW is here?* She was confused.

Conor looked around the garage for a moment then stopped.

A fetid, sickeningly sweet odor wafted over them on a breeze blown through the open kitchen door where Hannah stood. Elise gagged and bent over, covering her mouth and nose with a hand. She felt the bile rise from her stomach and the heat radiating off the asphalt sear her face. Conor took a step inside the garage then turned on his heel, taking her by the shoulders and pushing her back.

"Don't look. No, Elise," he said firmly. Over his shoulder he called to Hannah: "Call the police."

CHAPTER TWENTY-TWO

*B*efore the police arrived, Elise threw up behind the rosemary bushes twice. Conor held her hair back as she retched. A few dry heaves then she felt a little better. She stood up slowly, holding Conor's arm for balance.

"Let's go inside. Come on," he said gently. "This way."

He sat her down on the sofa and went to the kitchen. She heard him talking to Hannah, and Hannah crying. She wanted to console Hannah but couldn't remember why. The horrible odor had wiped out her senses.

Conor returned with a glass of cool water and sat beside her on the sofa. "Drink slowly."

She sipped the water, feeling it cool her insides. "Thank you. You have a good bedside manner for a golfer."

"My mother is a doctor. She taught me everything I know."

Elise balanced the glass on her knee. "Did she teach you what that smell was?"

He squeezed his eyes shut for a second then said quietly: "Had to figure that one out for myself." He glanced at her. "It's Ari, Elise. *Was* Ari."

She felt a sob rise in her throat and took a quick sip of water. "I—I thought it was an animal, a—a—beaver or something. A wild boar. Ari? Are you sure?"

He shrugged. "Pretty sure. He's been in there a while."

"Oh, god." The scent memory came over her in waves. She clamped a hand on her nose but it didn't help. "How horrible."

"Right." Conor stood up. "I can't wait for the Bill. I have to get back."

"The what?"

"Coppers."

Elise shot up from the sofa and took his forearm. "No! Please don't go, Conor. The police will want a statement from you, won't they? I can't do it. Hannah can't. You're the one who saw him. Please, Conor." She took a step closer to him and pleaded, whispering, "Please."

He looked unsure. She thought he would bolt out of here, get away as fast as possible. She understood that impulse. Most men would get the hell out. But she and Hannah might fall to pieces by themselves. Elise turned to Hannah.

"Tell him, Hannah. He must stay for the police."

The housekeeper was slumped, chin in hand, in a dining chair near the kitchen, one elbow on the dark wood table, one foot in an awkward angle. She blinked at Elise, a blank horror on her face. "What will I do? Where will I go?" she muttered.

Conor was watching Hannah then turned back to search Elise's face. "You're right. Someone will have to give a statement." He took Elise's hand then dropped it like it was hot. "All right, I'll stay. Don't cry." He touched his own cheek to indicate a tear that Elise didn't realize was trailing down her face. "Both of you. Pull up your garters, girls. We'll get through this."

The first policeman who arrived was a *gendarme* from the village, sent to secure the scene. He closed the garage door and set himself up in the shade of the front of the house and commenced smoking cigarette after cigarette. "For the smell," Conor remarked.

They waited over an hour for the two policemen from the *Police nationale* in Aix-en-Provence to make their way to this remote spot (fifteen miles away!) where nothing ever happened. That's what one *policier* said as he began the interview with Elise. Nothing ever happens out here. In Marseille, okay, sure. Even, once in a while, in Aix. But never here.

Elise blinked at the policeman, focusing on his long fingers better suited to piano than police work. He didn't wear a uniform so she assumed he was a detective. He gave his name as Yount. Like policemen everywhere he scribbled in a small notebook. He made her nervous. Where was Conor? She saw him outside, alone, sitting under the umbrella. At least he had stayed.

"*Madame?*"

"*Oui?*"

"*Parlez-vous français?*"

"*Très mal.*" She pointed at Conor. "He speaks English and French. *Il parle anglais et français.*"

Detective Yount looked annoyed but went to the patio door to call Conor inside to translate. Yount pointed to a chair to one side of the sofa for Conor. Yount asked questions and Conor translated back and forth.

"How do you know M. Delcroix?"

"I met him at a lavender festival in the Luberon, a few days ago. A week, I guess, on Sunday. Then on Tuesday, I left the farm and he gave me a ride here to stay until. . .."

Elise faltered, looking in Conor's eyes. "Until what?" he asked.

"Until I figured out my next move."

"Your next move? Like moving houses?"

"My life. I am figuring out my life."

Conor stared for a second then translated for the policeman. "He asks, when did you last see Delcroix?"

"The day I arrived, Tuesday. Hannah had made us lunch and we ate outside. Later we had supper, some cold soup, about eight. Then he left. He said he'd be back but he never came back."

Conor translated and listened. "Clearly he did come back."

"We didn't know. Neither Hannah nor I knew he was in the garage. We never heard a car. We would have called a hospital or the police or . . .."

Conor translated and appeared to be giving the detective his own take on their story. He turned to Elise. "I told him you are an honest person. I believe you."

"Well, thanks. I guess. Ask him, what happened to Ari? How did he die?"

She listened to them chatter back and forth, trying to pick out words. Finally, Conor nodded. "There will be an autopsy. It appears to be foul play." Her mouth dropped open. She had assumed he'd killed himself like his make-believe wife or come home drunk and passed out. The usual things.

"But how?" she whispered.

Conor glanced at the cop and lowered his voice. "Gunshot. To the head."

ELISE DIDN'T REMEMBER the rest of the questions. She hurried through her answers, trying to keep her mind from returning to what must have been—was definitely in her imagination—a horrific scene in the garage. Was he in his car? Had he shot himself? No, that wasn't possible. Was it? Wouldn't they have heard a gunshot?

At some point Conor asked for her phone and plugged it into the charger he'd brought back. She was going to have to call her sister now. Merle would be shocked but her boyfriend was a cop. She'd seen things. Merle was a rock. She could hold things together, support Elise if—no, *when*—Conor went home.

She stepped into the kitchen. The detective had told her he was done with her for now and turned his attention to Conor. She couldn't follow the conversation. It was too fast, too detailed, using words far beyond French 101.

She found the bottle of rosé in the refrigerator and poured herself a glass. She drank it in gulps, trying to breathe. She stared at the door to the garage and imagined she could smell through it. Was that possible? How do you keep such a strong odor from invading the door, permeating the walls, the whole house? Why hadn't they smelled anything? Why hadn't they tried to find Ari? Why had they just lain around the pool and sipped rosé when Ari was missing?

Why hadn't they called him? Hannah never seemed concerned. No one had come to the house to look for him. No one called. No one had missed him. Not even Elise herself.

She pressed her forehead against the refrigerator and tried not to cry.

He had been dead for days and nobody even cared.

As the sun faded from the sky, turning the mountains purple and the sky scarlet, the red ambulance rolled up, courtesy the *sapeurs-pompiers,* the local firefighters. It backed into the garage door. Conor watched from the front window that overlooked the driveway. The big van with yellow stripes on the front blocked his view of the action but he didn't care. He'd seen enough. As they pulled out again, the policemen, the crime scene officers, and the *gendarme* got in their respective vehicles and finally about eight o'clock, everyone had gone.

Conor went to the kitchen and pulled out fruit salad and cheese. He placed it on the coffee table in front of Elise. She had drunk three glasses of rosé on her emptied stomach and was quite bleary.

"Eat something. Please. Elise!"

She startled at his command. "Yessir." She felt numb and it was nice.

He sat down on the end of the sofa and held out a piece of cheese. "Here. Eat this."

She did as he said, nibbling on a piece of white cheddar. He gave her a bunch of grapes. She ate one.

"Who can I call for you? Is your phone working now?" He went to where he'd plugged it in, in the kitchen. "All charged." He tried to hand it to her. "Call someone. Is your sister still in France? Her name is Merle?"

Elise struggled to a more alert pose. "My sister? Yes. Merle. How do you know her name?"

"She came to the lavender farm, looking for you. She was very concerned."

Elise looked up at him. He'd stayed all day with her. She felt an outpouring of gratitude toward him. "Thank you, Conor."

"For what? For not spilling your secret location?"

"Oh!" She laughed, making his scowl soften. "You can keep a secret, can't you. Look, I'm sorry I ran off. Obviously sorry about everything to do with Ari. I wish I'd never met him although he didn't deserve to get shot, did he?" She looked at Conor, still holding her cellphone. "Did you have a glass of wine or did Hannah and I drink it all?"

"Hannah's gone to bed."

"Then there's more wine for you and me." Elise struggled to her feet.

Conor caught her arm. "I had some wine. You had some wine. Now we make a phone call."

"The cops won't let us stay here, is that it?"

"They didn't say. But I imagine, if I was you, I would want to leave as soon as possible."

"Definitely. Can you smell it...?"

"It's a memory of the odor. It happens when it's that strong. I have good ones, of lavender."

"You would, being around it all day. Do you smell like lavender now?" She pulled the shoulder of his shirt to her nose and sniffed. "Nope. You smell like the garage."

He pushed her gently back onto the sofa. "I'm calling your sister now." He asked her for her phone code. "Here we go. Merle." He tapped her name.

Elise looked up at him, looming over her. "Is she there?"

He nodded. "No, it's not Elise. Is this Merle? Yes, this is Conor Albion, we met at the farm. She's fine. She's right here." He handed Elise the phone.

"Merle? Yes, it's okay. I'm fine. Okay, fine, no problems. Conor's here. Oh, near Aix-en-Provence at the home of a friend—I know, I'm horrible. I'm a stupid, brainless, selfish brat. I should have called. I should have answered your texts. I don't know why, I just—I'm sorry I made you worry, I'm so sorry. I—I—"

And she burst into tears.

Conor grabbed the phone as it fell from her hand. He sat down and pulled Elise into his shoulder. "Merle? Yes, you should come. As soon as you can. Tomorrow is good. There's been an accident. No, she's fine.

The man she was staying with was found, um, dead. In the garage. Yes, pretty awful. Yes, I'll text you the address."

She felt his hand on her hair and a calmness that flowed through it. She was not alone. She blinked away her tears. She whispered again, "Thank you, Conor."

He wiped her cheek with a thumb. "All in a day's work, luv."

CHAPTER TWENTY-THREE

The next morning Merle drove at breakneck speed to pick up Pascal at the Toulouse railway station. It was still early as he'd caught a 6:30 train from Bordeaux. She'd called him the night before and explained what she knew about Elise's situation. He offered to go to Provence with her and she was grateful. Not that she would be traveling alone if he hadn't.

Scott lay stretched out on the back seat, asleep. He had insisted on accompanying her. What could she say? *Just because I made you sleep on the sofa doesn't mean I owe you favors?* He could be very stubborn and a little testy, showing a flare of temper when he learned that Elise had been staying at the home of some other man, dead or not.

The real surprise the night before had come from Scott. According to him, he had asked Elise to marry him and she had said yes.

Merle had blinked hard. "What? She said yes? She said she would marry you?"

"She did," Scott had reassured her. "You don't have to act so shocked. She's no spring chicken. She might never get another proposal, right? Then..."

"Then what? Don't do that, Scott. The not-finishing-your-sentences is killing me."

They were outside in the garden in the dark. Overhead the stars popped out in the purple sky. The peak of summer had arrived, with sunflowers and artichokes and melons in the markets. Scott was drinking her red wine; Merle had switched to herbal tea. The air was sweet with jasmine.

"Then she changed her mind," he had said angrily. "Just like that."

"I see." Merle could see how Elise would say yes, then no, to Scott. He was a nice man, pleasant although not particularly good-looking, with his freckles and skinny arms. But he was intelligent. She could do worse, Merle mused.

At some point all the other Bennett sisters had told Merle that Scott was too good for Elise, that she obviously didn't deserve such a solid catch. But now, being around him for a day or two, she could see what Elise no doubt saw: an angry, uptight man who could be unpleasant and had control issues.

"When did this happen?" Merle had asked gently, trying to probe the timeline.

"In May. We were on some garden tour she wanted to do, looking at people's backyards like peeping toms. Not my thing but since she liked it, it had to work, I figured. In a rose garden, I got down on a knee and gave her a diamond."

"Really." Elise had not mentioned this to any of the sisters.

"Yes, really. She accepted, then a week later she said she'd changed her mind and never wanted to get married to anyone, ever."

"So maybe it's not you, Scott. It's Elise. Have you thought of that?"

"Of course, I have! That's what she said, that old chestnut, 'It's not you, it's me.' But it's ridiculous." He was shouting then, pacing the garden, throwing his arms around. "She's being ridiculous. Of course, she wants to get married. All women want to get married."

"Do they? I'm not sure of your population sample, Scott."

He had turned on her, his face hot. "You're so sure of yourself, aren't you? Jesus."

"I'm just saying," Merle had stated, keeping her voice even, "that all women do not want to get married. I know that for a fact. My oldest sister, Annie, had a fabulous wedding planned in the Highlands, in

Scotland, and she didn't do it. She couldn't. She never wanted to get married."

Scott had cocked his head, listening. "Well. One woman."

No point in arguing with him. "We're pretty independent, we Bennett sisters."

And now, as he snored in the backseat of the Peugeot, still a little drunk from the night before, Merle watched him in the rearview mirror as she parked at the train station in Toulouse. She slipped out of the car and shut the door carefully. Before she reached the station, Pascal appeared, grinning, walking toward her with a duffle bag over his shoulder. A quick hug was all they time for, then he hurried her back to the car.

He slipped behind the wheel as she got into the passenger seat. He turned and looked at Scott who was sitting up, blinking. "What have we here?"

"Pascal, meet Scott. Elise's former fiancé." Merle rolled her eyes at Pascal. "He insisted on coming."

Pascal turned the ignition. "Well, let's get going then."

Scott was silent, thankfully. Pascal asked Merle about Tristan and when they were going to see each other. It had been planned for the next day but now that was uncertain, with going to rescue little sister in Provence.

"And the girl? Willow? What happens with her?" Pascal asked, fascinated by the generational drama of the Bennetts.

Merle sighed. "She hasn't told Stasia yet. She made me promise not to call her for a couple days. But I think tonight I will. I don't like keeping this from her, as much as she is going to go ballistic. But it depends on all this."

"What do we know?" Pascal asked. "About *all this.*"

"Not much. Just that Elise was staying at this man's house and he was found dead in the garage."

"It is a police matter then?"

"Possibly."

"Then it will be in the news. Try to find something on your phone while we drive."

When they stopped in Montpellier for coffee, Scott revived himself with a venti latté at a Starbucks that seemed to reassure him with its green queen logo and American-ness. Back in the car Merle finally found something in the news about the death.

"Here's a short article in the Aix-en-Provence newspaper," she announced as Pascal left the main highway at Nîmes. She scanned it quickly.

"Read it," Pascal said.

"It's in French. I can translate it but I'm—"

"I will stop," he said, pulling quickly onto the shoulder of the road and stopping with a jerk. "Give me the phone." He read the article quickly, handed her back her phone, then turned back onto the road. "It is a police matter. They think homicide but haven't ruled out suicide." He glanced in the mirror at Scott in the back seat, then back at Merle. "His name is Arsène Delcroix."

"Do you know him?" she asked quietly.

"Delcroix, Merle. The same name as our landlord."

"Oh. Is there a connection?"

"This is France, *chérie*. There is always a connection."

THEY FOUND the house after several wrong turns. It was tucked in the hills south of Aix, on a narrow country lane near a hilltop village. It was a pretty location, surrounded by lavender fields and old cedars and rose bushes. The house was low and rambling, stuccoed in a warm tan with an orange tile roof and green shutters. It was after one in the afternoon and they were glad to get out of the car, despite the midday heat and the three police vehicles blocking the driveway.

Pascal split off to talk to the cops while Merle and Scott approached the front door. Merle knocked. A tall young woman answered the door, flushed and obviously upset. *"Oui?"*

"Je suis la sœur d'Elise Bennett," Merle said haltingly, looking into the dim living room. *"Elle est ici? Je suis* Merle."

A look of relief crossed the woman's face. In English, she said, "Come in, please. She is waiting for you." She squinted at Scott fiercely. "And you are—"

"Scott Orr. A friend of Elise's." He glared back at her, daring her to bar him from entering. She slowly stepped aside and let him enter, then shut the door behind them.

"She is outside. This way," the housekeeper said. She turned to Merle. "I am Hannah. I work for monsieur—the deceased monsieur."

"I'm so sorry, Hannah," Merle said, touching her arm.

"I don't know what I will do now," Hannah said. Her eyes misted. "I have been here for five years. What about my visa? Where will I live?" She stood at the patio door, unable to make herself open it. Scott reached around her and slid open the door.

Merle turned to Hannah. "I'm sure you'll figure it out. Have you called your family?"

"What to say? I don't even know what happened."

"Just wait then. See how it works out." Merle patted her shoulder. "Be strong."

Scott stood outside on the terrace, staring silently at Elise. She sat across the pool, under an umbrella, with her elbows on her knees, head in hands. Beside her sat a man, talking on a cellphone. Merle squinted. She recognized him as Conor, the man at the farm who had called her last night. What was he still doing here? And how was Scott going to react? The negative energy around him felt electric.

Merle turned to the ex-boyfriend. "Why don't you wait here? Let me talk to her first."

Scott frowned but nodded, thrusting his fists into the pockets of his baggy shorts.

Elise looked up as Merle rounded the corner of the pool. She stood and walked toward her sister. Merle could feel Elise trembling in her arms and rubbed her back. "Are you okay?" she asked gently.

Elise stepped back, nodding. "Yeah. Just, you know, a bit shaky."

"Naturally." She took Elise's arm and pulled her back into the shade of the umbrella where she sat down again. Merle rounded the metal table and pulled out a chair. "Conor." She nodded at him. He returned the gesture. "What's happening?"

"They're searching the house," he said. "I think his mobile may be missing."

"And maybe his wallet," Elise added.

"They towed his car off this morning."

"Have they said any more about what happened to him?" They both shook their heads. "But you know how he died?"

Elise looked at Conor. He turned to Merle. "Gunshot to the head."

Merle winced. "Oh."

Elise raised her eyebrows as if there was more to the story. She glanced back at Conor with something like wonder in her eyes.

"Elise? Look at me," Merle said. "Scott is here."

She blinked, not comprehending. Merle tipped her head toward him.

Elise looked back at Scott. "*Merde.* What in the name of—?"

"Okay, look. He thinks he can talk you into getting back together. He showed up at my house unannounced. There's been some drama there too, with Willow. But now you have one task—to send him on his way, Elise. That is, if that's what you want." Merle glanced at Conor who was at least pretending not to listen.

Elise sighed. "I can't believe he came to France to find me."

Conor stood up suddenly and walked to the other end of the pool, concentrating on his phone. Merle whispered, "What about him? Conor."

"What?" Elise blinked hard, trying to keep up.

"He stayed with you last night?"

"Because I was hysterical. Obviously." Her eyes flicked toward him. "He slept on the sofa."

"Right. Okay. You better talk to Scott. Set him straight, Elise." She leaned in close. "Don't give him hope."

Elise rolled her eyes. "I told him once or twice already."

"It looks like you have to do it again."

CHAPTER TWENTY-FOUR

*M*erle watched her sister rise slowly out of her chair, hesitate, then turn toward the house. Scott straightened, seeing her come toward him, his face wary but hopeful. Ah, love. This was going to hurt.

Conor was watching them too, although he was trying hard to pretend he didn't care. It seemed obvious to Merle that he had feelings for Elise. Otherwise why would he have not gone home yesterday, or this morning? He was still here because he wanted to be. And no one really enjoys being at a crime scene.

Elise stood a few feet away from Scott and crossed her arms defensively. He moved a step closer and she backed up. *Get the message, Scott.* This dance with two suitors reminded Merle of the time her awkward boyfriend, James, had shown up in Malcouziac unannounced. Although Scott wasn't quite as ridiculous as James, there were some parallels. Neither was good at reading the romance tea leaves.

Scott was talking earnestly to Elise now, as if he'd finished listening and was giving her an earful of why she should come back to him. It was painful to watch.

His voice rose. "What are you talking about? Of course, I love you. I'll always love you, Elise. I told you—so many times. Don't you believe me? There have been some bad times, I admit, but I'll make it up to you, I will. Everything will be great, you'll see! I've changed, I have. I will."

Elise took another step back and put her hands on her hips. "Stop it, Scott. You're not listening to me—"

He took another step closer to her, his eyes a bit wild. "My darling girl. You look so beautiful. We're meant for each other. You know we are—" He stretched his arms out toward her and again she stepped back.

"Stay away from me, Scott."

"But, sweetie—"

In a flash Conor had moved into the scene, stepping next to Elise. "She said to stand back, man."

Scott flushed, his temper rising. "Who the fuck are you? Get away from my fiancée."

Conor glanced at Elise. "We broke up months ago. He can't accept it."

"But, Elise, my—"

"Don't," Conor said in a low, angry voice. "Seriously. You're embarrassing yourself, mate. It's over. Accept it. Go home."

Scott reddened even more. His ears flared scarlet. His jaw twitched and suddenly he lunged at Conor who deftly sidestepped. Scott stumbled and, with a little shove from Conor, fell head first into the pool.

Elise covered her mouth with her hands. Eyes wide, she glanced at Conor and chuckled. She whispered, "Thank you."

Scott flailed in the deep end. Being fully clothed he had trouble swimming, or maybe he was just not a good swimmer. Merle stepped over to the ladder, halfway down the side of the pool. "Over here, Scott," she called. "You can do it."

His ears below the surface, he dog paddled to the ladder and clung to it, gasping. Merle reached a hand down to help him up. He took her hand and with his other on the ladder, hauled himself out of the pool. He looked like a drowned rat, his reddish hair plastered to his forehead, his t-shirt clinging to his bony torso, and his shorts slipping down his backside.

"I'll get you a towel," Merle said cheerfully. "Was it refreshing?"

. . .

HANNAH BROUGHT out fruit and cheese and another ice bucket with a bottle of rosé, telling them that Monsieur Delcroix had a vast wine cellar and would not want them to go thirsty. Pascal appeared just in time for snacks and wine, his French nose leading him to the table at the right moment. Merle squeezed his hand and sat him next to her on the terrace, with Conor and Elise on the other side of the table.

Scott was hidden away inside somewhere. Hannah had taken his wet clothes and put them in the dryer. At least they had an hour or so without his company.

"I will order him an Uber when he's dressed," Conor said.

"Where will you send him?" Elise asked.

"Anywhere. The train station in Aix perhaps."

Pascal had been filled in briefly. "Good plan," he said, nodding at Conor. "You look familiar. Have we met?"

Conor shook his head. "I don't think so."

"Tell him," Elise told Conor. Before he could answer, she blurted out: "He's is a professional golfer. You might have seen him on television."

"That must be it." Pascal appraised him. "I do watch golf. Mostly it helps me fall asleep when Merle is not with me."

"Pascal," Merle scolded. She looked at Conor. "He's French. Not that many French golfers, are there?"

"Not many," Conor agreed. "I'm only half French. I learned to play in England."

"I am sorry for your non-French half," Pascal said with a smirk.

"Tell us what's going on," Merle asked Pascal.

He took a sip of wine and sat back in his chair. "It appears that monsieur has been murdered."

Elise gasped involuntarily. "Are they sure?"

Pascal nodded. "It does not appear that he died here, in the car at the house."

"He was moved?" Merle asked.

"So it would seem. No weapon was found in the car or garage. And yet it is apparent that he was shot with a pistol of some sort. They will discover that in the autopsy." Pascal looked at Elise, then at Conor. "Are you aware of what monsieur did for a living?"

"No," Elise said.

Conor wagged his head. "I've heard some rumors." They waited. "It was said in Bellemont that he was some kind of gangster—er, mafioso in Marseille. I have no idea if that is true."

"Maybe Hannah knows," Elise said.

Merle flicked her eyes toward the kitchen. "I doubt it. But he must tell her some story."

"Can you ask her?" Pascal asked Elise.

The youngest sister disappeared into the kitchen, carrying her wine glass. Pascal then turned to Conor. "What is your connection to the man?"

Conor straightened and cleared his throat. "We have met, in the village, over a few years. He spends much of the summer there. He is always around, chatting up girls. Ask Hannah; she told Elise that was his reputation here as well. As a *dragueur*."

Pascal nodded thoughtfully. "Apparently, yes. Even the Aix-en-Provence *policiers* knew that about him."

"Maybe a jealous husband?" Merle suggested.

"Anything else?" Pascal asked.

Conor squinted. "That's it."

"No other connections?"

"I'm only here for a few weeks in the summer to help with harvest. Then I go back on the tour, or home to England."

Pascal looked at him thoughtfully. "Well, the detectives—the *Brigade criminelle*—they are looking into his Marseille connections. It is the logical avenue."

"Is he—was he—in the mafia?" Merle asked.

"What is that anymore?" Pascal said. "Smugglers and drug dealers? Possibly."

"So, it's not the 'French Connection' anymore?"

"Like the film? Well, a little, yes. It is Marseille after all."

"That was heroin, right? Is there still heroin being smuggled through Marseille?" she asked.

Pascal looked at Conor and raised his eyebrows. "You think?"

Conor nodded. "If I had to guess."

"And plenty of other things, including grapes from South America and cheese from all over the world."

Elise returned from the kitchen and sat down. "Hannah says she isn't sure what he does—did—for a living. There was always lots of money. And sometimes what she called 'unsavory types' here for card games with lots of cigars and American bourbon and girls who looked like sex workers."

Pascal said, "Thanks, Elise."

Conor put his napkin under his plate. "I should be going. The police don't need me anymore, do they?"

"They'll be in touch if they need more."

Conor stood up. Elise got up too. "Thanks for everything, Conor. I don't think I could have coped with all this without you here."

He looked at her solemnly then nodded. "Bye then." He turned and walked toward the living room door.

"Elise," Merle whispered. "Go."

She blinked, halfway back to her seat. "What?"

"Walk him out to his car, for heaven's sake." Merle scowled at her. "He stayed here for you. He protected you from Doofus Scott. He *likes* you. Wake up."

Pascal smiled up at Elise and nodded. "So it appears."

"Oh," she said then turned to follow Conor into the house.

"What is wrong with that girl?" Merle muttered when she'd gone.

"Not much, according to the golfer."

"WAIT! CONOR!"

Elise ran down the driveway after him, catching him as he turned onto the lane. He paused, looking back.

She gasped for breath, smiling at him. The afternoon sun outlined his shoulders, turning his wavy hair auburn. For a moment she couldn't see his expression then she saw he was still fiercely serious, watching her come toward him.

"Whew, you walk fast. Where's your car?" She looked at three or four police vehicles lining the lane.

"Over there." He gestured toward a beat-up green Deux Chevaux, the ancient Citroën that was everywhere in France, as common, plump, and lovable as a puppy. It was half-hidden in a hedgerow. "It's the farm car."

She did a double-take and smiled. "I love these." She walked across to it and looked inside. One of the fold-up windows was missing and it looked like a flock of crows had sat on it all night, leaving their marks.

"Ari told me a lie, about his nonexistent wife who had one of these then killed herself in it." Elise winced. "Not a great story now, is it. But yours is so cute. I wish—"

He stood next to her, rubbing a rust spot on the door. "You wish?"

"I wish I could go for a ride in it. But I guess with my sister here and all this mess with Ari, maybe not." He nodded, looking down the lane beyond her. "Thank you, Conor. For everything. For staying with me, for calming me down, for holding back my hair while I puked."

He smiled. "All in a day's work."

"And for coming to my rescue with that dumb-ass, Scott. What a dope." She put a hand on his arm. "I can't believe he came to France. I told him so many times—Thank you for nearly drowning him."

He looked into her eyes then. "You're done with him? You're sure?"

She smiled up at him. "Who wants to know?"

"Just a guy."

"A guy who. . .." She asked teasingly.

". . . Is dying here. Elise, please."

She touched his chin. "Kiss me, Conor. And we'll see what happens."

He pulled her close. "Did you kiss Arsie Ari?"

"No." She laughed. "Did you?"

"Definitely not."

CHAPTER TWENTY-FIVE

*W*hile Elise was gone, Hannah stuck her head out the kitchen door. "Need anything?"

Pascal half rose from his chair. "Can you come here, Hannah? I have a couple questions about Monsieur Delcroix."

"I talked to the detectives twice already, monsieur." Hannah wore a black t-shirt and slacks, semi-funereal attire, Merle assumed. Or maybe it was a uniform, hard to say. Her face was rigid with nerves as she rounded the pool toward them.

"He's not working on the case, Hannah," Merle said. "Sit down for a minute."

She sat gingerly, skittish as a cat, eyes wide at Pascal. Merle patted her hand reassuringly and told her everything was fine.

Pascal asked, "Did you know or meet any of Monsieur Delcroix's relatives?"

"No sir. I don't think so."

"Friends then. Or enemies."

Hannah frowned in thought. "No enemies. I guess some friends. They would come to the house and play cards once in a while."

"Can you remember their names?"

"Mostly first names only. There was an Ahmad, some Saudi prince or something. And a Jean-Marie like that Nazi. But wait, there was one with a last name. They called him the *capitane* of the card games. Um," she said, squeezing her eyes shut. "*Capitane* Koch. That's it. Like the sailor."

"Captain Cook?" Merle asked. She nodded.

"Where was this man from, do you remember?" Pascal asked.

"Somewhere south, Marseille maybe? I don't know. Monsieur said he had a big boat, like a yacht. Maybe that's why they call him *capitane*."

"So somewhere on the Med?"

"I assume. Oh. I think it might have been Saint-Tropez. Is that on the water?"

"It is. So how did Miss Bennett and he come to arrive here? When was that?"

"Three days ago or so? On Tuesday, I think."

"Almost a week then. Where was Monsieur Delcroix before that?"

"In the Luberon. He likes it there."

"He has a home there?"

She shook her head. "He stays with friends. Mostly with this rich lady, Louise somebody. She has a huge château with a big wall around it. Very private, he says. I guess that's why he likes it."

"He's a private man?"

"Oh, yes. Almost secretive. I was never to have anything to do with his personal affairs, his money, his cars. I couldn't use his computer, his mobile, nothing. I had to have my own. He would give me cash each month, no checks."

"For household expenses?"

"For those he had accounts in Aix. He had them deliver groceries and wine, once in a while something bigger like plants for the garden or new clothes. He would reimburse me if I made purchases for him in the village. And paid me cash for my salary."

"Can you tell us how much he paid you, Hannah?"

"I'm not—" She looked at her hands. "I guess it doesn't matter now." She sighed. "He paid me four-thousand euros a month. Because of me being so reliable, he said. But no health insurance. I am not French, you see."

"That was generous of him," Merle said. "Except for the healthcare."

"I know! What if I got sick?" Her eyes widened. "But I didn't."

"Were you able to save some of your salary, Hannah?" Pascal continued.

"Oh, yes. I have no expenses. I take no trips, of course, as he needed me here to keep everything safe."

"He was concerned? Did he keep valuables in the house? Cash? Jewelry?"

"Um." Hannah glanced away. "Well. There is a safe."

Pascal stood up. "Show me, Hannah."

HANNAH LED them into a small office off the hallway to the bedrooms. It looked like the policemen hadn't bothered much in here, except to take away a computer from the desk. The outline of it stood in the dust. Bookshelves lined two facing walls with a window on the outside wall. Two large paintings hung on either side of the window. Pascal walked immediately over to them. They looked like original oils, and expensive. They might be Gustav Klimts, Merle thought. Beautiful pinks and pearly golds.

He felt around the frame of the maybe-Klimt.

"No, no," Hannah said, pointing at the bookshelves on the right. "Over here."

She stepped up to the middle bank of shelves and counted the books on an eye-level shelf with her finger. She stopped, pulled out an ancient green hardcover book and ran her fingers inside the slot where it had been. There was a loud click. The full shelving unit, some eight feet tall and three feet wide, sprang open along the right edge.

"I'm not supposed to know about that," Hannah said guiltily. "But five years I'm here. I see things. And when I am alone for weeks, I figure it out."

Pascal grabbed the edge of the wooden bookcase and pulled it wide. Behind it, set into a wall, was the safe, with a rotating combination, some three feet wide by three feet high.

Hannah said, "I do not know how to unlock it so don't ask me."

He looked closely at the safe. "Wait here," he told the women. "Don't touch anything."

Merle backed into the hall, watching Pascal go out the front door. Elise came in the door and looked around. "Merle?"

"Back here."

Elise appeared to be glowing. It made Merle smile. She rushed down the hallway and looked inside the office. "What's this?"

"A safe. Did he tell you about it?"

"No. But we were only here a few hours together."

Merle took her hand. "I'm glad you didn't go out with him that night."

Elise frowned. "Me too. Where did Pascal go?"

Before Merle could answer he returned through the front door with two of the *Brigade criminelle* detectives from *Nationale*. The women backed out of the way and watched as they examined the safe, berating each other for not finding it during the search. Pascal nodded, mentioned Hannah, and they scratched their heads. Then they all left, leaving the bookshelf out of place and stretching a crime scene tape across the closed office door.

"*N'entrez pas, mesdames,*" one *policier* entreated, wagging a finger. "No entry."

IN THE KITCHEN, Hannah discovered yet another bottle of wine chilling in the refrigerator. "*Quel surprise,*" she said. No one refused.

"We need to find a hotel," Pascal told Merle as they settled back in the shade of the umbrella outside. "It is too late to drive home tonight."

"I know just the place," Hannah said. "I will make you a reservation. It is close by, in the village."

"Thank you, Hannah. Two rooms if possible." Merle watched the young housekeeper, who seemed to have her definite ups and downs today, as she scurried inside to make the call.

Pascal took his wine glass and went back outside to talk to the cops. Merle looked at her sister. "Well?"

"What?" Elise took a sip of the *sancerre*. "This is good, isn't it? Buttery."

"Don't be coy. What happened? With Conor."

"Ah, Conor." She smiled at Merle. "You're dying to know, aren't you? Well, you were right. He likes me."

"And do you like him?"

"I wasn't sure. You don't know what's gone on, Merle. He was quite short with me, pretty cold and rude really. On the farm and so on."

"So? Were you rude to him?"

Elise shrugged. "*Peut-être*. Playing hard to get. It's so tiring. I guess he was jealous of Ari although I have no idea why."

"So spill."

"I wasn't really sure if I liked him, is what I was trying to say, until I kissed him."

Merle whooped. "I knew it."

"Then, sister dearest, I was positively sure. Ooh la la. What a kisser." Elise's eyes went soft. "He's a hottie, isn't he? Those shoulders! But he might have a girlfriend, some Duke's daughter, Lady Stick-up-her-Behind. I saw them online at a lah-dee-dah horsey thing."

Merle scoffed. "If he had a girlfriend—which I doubt—he doesn't have that one anymore. I guarantee it."

Scott opened the sliding door to the living room door and squinted into the shafts of afternoon sunlight. He was fully clothed again, in his wrinkled cotton shorts and t-shirt. He appeared to be dry. His hair had been combed, his freckles polished. Elise and Merle looked at him, then at each other, and both swore under their breath.

"Conor was going to get him an Uber," Elise whispered. "What are we going to do with him?"

Merle put up an index finger and stood up. "Scott." She walked quickly over to him.

"Pascal wants to talk to you out on the driveway. Come with me."

As he left, he glanced at Elise, his eyes pained and sad. She had turned her back.

CHAPTER TWENTY-SIX

lthough Hannah insisted she had to stay at the house to safeguard Ari's belongings, the three of them, Pascal, Merle, and Elise, talked her into having dinner with them. She knew, of course, just the place. They all got into Merle's Peugeot about seven in the evening, after the *policiers* had finished for the day.

Scott was gone. He had been given a lift to Aix-en-Provence courtesy of the first *policiers* to leave the scene. He still had his wallet, although it was damp, with credit cards, identification, and cash—everything he needed to get a train ticket. He was going back to Malcouziac to get his bags then on to Paris and home. That's what he said anyway. Pascal had given him some straight talk about women, he told them, laughing.

The village was ancient and quaint and lovely in the evening air, the stone facades of the buildings around the central *place* radiating the day's heat. Hannah led them through the square, down a side street to a small, quiet restaurant, the type of place Merle would have picked out in a heartbeat, the elegant menu posted and the delicious smells wafting out the door. It would be a nice finale to a long, tiring day.

"You sit," Hannah said as the maitre d' led them to a table. "I will join you in a few minutes. I have to see someone. You understand?"

"Of course," Elise said. "Should we order?"

"Yes, yes," Hannah said, already half out the door.

"She has a boyfriend here," Elise explained as they arranged themselves at the small table. "He owns a bicycle shop."

"I wonder that he didn't come out to see her today," Merle said. "Do you think the village even knows about the—"

"Shhh," Pascal whispered. "Don't upset the digestion."

The restaurant's dining room was washed in blue light, with pale walls and a scattering of mirrors and artworks. It was a relaxing atmosphere, serene and hushed. Not a place to discuss murder.

They ordered from the oversized menus and ate leisurely, with little conversation. They were all too tired. As they finished dessert, with still no sign of Hannah's return, Merle heard her cellphone buzzing in her purse.

It was Stasia. "Oh, shoot," Merle muttered. "I didn't get a chance to call her and now here she is."

"You better take it," Elise said. "Go outside."

Pascal nodded. "Don't worry. We will finish your *chocolat*."

Merle answered as she walked to the narrow street. "Stace! How are you?"

"Just peachy. Absolutely fucking peachy."

"Ah." Merle leaned against the still-warm stone of the building across from the restaurant. "So you heard."

"Did I ever. You didn't call and tell me though, Merdle. Really?"

"I'm sorry. She made me promise."

"Well, it doesn't matter now. The boy's father has been on the line, ripping Rick a new one. Honestly, who are these people and why do we care about them?"

"I was wondering the same thing. Who are they?"

"Wait, I'm going out onto the porch. Is it nice there? The fireflies are here. It's a bit magical in the yard."

"It's hot here in Provence. I found Elise. Or she found me. Anyway, she's fine."

"Was she lost?"

"She was a bit lost. But she's okay. So what's the deal with Teague??"

"His father is some muckety-muck hedge fund manager in Boston. She's a professor, I think, of something. Mostly they are pissed off."

"Really mad? At Willow or at Teague?"

"At both of them."

"I know you must be furious, Stasia. No wedding and all...."

"I was, at the beginning. But that didn't last long. The parents, Mr. and Mrs. Stanley Hoover the Third, have decided they are going to have the marriage annulled."

"Oh no. Poor Willow."

"Don't start on 'poor Willow.' She got herself into this mess."

"Right. But they did seem like they were in love."

"Did they? Seriously?"

"He said it. 'We love each other, Miss Bennett.'"

The swing on the porch creaked a few times. "Well, that's something, I guess." Stasia's voice was low and hurt.

"How old is Teague anyway? He seems young."

"Barely twenty-one. Still at Boston College, in the middle of his junior year. With no visible means of support beyond his trust fund."

"What a mess. I'm sorry. Are they still at my house?"

"Where are you? I figured you'd be there, supervising."

"Sorry. Emergency in Provence." She hesitated. Did Stasia really need to know about the violent demise of Monsieur Delcroix? "There was a problem with the man Elise was staying with. But it's all good now. She's safe."

"Did she run off with another Frenchman? That cow."

"It's working out all right, Stasia. Don't worry."

"You're not going to explain, are you? Well, that's fine because I have enough on my plate. We have to get those kids back here, separately or together, and figure out an annulment."

Merle sighed. "I'm so sorry, Stace."

Her sister moaned and groaned and swore a little more, then rang off. Merle stared at her cellphone, wondering if these busybody parents really knew what they were doing. That included Rick and Stasia. Willow was almost twenty-three, going to law school soon. Should her parents be running her life? She obviously didn't want them to. But did she have a choice in the matter?

Merle looked up and saw Hannah walking quickly down the narrow lane, holding onto the hand of a rangy young man. She smiled broadly as she spied Merle.

"I've missed dinner, haven't I?" Hannah took a big breath. "This is Régis. My boyfriend."

Merle smiled and shook his hand. "*Salut*, Régis." His hand was darkened with oil. His greasy dark hair fell in his eyes and he had multiple tattoos on his arms. He had charm though and a nice smile. "The bicycle shopkeeper?"

"*Oui.* That is right," he said haltingly in English. "Hannah teach me *anglais*. I am bad."

"You're doing very well," Merle said encouragingly.

Hannah said, "Can you tell them I had to go? I'm going to stay here, with Régis. He doesn't want me to stay at the house, not with a murderer on the loose."

"That's sensible." Merle wished the two of them well as they turned to go. Inside the restaurant, she joined Pascal and Elise in time for a few sips of coffee. "I order you *décaf*, as you like," he said. "Did sister give you a rant?"

"Not really but she is upset." Merle sipped her lukewarm coffee. "The parents are going to get the marriage annulled."

"What? Is that fair to the young lovers?" he protested.

"Yeah, don't they have a say in it?" Elise asked.

"It's the boy's parents, I think, although Rick and Stasia are going along with it. Teague's parents are rich, it appears, and hold all the purse-strings. He's only twenty-one."

"Old enough to vote," Pascal said.

"And go to war," Elise added.

"But not support yourself without your trust fund apparently." Merle looked at each of them. "Are we going back to Malcouziac tomorrow?"

"It is up to Elise," Pascal said.

"Are you done here?" Merle asked. "We can't stay at Ari's house. We're just in the way of the investigators."

It was agreed. They would head back to the Dordogne in the

morning. As they walked through the warm night to the car to get their bags, Merle took Elise's arm. "What about Conor?"

"I don't know," Elise admitted. "We didn't make plans. It seemed useless."

"Plans are never useless. They just don't always work out."

Elise turned to her sister. "It's ridiculous to even think about seeing him again. I mean, how would that happen? Where? He travels all the time, all over the world. I feel like like a fool—why bother, you know?"

Merle let Pascal go a few steps ahead. She lowered her voice. "Seeing a hottie again, one who kisses like a dream and is crazy about you? You're right, that is a bit of a bother."

Elise squeezed her arm. "Oh, Merle. It never works out for me."

"Don't give up, honey. Never give up."

CHAPTER TWENTY-SEVEN

THE DORDOGNE

*B*y the time they got back to the Dordogne, lugging bags through the streets to the stone cottage Merle had named *La Maison Chanceuse,* the Lucky House, they were all hot and exhausted. The trip hadn't been any shorter than the previous ones. Elise in the back seat, moping about something she wouldn't specify—the end of her adventure, the lavender she forgot to bring back, going back to work, and no doubt Conor—was a buzz-kill. Merle tried to engage her for the first hundred miles then gave up.

Pascal unlocked the door and ushered the sisters inside. He dropped his duffle and listened for sounds of the occupants. "Tristan? Are you here?"

"Hey." He came bounding down the stairs and gave Pascal then his mother many kisses. He was careful with Elise but when she brightened at his smile, she too got the hug and kiss treatment. "You're back." He looked out the door to the street. "No Scott?"

"Didn't he come back for his bags yet?" Merle asked. "He said he would."

"Nope. Hey, come and see Willow and Teague. They're in the back." He led them through the kitchen. "They love your garden, mom."

A cheap lounge chair had been set up in the shade under the acacia tree. A tangle of limbs, arms and legs, were visible. As they stepped into the garden, Willow and Teague jumped apart, faces red and obviously in the foreplay stage of marital relations. Teague stood up, straightening his shorts. "Miss Bennett." He glanced at Pascal.

"And you are the infamous Teague, I suppose," Pascal said loudly, as if the boy were hard of hearing. "And the adorable Willow." He crossed his arms.

"Hi, Pascal," Willow squeaked. "Aunt Merle." The strap of her sundress kept falling off her shoulder. She was sunburnt, or just embarrassed.

"So," Pascal continued, glowering at them. "You two tied the knot. Here at the church?"

"Yessir," Teague replied, eyes darting.

"Were there witnesses?"

Willow and Teague looked at each other. "There was a priest," Willow said.

"No witness? No family members, no friends?"

"There was Scott," Teague said.

"Did Scott sign the big bible as a witness?" Pascal demanded.

Merle hid her smile. She could see where Pascal was going with this.

"Um." Teague shrugged.

"And you registered the marriage at the provincial offices in Périgueux? And all the blood tests and official health things?"

"Health things?" Teague said.

Pascal ignored him. "And the honeymoon suite is at which hotel in town?"

"Honeymoon suite?" Teague repeated.

"We—Aunt Merle said we could stay here," Willow stammered.

"And that has come to an end. Because I am here. Your aunt is here. We need our bedroom. Plus, your *tante* Elise and your cousin need beds. You understand, sweet Willow?"

She nodded. "Of course. We'll just—"

"And remove the sheets before you go." Pascal watched them as they gathered up shoes and towels and hurried into the cottage to pack. He called: "Bring them down to the laundry."

"That wasn't necessary," Merle said.

"But you liked it, didn't you?" Pascal had a big grin on his face. "They had their fun. They will be going home soon anyway."

Merle had texted Tristan from the road and asked him to buy a chicken at the grocery and any sort of vegetables. He had done marvelously, finding a plump hen, asparagus, Brussel sprouts, tiny new potatoes, and a bunch of dill. Merle gave him a congratulatory hug for all that and stared, exhausted, at the ingredients. Pascal came up behind her. "It is a feast. Good work, Tristan."

Her son peered into her face. "Mom looks tired. Maybe we should take over. Let the sisters catch up."

"A perfect idea. I think the sisters may have talked themselves out but that is nothing to having your two favorite men prepare you a meal." He put his arms around Merle and kissed her neck. "Pour some wine for your sister and yourself and we will make cuisine magic."

Before the cooking could begin, Teague and Willow clomped down the stairs with suitcases and armfuls of sheets and towels. Tristan stepped up to take the laundry from them. "That inn is always a good place. You've seen it, right? Hotel Quimet. By the *place*, with the yellow front," Merle said

Willow had regained her composure. "Don't worry about us. We're adults." Teague was hiding by the front door.

Pascal raised his eyebrows. "Come back for dinner if you wish. Eight o'clock."

"Don't wait for us," Willow sniffed and led Teague out the door into the street, dragging their rolling bags behind them. Merle and Pascal went to the front window and watched them arguing as they walked. Willow threw one arm up in the air angrily, yanking on her bag with the other.

"Oops. First fight," Merle said.

"More like fourth or fifth," Tristan muttered.

AFTER DINNER they all collapsed into bed. At eleven-thirty Merle heard her cellphone ping with a text. Stasia announced she would be arriving in Malcouziac the next day. Then, several hours later, they heard banging on the front door.

"What is it?" Merle asked Pascal as he pulled on his pants.

"We'll see."

Pascal shone the flashlight through the door's windows and the crack in the shutters. A reddened, freckled face with a dirt smear across the forehead peered at him. "Please, sir. It's Scott Orr. Remember me? Scott?"

"I remember," Pascal muttered as he unlocked the door shutters. He stood squarely in the door frame, blocking entry to the house. "What is it, Scott? You've managed to wake up the entire house." He looked at his watch. "It is three in the morning."

Scott slumped. He looked dirty and tired, still in the shorts and t-shirt he'd been wearing when he left Provence. "You wouldn't believe it if I told you. What happened, I mean. The train, then getting here." He put on a sad-eyed face and looked over Pascal's shoulder into the house.

"There is no place for you here, Scott. But we have your case ready." He leaned down to pick up the suitcase set by the door for just this moment. "Good luck. Enjoy your time in France."

Pascal pulled the shutters closed as Scott sputtered, "But—but what? Sir? Monsieur? Please, can you help me?"

Pascal paused, threading the chain through the padlock. "What?"

"Where will I go? It's so late. Where can I stay?"

"I would try the inn by the square. Your cousin stays there with his beautiful bride, I believe. *Bonne nuit.*"

Merle rolled over when he got back in bed. "Everything okay?"

"Only Scott. He is gone."

MERLE FOUND Elise in the garden the next morning, nursing a cup of coffee. She glanced up at her sister with dull eyes.

"How did you sleep?" Merle asked. She shrugged. "Scott came by for his stuff. Pascal sent him packing."

"Good," Elise muttered into her mug. She heaved a big sigh. "I should go home, Merle. There's nothing for me in France now."

"I understand. When is your plane ticket?"

"What's today? I think it's in three days."

"Do you want to try to change your ticket?"

"I have to get to Paris anyway. That'll take a day."

Merle nodded. "Did you get a text from Stasia?"

"Can't wait to see her," Elise said drily. "Today, right?"

The morning sun hit the wall that overlooked the orchards and pastures below the village, lighting up the little apple tree. Merle sat down on the metal chair, feeling the sunshine warm her shoulders. "So—"

Elise glanced up. "What?"

"What about Conor? Have you heard from him?"

"It was just a passing thing, Merle. Forget about him. He's just a cute guy in corgi boxer shorts."

Merle laughed. "What?"

"He captured the bat in my room. We were all in various states of undress. It was the middle of a hot night."

"And his boxers have little corgi dogs on them? That's kinda hot."

"Well." Elise smiled and raised her eyebrows, then slumped over her coffee mug again.

They sat in quiet morning contemplation for a few minutes. Then, they both got texts on their mobile phones, one ping after another. They dug out their phones from various pockets, read the messages, and said in unison: "Stasia."

Elise said, "Miss Drama has arrived. Where is she?"

"Bergerac. She'll be here at exactly eleven-oh-five."

Elise stood up. "Do I need to be present?"

"No, she's here for Willow. Oh, she's bringing Teague's mother. Greaaat."

Elise was almost inside the house again, mentally preparing for her hide-out from the mothers, when her phone pinged again. Merle looked back at her. "Stasia?"

Elise shook her head, a smile creeping across her face.

She put her phone against her chest and ran up the stairs. She wanted to read the message in private, whatever it was. As much as she was cheered by hearing from Conor, she had a fair idea it would be a 'Dear Jane' type text, a sorry-but-not-gonna-happen. He was a very serious person, not a silly romantic. He had to feel the same way she did, that their circumstances prevented them even seeing each other again, let alone kissing at length on a sunny lane in Provence. Still, her girlish heart betrayed her.

Weirdly, it was neither the good news, nor the bad news, she expected.

CHAPTER TWENTY-EIGHT

*E*lise stood in the door of the bathroom as Pascal was shaving. She read him the message from Provence.

"Bonjour. I hope your trip to the Dordogne went smoothly. And no Scott sightings. The farm is in an uproar. I need to tell you that my cousin's husband Guy has been taken in for questioning in the death of Delcroix. The coppers are such keufs here, this is total bollocks. I will call when I know more. À bientôt. Conor."

SHE SQUINTED AT HER PHONE. "What's that mean—'*keu*fs'?"

In the tiny bathroom Pascal watched her in the mirror, rinsed his razor, and shut off the water. "What is this? The farmer?"

"Guy. Monsieur Vernay. He's married to Conor's cousin Vivianne. They run the lavender farm."

"But what is his connection with Delcroix?"

She shrugged. "Should I call Conor?"

"*Bien sûr*. We need information," Pascal said, wiping his face on a towel. "And don't call a *policier* a '*keuf.*' It won't go well." Elise ran back into the garden to make the call. Merle stepped back to let her pass.

"What's happening?" Merle asked.

Pascal made for the stairs. "The farmer has been detained for questioning in the murder. I need to make some calls."

Merle stood in the cross-section of Elise and Pascal, both dashing off to make important calls. This day, so peaceful at the start, the four of them cozy at home, Tristan making coffee then off for a run in the countryside, Pascal nuzzling her neck—it had turned chaotic. She rubbed her eyes. She needed more coffee.

She'd brought an American-style drip coffeemaker over a few years before, just for these occasions, when a house full of guests all needed caffeine and they needed it now. Unfortunately, they had emptied the pot, all twelve cups. And the bag of coffee beans was empty. Merle tied on her shoes and called upstairs: "Going to the grocery."

No one answered.

Walking the cobblestone streets of the village, making sure to miss the holes where stones had gone missing, slowing to admire the colors of the flowers in boxes, waving at neighbors and acquaintances: it was like a meditation, much needed today. At the bottom of Rue de Poitiers, she turned right instead of going toward the grocery. She turned right again and knocked on the door of her friend, Albert.

The old priest opened the door wide and blinked at her, his smile widening. "*Mon amie! Bonjour!* Come in, come in."

"Can I wait until I get back? I'm headed to the *petit marché* and wondered if you needed anything."

Albert rubbed his round, bald head and decided the only thing he needed was goat cheese. Oh, and white peaches, if they looked decent. And some sliced ham. And, don't forget the baguette. Always the baguette. Merle smiled, making a mental list.

"Is that all?"

"Tomorrow, I walk over myself."

Albert looked like he'd been napping. His sparse gray hair stood at all angles and he was wearing his ever-present blue jumpsuit, the kind plumbers wore to fix your pipes. As a uniform, it was convenient. And possibly comfortable enough for bed.

Stasia is coming, Merle reminded herself as she walked toward the center of Malcouziac. She'd have to make several stops to get all of Albert's items plus her own dinner fixings. The baguette at the *boulangerie*, peaches at the produce market. It was fine. It kept her mind off whatever was happening in Provence.

Stasia said she was traveling with Teague's mother, a woman named Holly. What exactly was Merle's role here, just steer them to the young couple and hope for the best? She hoped that was all that would be required but knowing Stasia there would be a few scenes. She hoped to avoid them.

By the time she finished her marketing it was ten-thirty. Thirty-five minutes to Stasia touchdown. She spent a few minutes chatting with Albert, told him to come over for dinner, and made a quick exit out his back gate, across the alley, and into her garden.

STASIA WAS IN THE COTTAGE, yoo-hooing at the top of her lungs, before Merle even heard the arrival. She was in the kitchen, putting away groceries. She stuck her head to the right, looking through to the living room and acted surprised that her incredibly punctual sister was ten minutes early.

"Look at you, traveling the world at the drop of a hat!" Merle wiped her hands on a towel and went to give her sister a hug.

"What a whirlwind," Stasia said. "I feel like a damp rag."

"Do you want a shower?"

"Oh, no, it's not that bad. They gave us those lovely hot towels on the flight." Stasia turned to the woman standing behind her. "This is Holly Hoover. Holly, my sister Merle."

The women shook hands. Holly straightened and tried to smile but she looked like she'd been run ragged, possibly by both Stasia and Teague. Her dull brown hair stood out on one side of her head, her eyebrow pencil had smeared on the left brow, and her tan skirt and polka dot blouse must have once been prim and proper. Now they looked like she'd slept in them, which she no doubt had.

"You made good time, Stace," Merle said cautiously. "When did you leave New York?"

"Yesterday, around noon. Not ideal for arriving in Paris. There are no trains in the night, did you know that?"

"I did. But you made it. Come in, I'll get you something to drink." She led the two women out into the garden. There was no sign of Elise. Holly seemed to perk up, gazing at the flowers and fruit trees and sunshine. "Water? Wine? Coffee? Something stronger?" Merle asked.

"Just water," Stasia answered. "We have a lot of work to do this afternoon." They sat down on the green metal chairs. "They're not—" Her eyes flicked to the upstairs windows.

"No. They're staying at Hotel Quimet, I think. We asked them to move. We needed the beds."

Fifteen minutes later, sipping their cool drinks and moaning about their unmanageable children until Merle was hoping for a distraction, one came in the form of Pascal. He called her name, then stepped out the kitchen door. He stopped at the sight of Stasia and Holly.

"Ladies."

Stasia jumped up and ran over to give him a big hug. She immediately released him and went back to pouting in her chair. Merle watched the comical display of pretend emotion and said, "And this is Holly. She is Teague's mother. They're here to straighten out *les jeunes*."

"Ah. Welcome." He nodded as if to say, 'good luck with that.' "Can I talk to you inside, blackbird?"

Merle followed him into the parlor. "I guess I have to ask them to stay for dinner," she whispered. "I already asked Albert. We may have to borrow some chairs."

They stood close together between the furniture, voices just above a whisper. "This is about the Delcroix business," Pascal said. "*Nationale* opened the safe. Inside they found documents related to a loan that Ari gave to Guy Vernay, using the lavender farm as collateral."

"A big loan?"

"About four-hundred-thousand euros."

"What did they need that for?"

"Paying off a mortgage or something like that. Farming, it is risky. At any rate, the note was to come due August 1."

"In a few days."

He nodded. "Puts him in a bad spot. But that's not the worst of it. There were computer disks also in the safe, with video from a surveillance system at the house. It showed Guy Vernay arriving on the doorstep."

"When? Was it dated?"

"That, I don't know. But the *Brigade* detectives think it's enough, for now."

"Does he have an alibi for whatever date it was supposed to have happened?"

"Maybe, maybe not. The coroner hasn't determined an exact time of death yet. The body was in bad shape from the heat."

Merle winced. She could only imagine. "Is Elise talking to Conor? What does he say?"

"He is angry, concerned for his family. It is the talk of the Luberon, as you can imagine. There has been some bad blood between the Vernays and other lavender producers, he admitted. Accusations of pesticides and chemicals when they advertise their product as 'organic,' of cutting corners, of using students as free or cheap labor and not paying taxes on them."

"Sounds tricky."

"Elise wants to go back to the area. Conor has invited her, it appears."

"Oh, sweet. But why? What can she do?"

"I don't know. You talk to her, blackbird. I am off to make some more calls and see what I can find out about the murder." Pascal gave her a quick kiss, pocketed his mobile phone, and left the cottage on foot, head down, concentrating.

Merle wondered if he missed the action of field investigation now that he had a desk job in Bordeaux. He seemed to make little chores for himself, surprise visits to vineyards when nobody asked about them. He helped his boss with a homicide investigation last year. He still talked about it once in a while, with a little gleam of excitement in his eye, even though the wine business was in his blood.

Tristan returned from running, sweaty and starving. Merle sent him to the bathroom to clean up and told him his aunt Stasia had arrived and to try to be nice. He jumped up the stairs three at a time and returned with his clean clothes. When he shut the door to the bathroom, she peeked into the garden. Stasia and Holly were calm, talking quietly between themselves, smoothing their blouses and dabbing their noses in the heat. They would be fine for a few more minutes.

Upstairs, Merle found Elise sitting on the edge of one of the twin beds in the loft, staring at her cellphone as if willing it to ring. She startled at Merle's appearance. "Hey."

Merle sat on Tristan's bed. "Stasia's here. With Teague's mom. They look shellshocked."

"Jet lag."

"Or the suddenness of flying across the Atlantic to save your children from themselves."

Elise rolled her eyes. "They're not children. It's ridiculous."

Merle let that one lie. "Pascal says you've been talking to Conor."

She nodded. "Uh-huh."

"You don't sound excited."

"There's been a murder— where I was staying. I'm not excited about that. Plus, I feel like it's just another fool's errand, another thing to get my hopes up, then dash them. It's not a good time for him. He's angry and confused. His family is falling apart."

"You got to know them pretty well then?"

"I wouldn't say that. We saw Vivianne at breakfast, then at dinner. She didn't speak English though and me, you know, with my two percent French. The farmer, Guy, was like a manager, just assigning chores to everyone. I spent very little time around him, or the kids."

"What does Conor think?"

"He didn't know about the loan. Pascal just told him about that. He was shocked. He thought the farm was profitable. It always seemed so well-run. They inherited it so why was there a loan? It's been in the family for generations." Elise looked up at her sister. "I saw something one night. Now I think it was Ari coming over to rag on them about the money. I was going to the kitchen to get some wine late one evening. Two men were arguing then they ran out the back door, into the shadows. It gets really dark out there. One had to be Monsieur Vernay because he was tall, but I couldn't see the other one. I went into the kitchen and Vivianne was crying. Like sobbing uncontrollably. She wouldn't tell me what was going on so I just got my wine and left."

"Awkward," Merle agreed. "Not what you expect at a place of heavenly flowers."

Elise smiled. "Monsieur Vernay said that all the time. Like he was trying to convince himself of the magnificence of the farm."

"It *is* pretty fabulous. Do you think Ari coveted it?"

"Hannah said he wanted a lavender property. So yeah, quite possible."

Merle waited for Elise to say more, to change her mind about Conor, to get out of her funk. The second hand on Merle's wristwatch went around the dial. It was silent in the house, except for the shower running downstairs.

She rubbed her eyes. What a morning.

CHAPTER TWENTY-NINE

Stasia and Holly stood motionless, waiting for Merle in the parlor when she came down the stairs. Merle hadn't gotten far with Elise. It was sad to see her so pessimistic about everything, especially about a hot golfer. Something wasn't right. The only time she'd seen Elise smile was after he kissed her in Provence.

"Merle." Stasia looked furious, ready to lower the boom. "Can you take us to the hotel? We can get lunch there and talk to Teague and Willow at the same time."

"Sure." Merle headed for the front door. The women grabbed their rolling bags and pulled them out the door. "This way," Merle said, motioning them down the street. She was several steps down the *rue* when she realized they weren't moving. She turned back.

Stasia called, "Where's your car?"

"Parked in the city lot." Merle walked back. "Where's your car?"

"We came by taxi," Stasia said.

"What—all the way from Bergerac?"

Holly nodded while Stasia pinched her lips together. "Three-hundred euros," she whispered.

"I paid for it," Holly said. "It was quicker."

"Wow, I—" Merle was going to say she could have picked them up but that would be a lie. "So, can you walk to the hotel with your suitcases?"

"How far is it?" Holly asked, sniffing at the idea of it.

"Five blocks."

Stasia turned to Holly. "It'll be okay. Come on."

With huffs and curses and bags going sideways they managed to make it to Hotel Quimet with no injuries. Merle held the door for them. "Have a nice lunch. Talk later," she called.

Stasia stopped abruptly. "We need you in here, Merle. For the *français.*"

Merle was negotiating with the front desk clerk, translating for Stasia, figuring beds and nights to be stayed, the whereabouts of Teague and Willow, when they heard raised voices in the lobby. They turned to see Holly standing in front of a slumped Scott Orr, cowering in a chair with a filthy leg dangling over the arm.

"What is the meaning of this, Scott?" Holly demanded. "You were meant to be traveling with Teague, not setting him up to elope. And what in heaven's name happened to you? You look like you've been dragged through the mud."

Merle turned back to the clerk, ignoring the drama. "You have two rooms?"

The clerk told her yes but they were not on the same floor and rather small. Stasia threw down her credit card. "Passports," Merle reminded her, glancing back at Holly.

Stasia walked to Holly and returned with her passport. "It seems Scott is Teague's cousin?"

"Yes, we've had the pleasure. He's been here for a few days. Remember him? Elise's ex?"

"What? I thought they were engaged."

"Did she tell you that? She never told me."

The clerk interrupted with two key fobs. He squinted at Holly and Scott. "*Monsieur, cet homme là-bas? Il n'est pas bienvenue ici.* He is not welcome. Last night he was abusive to the manager. He is filthy. Does he belong to you?"

"Oh, no," Merle said. "Absolutely not."

"Can he come up and take a shower at least?" Stasia whispered.

Merle shrugged and smiled sweetly at the clerk. Of course, they could sneak him up. She on the other hand was out of here. The sisters stepped over to Holly.

"All set," Stasia said. "They're in Suite 310. Right?"

Merle nodded. "Dinner tonight?"

Stasia shook her head. "There's too many of us. We'll talk later."

Merle gave her hug, glanced at the pathetic spectacle of Scott, and widened her eyes at her sister. "Good luck."

ALBERT JOINED THEM AT SEVEN, bringing his usual bottle of plum *eau de vie* made from the fruit of his backyard tree. Merle suspected he would never run out of *eau de vie*, having seen bottles that looked fifty years old emerge from his *cave*. The stuff was almost toxic, strong enough to strip the hair off a monkey's back, according to Albert, but Pascal always had a little, adding water to it on the sly.

Pascal managed to keep the conversation light until they were finished, eating cheese from a round wooden serving board. He passed the tray to Albert and recommended the Comté. "You can never go wrong with a Comté," he said. He glanced at Tristan. "You will clear tonight, or should I?"

Tris got the hint, popping his last bit of cheese into his mouth and gathering the plates and flatware. He carried them to the kitchen and ran water in the sink. Pascal raised his eyebrows at Merle. She leaned in.

"What have you discovered, my sweet?" she whispered.

"Well, the *Brigade* still keeps Guy Vernay. They are sure that he has done something, or hired someone, or something. It appears he has an alibi for the night they think Delcroix was killed, the first night he and Elise went to the house near Aix."

"What's his alibi?"

"Not the best—sleeping with his wife. But there was a disturbance in the students' quarters. Someone had found a rat in their room and, well, you can imagine the scene. Guy went up there, as did his son, Lucas, and most of the male students helped round up the beast, cornering it in the back stairwell. A student used a broom to get it into a box held by Guy. They are experts at rat-catching in Provence."

"Elise said they had a bat incident, quite similar."

Elise nodded. "I opened my window. Against the rules but it was so hot and stuffy and my fan broke. Actually, Conor was the one who got the window open. The bat flew in sometime in the night. Then the same thing happened. Guy and Conor came upstairs, everyone was out in the hallway in next to nothing." She raised her eyebrows at Albert. "One girl sleeps in the nude, we discovered."

"Rats and bats and naked girls," Albert said, smiling. "Such excitement."

"So, he's fine?" Merle asked. "They'll release him?"

Pascal shrugged. "Not immediately. You know they can keep someone for days without charging them. It's the French system."

"I remember," Merle said. She had been detained on her first visit here but only had to spend one night in the tiny cell. The food at least was delicious.

"But if he has an alibi, with all those people vouching for his where-abouts," Elise asked, "why are they keeping him?"

"The timing of the event is still a little soft," Pascal said. "Still a guess."

"Did you talk to Conor again? What does he say?" Merle asked.

Elise shook her head and ate a bite of ashy goat cheese. "I didn't."

"Tell Pascal what you saw that night," Merle urged her.

Elise recounted the story of the two men arguing and the crying Vivianne. Pascal asked if she thought the second man was Ari. "I never got a good look at him in the dark. He was shorter than Guy, that's all I could tell."

"So, it could have been one of the students."

"Whoever it was spoke really good French," she said. "The students didn't."

"So, who else was on the farm?" Pascal started counting on his fingers. "Males, let's say. The son. Conor. Who else?"

"There's an old man who works in the distillery."

"That's three. Anybody else?"

"Maybe another farm hand. I think at least one more, maybe two."

"Okay, four or five suspects for the argument, if it was someone who worked there. You can't remember anything they said?"

She shook her head. "Couldn't understand it. Sorry."

"But what about Vivianne?" Merle asked. "Can we ask her who it was and what they were arguing about?"

"We might be able to," Pascal said. "But Elise definitely can."

LATER, under the dome of stars in the dark, fragrant garden, Merle sat forward in a metal chair to gently ask Elise, "What if it turns out to be Conor?"

Elise had been staring at the Milky Way, bright in the moonless sky. "What if what?"

"The person Guy was arguing with. Is it possible?"

"Sure, I guess. But if it's not Ari, what does it matter? Having an argument isn't the same as shooting somebody in the head."

"If Conor caught the bat that night, when it flew in your window, why didn't he help with the catching of the rat that night? Where was he?"

Elise's eyes widened. "You mean—"

Merle nodded. "He has no alibi, if that's the night it happened."

A wave of concern crossed Elise's face.

"How did Conor know you were at Ari's?" Merle asked.

"Oh. Well, the night before I left, I went to dinner with Ari in a little village nearby. Did I tell you that? I was so excited to have dinner away from the crabby little creeps at the farm. They basically had shunned me, wouldn't even speak to me. I got all dressed up. As I was waiting for Ari to pick me up, Conor bumped into me in the front hall." She sighed. "I was always running into him. Like he was following me."

"He must have been looking for a way to talk to you."

"Maybe. Anyway, Conor wanted to know what I'm doing dressed up and I told him I'm going to dinner and it's none of his business. He was really snippy about it. I see now he was jealous but then, I didn't know."

"Did he ask if you were going with Ari?"

"I told him. He'd seen us together at the *fête* the day before. He really blew up about Ari. He said, 'Do you know who he is, what he's done?'"

"What's he done?"

"I never found out. I guess Conor meant that he was a gangster or some kind of thug."

"Do you think Conor hated Ari? Enough to harm him?"

Elise blinked. "Um. No?"

Merle looked at her for a long moment. "Are you going back to Provence?"

"Should I?"

"I think we have to go back."

Elise's eyebrows spiked in the middle, the way they'd done when she was little. "For Conor?"

Merle nodded. "For Guy. And yes, for Conor."

CHAPTER THIRTY

*E*arly the next morning, while Merle was making coffee, Stasia called. Merle had been wondering what was happening over at the hotel, whether anyone was speaking, had run away, or been bloodied. But their own dinner and late-night conversations had blotted out most of those concerns.

"Hey, what's up?" Merle asked, trying for cheerful.

"Oh, holy hell." Stasia sighed. "What a mess. So many slammed doors, yelling, cursing, refusing to talk, refusing to listen—you'd think it was a French farce. Oh, wait."

"Is Holly really upset?"

"A mild term for her state of mind. She must be used to being obeyed without argument. No wonder Teague ran off and got married. She even scares me."

"How are you doing?"

"Well, I've had about four hours of sleep in the last three days so—mostly running on caffeine fumes."

"Ugh."

"Yeah, not pretty. Look, I have a favor. You're so good at mediation. Could you come over and play that role for me? I've completely lost my objectivity. I want to kill everyone."

Merle hesitated. She had a tentative plan to whisk Elise back to Provence, along with Pascal and Tristan if possible. But maybe it could wait until afternoon.

"Sure. I'm happy to help, if I can."

"Oh, thank you. Can you come over right now?"

"Give me an hour, Stace. I'll be there at nine."

WHEN MERLE ARRIVED at Hotel Quimet, wearing her red blouse that she hoped would say 'stop' to all screamers, with a black skirt and sandals, she paused inside the doors to let her eyes adjust to the dim, slightly grimy lobby. It smelled like bacon and mildew. What room was Stasia in again? She would have to ask the clerk. A different one was now on duty, a young woman with dark hair and dramatic eye makeup.

She smiled at Merle in a professional way. "Bonjour, Madame."

Merle asked to be connected to Stasia's room on the house phone, that old-fashioned black instrument gathering dust at the end of the counter.

"Ah, you are Miss Bennett's sister?" The clerk inquired, somehow thrilled to have inside knowledge.

"Yes," Merle said warily.

"The party is in the breakfast room. Off to the right side. You will see them when you go through."

There were only three other tables of guests in the breakfast room, a large dining area with round tables for two or four guests. Except for one table in an alcove, where five Americans sat in a circle. There was an empty chair for Merle.

She did a quick examination of their faces as she approached. Stasia looked dead tired. Teague and Willow, sitting close together in the middle of the group, looked defensive but alert, fingers drumming the tablecloth. Scott sat to Teague's right. Why was he still here? He should be on a train to Paris by now. Merle felt her anger rise a little. *He better not come over and hassle Elise.*

Holly Hoover sat ramrod straight in her chair in a yellow twinset. Her jaw was tight, nostrils flared, and she looked like she might bite your head off, given half a chance. Merle sat down beside her, with Stasia on her right.

Let the games begin.

"Good morning, everyone," she said, trying to sound neutral but in charge. Like a judge, that was it. She would play judge this morning. She wanted to tell them all to be seated, like a bailiff would, but they wouldn't get the joke. "Can I get some coffee?"

Stasia immediately raised a hand for the waiter who trotted over. He was young but worldly enough to have figured out you do not cross Stasia Bennett. "My sister will have—?"

"Café latté. Double. *Merci*."

"Do you want to wait until you get it to start?" Stasia whispered.

"No. It's fine. Let's begin." Merle glanced at her for instructions but none came. "Okay. So, we have a problem. Willow and Teague want to stay married. Their parents want to get it annulled. Is that the long and short of it?"

Teague, Willow, Stasia, and Holly all responded immediately, voicing their objections to either what she said or what the words implied. Merle held up her hand like a cop and they shut their mouths. "Okay. I know you're all passionate about this. How about we go around the table and everyone give me their best argument for whatever outcome you want? Okay? You start, Stasia."

Stasia gave a rather weakly-argued case for law school and practicality over stupidly falling in love and stupidly getting married on a whim. At least she didn't raise her voice.

Next it was Willow's turn. "This is very simple. I am an adult. I have dominion over my own life, my own future. I can go to law school and be married. Ruth Bader Ginsberg did it. Teague can still finish college wherever he wants. He can transfer. He can get a job. I only want him to be happy. And be with me, of course."

She squeezed his hand and gave him an encouraging smile. Then Teague was up.

"Well, I—" He paused, eyes dark, brows low, and shook his head. Then he leaned back in his chair and crossed his arms. "This is bullshit. I don't have to tell you anything. You're not even involved in this."

He glared at Merle. Instead of hate, she saw fear in his eyes. He was way over his head here. That's why Scott had stayed. Teague probably asked him to.

"Teague," his mother hissed. "You said you would participate. We're trying to work this out."

He stood up angrily, throwing his napkin on the table just as the waiter arrived with Merle's coffee. "Then go right ahead. Work it out. But leave me and Willow alone." He grabbed her arm. "Come on."

"Ow." Willow squirmed out of his grip. "Sit down, Teague. Be sensible."

Wounded, Teague sat, keeping his chair far from the table and arms crossed. Merle looked around the table. No one appeared ready to engage him. That left it in her court.

"So, Teague. What is your plan about college?" He shrugged and looked away, out the window. "Do you plan to transfer somewhere closer to Willow's law school? Do you have a job lined up instead? What about an apartment? Have you put down a deposit somewhere?" Again, a deafening silence. "Okay, Scott. What do you have to offer here?"

"Ah, well. Nothing really." Scott blinked a number of times. He had taken a shower, it appeared, and changed his clothes. "I'm just the wing man, you know. Teague's my friend, and my cousin. I was just doing this as a favor for him, you know? And so I could see my girlfriend of course." He glanced at Merle. "Okay, my ex-girlfriend. I admit it, we're probably done."

"Progress. Good work there, Scott," Merle said. "What did you know about Teague and Willow's plans to get married over here?"

"Ah, nothing? He wanted to come to this village which I thought was kinda weird since that's where I wanted to go too. He told me he was going to meet somebody but I figured it was somebody else." Scott gave Teague a guilty side glance. Teague rolled his eyes. "What, man?" Scott pleaded.

"Someone else?" Merle asked. "Like someone else in particular?"

"Well, I..."

"Finish your sentence, Scott," Merle commanded. "Who is the someone else you expected him to meet?"

"Ah," he said nervously. "A different girl. You know. Not Willow."

"Does this different girl have an actual name, Scott?"

Holly was watching and listening intently. She gave a little gasp. "Amber? You mean Amber?"

"Who is Amber?" Merle asked.

Stasia leaned forward and confronted her daughter. "Amber Tinsley? Your *friend*, Amber Tinsley?"

Willow turned red. She swallowed hard and glared at Scott.

"Shut up, you bastard," Teague said to his cousin, on his feet again. "Just shut up."

"Who is Amber Tinsley?" Merle asked again.

The married couple clamped their mouths shut. Teague sat again, head in hands. Stasia took a breath and turned to her sister. "Amber Tinsley was Willow's college roommate and best friend. Have I got that right, Willow?" The girl shrugged one shoulder.

"Amber Tinsley," Holly announced, "is the daughter of Justice Louis Tinsley of the Massachusetts Supreme Judicial Court. Amber is Teague's fiancée."

"*Was* his fiancée," Scott said with no trace of irony. "Words matter, Aunt Holly."

THE MEDIATION BROKE up soon after that. Holly was giving Scott a piece of her mind. Teague sank nearly below the table. Merle let Stasia drag her upstairs to her hotel room. She also had ahold of Willow, pulling her into the room and shutting the door. Merle sat on the bed, as far from the action as she could get. She'd been on the receiving end of a few of Stasia's righteous lectures. This wouldn't be pretty.

"Explain yourself, Willow. Now." Stasia had her hands on her hips. Willow had her arms wrapped around her waist, as if trying to hold herself together. "Amber was engaged to Teague?"

"It just happened, Mom. We didn't plan it. We didn't sneak around behind her back or anything."

"How did it 'just' happen?"

Willow sighed. "We were at a concert down by the river. Tons of people, just before school started last fall. We danced, we kissed. You know, the usual stuff."

"You danced with your roommate's boyfriend. And kissed. Then what? You had sex? Then she got engaged to him. Your roommate. And you kept seeing him on the sly?"

Willow rallied and looked her mother in the eye. "That sounds about right. Look, I'm not the love police. If he doesn't love her and they're not married, what's the big deal?"

Stasia stared angrily at her daughter. Merle muttered, "She has a point."

"Did he break up with her before he came over here?" Stasia asked.

"I don't know and don't care. That's not on me, one way or another," Willow said. Then she sat on the end of the bed with a bounce. "Actually, maybe it's better now that it's all out in the open."

"Willow. If he cheats on his girlfriend—on his fiancée—how do you know he won't cheat on you?" Stasia asked, swinging her arms around. "Is that the kind of man you want to spend the rest of your life with? Always wondering who he's with, what he's up to?"

Willow put her head up and flung back her long blonde hair. "No. It's not."

Stasia's mouth was still open to continue the harangue. She shifted her feet, lowered her shoulders. "What did you say?"

Willow pouted and crossed her arms. "I don't think I want to be married. Not to him anyway. He's a brat. So immature. He's in that fraternity with all those neanderthals."

"And he grabs your arm," Merle added.

"Right. He's so physical," Willow said. "I guess that's why the sex was pretty hot. But not much in the brains department. His GPA seriously stinks and he's a business major, of all things. Not exactly like RBG's fabulous husband, is he? He'll have to go work for his father."

There was a change in the air as these new facts settled. A lightness, almost like a breeze, lifted Merle off the bed and set her down again, imperceptibly. There was hope, a resolution. She glanced at Stasia. Her face went white and her knees gave out. She sank to the floor, her face in her hands. Her gasp was like air going out of a balloon.

"Oh, thank you," Stasia whispered hoarsely. She reached out to touch Willow's foot. When she looked up, mascara and tears streamed down her face. "My darling, darling girl."

CHAPTER THIRTY-ONE

*I*t was decided that Willow should be the one to break the news to Teague. It was her marriage, after all, no matter how much the mothers meddled. How to do this without creating a huge scene was another long discussion. At length the scene for the announcement was determined: Merle's garden, over champagne and rosé. The time was set for four o'clock and Willow sent Teague a text with the invitation for him and his mother. His only response was a thumbs-up emoji.

"What do you suppose they're doing now?" Merle asked her sister as the three of them went down the stairs and slipped out the back entrance of the hotel into an alley.

"Arguing," Willow said flatly. "He loves to argue."

Stasia shot Merle a look. Willow was obviously no slouch when it came to arguments. She would make a great lawyer.

Merle said, "His mother looked like she didn't take much guff off him. Had you met her before, Willow?"

"No. We didn't tell anyone. We wanted it to be a secret."

"Well, it surprised us all," Stasia said. "Your father especially."

Willow frowned. "I thought he'd understand. He always backs me up."

"Because he loves you," Stasia said. "But this he did not approve of."

"Well, it's over now. Everyone will be as happy as clams." Her voice was snide and sharp.

Merle stopped in front of her and turned around. "Even you, Willow?"

The girl took a deep breath. "Yes, Aunt Merle, I will be happy one of these days."

BACK AT THE cottage everyone split up to do some deep thinking, or possibly napping. Willow went for a walk. Stasia couldn't interest anyone in lunch at the café so she announced she would go collapse in her room. Merle found Elise in the garden, slumped over under the acacia tree. She sat down next to her on the low wall.

"Willow came to her senses. She's calling off the marriage." Elise just nodded, back in her silent shell. She looked pale and sad again. Merle took her hand. "Everything okay? Did you hear from Conor?"

"Yeah. He said nothing's changed. Guy is still in custody."

"Okay. Has Pascal been back?"

Elise brought her head up. "I almost forgot. He said to meet him at the café at two o'clock. Do you know what café? He said you'd know."

Merle checked the time. She had a half hour. "I know. Now, what about you? Did you get lunch?"

"I can feed myself, Merdle."

PASCAL WAITED at one of the outside tables closest to the fountain, at the café on the *Place de Verdun*. Named after a famous and horrifying battle in World War I that had the distinction of being the longest battle of the war at 300 days (according to the plaque set in the stone under the fountain), the village plaza was empty at this hour. Some days it was busy and filled with customers at the market, other days, tourists. But now, just the trickling of the water in the fountain could be heard.

"Did you start without me?" Merle asked, slipping into a chair under a red umbrella. A half-empty glass of red wine sat in front of Pascal.

"Some time ago, yes. I gave up and took myself off to lunch." He sipped his wine and winced. "Gone hot, I'm afraid. What happened with *les amoureux?*"

"Willow is calling it off. She got tired of him, I guess. Except for the sex." Merle wiggled her eyebrows. "What have you been up to?"

A waiter interrupted them and they both consented to a small glass of *sancerre*, strictly medicinal against the heat. Pascal waited until they both had their glasses and took a sip.

"Some news, *chérie*. I have a friend who is the harbormaster in Saint-Tropez."

"Of course, you do."

"He has helped the police many times, and my department as well. A good man. So, I ask him if he knows this Koch or Cook who possibly owns a yacht moored there. And, *voilà*, he does."

"What does he know about him?"

"His full name is Eduardo Koch." He spelled the name. "Pronounced like Coke. Some nationality, maybe German. He only knows the name of his boat and its size. Ninety meters. That's large, technically a 'super yacht.' Many levels, swimming pool or two, helicopter on board."

"So, he's super rich."

"Right. He does let people charter it with a crew."

"How much does that cost?" Merle asked.

"About a million dollars a week."

"So affordable. What's the name of the yacht?"

"*Armée d'or*—the golden army," Pascal said. "A strange name but then boats all have strange names."

"Did you look up this Eduardo Koch? Who is he?"

"I tried but he is not French. I cannot get into the Interpol database without some help. Which I will do if we get nothing out of him."

Merle sipped the *sancerre* before it could get warm. "'We' meaning 'you.' What are you thinking? We pay him a visit? Ask him about Delcroix?"

"I think the *Brigade* should do that. But if they are caught up with their theory about the farmer, what can we do?" He smiled at her. "The yacht is in harbor now but there is a manifest filed. The boat leaves in two days, off to Monaco and Italy."

"We must do what we can for justice," Merle said. She checked her watch. "We have some fireworks to watch at four. Then we go?"

"Tomorrow is soon enough. We can take the train to Marseille then rent something racy for the drive to Saint-Tropez and on to the Luberon."

"A racy car? You will hate that."

He grinned. "Strictly business."

WHEN THEY RETURNED to the cottage, wine and champagne in hand, Elise and Stasia stood together in the garden, in silence, while Teague and Willow were sequestered behind the stone laundry, formerly a *pissoir*. Tristan lounged on the low wall. Holly Hoover paced in front of the small apple tree, dragging her high heels in the gravel.

Merle held Pascal back as she scoped out what was happening. Stasia looked up, holding up a palm to say 'wait.' "Let's go get the glasses." They took their time, collecting wine glasses and champagne flutes, setting them on a tray, opening the champagne, using the corkscrew on the wine. Finally, nothing left to do, they stepped outside again.

Teague stood by his mother now, a hang-dog look on his face. Willow, it seemed, had broken his heart. Willow was near her mother, composed in a fresh sundress and hat. She looked serious but determined. The little girl who had been Willow had been replaced by a woman.

Pascal set the tray of glasses on the table. Merle deposited the bottles next to it. They stood back and waited. Finally, Stasia leaned in and whispered in Willow's ear. The girl frowned, then nodded. She straightened her shoulders and glanced at the Hoovers.

"Friends, family, I regret to inform you that the marriage will be annulled, as the mothers have requested. Teague and I agree. We rushed into things without completely thinking them through. I'm sorry, Teague, Mrs. Hoover. Mom. I'm sorry for everything." She didn't sound very sorry, mostly just glad it was over and done.

Holly Hoover, who apparently hadn't gotten the message from her son, slumped over and covered her eyes with a hand. Teague put an arm around her shoulder and spoke quietly. She nodded, then hugged him.

"And I'm sorry to have intruded on your hospitality, Aunt Merle and Pascal." She glanced down at her cousin. "And you too, Tristan."

Stasia patted her daughter's shoulder in a 'well done' gesture. "This wine isn't getting any colder." She stepped forward and poured a glass of white wine for Elise and her daughter, then turned to Holly Hoover. "Holly? White or bubbly?"

"Yes, please. Oh, bubbles." Holly seemed recovered now, her arm linked through Teague's. "And one for my son."

The romantic intrigue of Willow and Teague dissolved into a soirée with wine and champagne, in the best French tradition. There was very little drama, also a French tradition. The road of love is often a rocky one, they reminded each other. Tristan ran inside and brought out crackers and olive tapenade. The eight of them drained the four bottles in a half hour and the Hoovers took their leave, intending to fly home the next day.

Merle saw them to the door and wished them well. She turned back to the cottage, a happier place now that the entanglements were done. Pascal came into the kitchen with the tray full of glasses, followed by Stasia and Willow.

"Whew," Merle said to her sister as they stepped into the cool parlor.

"No kidding," Stasia replied. She glanced at her daughter who had flopped onto the settee. "Willow and I decided to stay a little longer in France. We're going to travel a little, see some new places."

"Good idea. Where do you think you'll go?"

"Maybe Bordeaux. Then down the coast to the beaches. Biarritz is nice, isn't it?"

Merle brightened. "You can stay at the townhouse in Bordeaux. We're going to Provence in the morning anyway. We won't be back to Bordeaux for at least a few days."

"Really? Are you sure?" Stasia glanced back to the kitchen where Pascal was washing wine glasses. "Do you need to ask him?" she whispered.

Merle walked into the kitchen and did just that. "He says it's fine. Just do the dishes."

CHAPTER THIRTY-TWO

PROVENCE

The train to Marseille left early. Rail travel was soothing, once the hectic pace of driving to the town, finding parking, buying tickets, locating the platform, and finding the seats was over. They sat facing each other, Tristan and Elise sitting forward, Pascal and Merle facing backward. It was a long trip so they got up and rearranged themselves several times. Tristan and Pascal played cards. Merle stood in the aisle, stretching. Elise kept her window seat, gazing at the scenery and towns as they passed.

It was mid-afternoon when they pulled into the Gare de Marseille Saint Charles rail station. Within minutes Pascal had located the car rental and was herding them into a shiny black Mercedes convertible. He put the top down as they threw their bags into the very small trunk. Tristan complained about the back seat so Merle and Elise got wedged in back there.

"Put something on your hair," Pascal told them as he wound out of the car rental area. "It's windy in the back."

Neither Merle nor Elise had anything to "put on their hair," no hat or scarf or hair tie. So, they spent the drive to Saint-Tropez holding onto their hair as Pascal hit the gas hard. There was some eye-rolling between them as they were battered by the wind.

The trip along the Mediterranean coastline, the famous French Riviera, the Côte d'Azur, was one of the most memorable things Merle had ever done in France. Pascal was clearly enjoying himself on the winding roads above the sea, near the sheer cliffs, under the blue sky. The sun shone on the water, sparkling and churning with white caps. Under normal circumstances, with another driver, this would be the longer route, the scenic one. But with Pascal behind the wheel it was spectacular and crazy fast.

Tristan was laughing hard, holding onto the dash as Pascal zoomed around corners. Elise and Merle in the back gave up holding onto their hair after a while, realizing holding onto the car and each other made more sense. They slowed as they went through Toulon and some villages perched along the Med, then sped up for the final stretch into the secluded harbor of Saint-Tropez.

The red roofs went on for miles, tucked into the cut in the hills, leading down to the water. Boats of all shapes and sizes lined the coast and the piers: sailboats, power boats, yachts, and cruise ships. Pascal had directions from the harbormaster and didn't linger at the pretty shops or ice cream parlors along the streets, not even slowing for girls in bikinis. He pulled into a lot by the piers, paid an exorbitant fee, and parked the car.

He held the door open and pushed the seat back forward. "Ladies." He finally got a look at Merle and Elise and his mouth dropped open. "Oh, Merle. Elise, I am sorry."

"About what?" Merle asked. She really didn't care how he drove; she was accustomed to his lead foot.

He waved his hands around his head. "Your hair, *chérie*—it is—"

Tristan stood on the opposite side of car, helping Elise out of the back seat. His eyes bulged and he began to laugh. "Oh, Mom, your hair." He looked at Elise and laughed more.

Merle felt around her head. Her hair appeared to be vertical, standing out from her head in every direction. She glared at Pascal and turned the side mirror to get a look. At the same time Elise yelped. She'd got a glimpse of her own hair.

For the next five minutes the men waited while the sisters found their hairbrushes and attempted something—anything—with their hair. Merle's was a snarled mess. She bent over and brushed it forward, then tried to get it to lie down. Eventually a truce was called.

"You should have said something," Pascal said apologetically. "I would have put the top up. I'm so sorry, Elise." He put his arms around Merle. "My crazy hair blackbird."

Pascal led the way toward the harbormaster's office, near the intersection of several long piers. The three of them waited outside while he went into the small white clapboard building to find out where Eduardo Koch's boat was moored. Tristan exclaimed about the size of the cruise ship. Elise stared blankly at the colorful sailboats out on the sea.

"This way," Pascal called, waving them down a long plank pier, through a gate, down another pier lined with yachts, two and three levels high. They seemed to get bigger and bigger as they walked farther down the pier. Finally, at almost the end, the yachts expanded to super yachts, with small helicopters on top and hot tubs on the decks. Women in bikinis laughed and drank, paying no attention to them as they passed. This must be the place, Merle thought. Where the fancy people party.

Pascal held up a hand, stopping them by the next to last yacht on the left, before the end of the pier. The point of the front poked overhead, a small flag with a 'K' on it attached to a pole. He walked down the side walkway to a locked gate. He turned back and told them to wait.

"These boats are amazing," Tristan said. "They must cost millions."

"They do," Merle agreed. "I wonder if this Koch person is even aboard. He could be off at a party or gambling in Monte Carlo."

"Pascal said the harbormaster called him to make sure he'd be there."

Elise said nothing, standing behind them. Merle turned and took her arm. "This won't take long."

Pascal was speaking into an intercom on the gate. A man in a white uniform walked down the deck above them, leaning over the railing. Pascal had his police identification out and seemed to be explaining it was all a friendly chat. The crew man talked into a walkie-talkie and another man appeared, older but also in uniform. More negotiations. They disappeared. After a few minutes, the gate buzzed and Pascal pushed it open. He waved at them, gave them a thumbs-up. In a few seconds they saw him walk up a gangplank and disappear into the yacht.

EDUARDO KOCH LAY on a lounge chair, slathered in oil, wearing a very small Italian bathing suit that left nothing to the imagination, as his mother would have said. He was muscular but with a round belly that poked up like a muffin. Very tan, he wore his black hair slicked back and dark sunglasses. He didn't move as Pascal approached. "*Monsieur? Pardon*," Pascal said finally, when no movement came from the prone millionaire.

Koch pushed up his sunglasses and stared at Pascal, unsmiling. Pascal stepped over and put out his hand. "*Bonjour.*" He introduced himself as a member of the *Police nationale* even though that wasn't technically true.

Koch sat up and swung his feet to the deck, wiping his face on a white towel. "What is it then?" He asked, annoyed at the interruption of his very important tanning session. His accent was not completely French, maybe a little German mixed in, or Russian. Around here, who knew.

Pascal apologized again and told him how the harbormaster was a friend who had given him directions to the yacht. He threw in a few compliments to the boat. Thus softened, Koch stood and walked to a bar at the side of the deck. "Something cold?" he asked, plunking ice cubes in a glass and pouring vodka over them.

"Merci," Pascal said. "Wine?"

Koch pulled a bottle of rosé from an ice bucket and glanced at the label. "This is what the women drink." He raised his eyebrows at Pascal who told him it was fine.

Thus fortified, they sat on padded chairs under an awning. The heat wasn't as bad here on the water but it was still blistering.

"I'm told, monsieur," Pascal began finally, "that you play cards with a man named Arsène Delcroix. Near Aix-en-Provence."

Koch frowned. "Who?"

"Ari, he may have called himself. Last name Delcroix. Or perhaps in Marseille?"

"Ah, Ari. Why didn't you say? Yes, I have beat him many times at cards. He is not bad but I am much better."

Pascal sipped the cold wine. "I suppose you have not heard." Koch frowned. "Ari is dead." He told the story quickly, dispassionately. Koch didn't seem too upset.

"Too bad. What's it to do with me?"

"We are looking for his friends and enemies, that sort of thing. Men he took money from at cards or did business deals with. Would you know any such men?" Koch shook his head. "Do you remember the men who played cards at Ari's?"

"I didn't pay them much attention." He stood up and refilled his glass. "Except a couple who were friends of mine." He gave Pascal two names which he wrote down: Pierre Herringer and Antoine Sever. "They came with me. They live in Nice, or sometimes on their boats here. Very wealthy men."

"Was there ever any argument between them and Ari?"

"Once in a while there is a hot head, but not those two. They don't care if they win or lose. You know the type. Life is a game and they've already won."

"Anyone else?"

"Someone named Thomas, perhaps British. Older man, in his seventies. Never got his last name."

"How about someone who lost a lot of money?"

"Oh, of course. It happens. Mostly, there was Guy."

Pascal looked up at millionaire's hairy back. "Who is that?"

"Somebody who lived around there. I never got his story. I really don't care about people's stories. We play cards and that's all. We aren't gossipy women." He spun back to Pascal. "He came almost every time.

He had dirt under his fingernails, I remember that. Not like the rest of us."

Pascal stood up, alarmed. If the lavender farmer lost a lot of money to Ari that gave him another reason to kill him. "Was his name Guy Vernay, by chance?"

"Sounds right. Late 40s, solid, dark blond hair that was never combed."

"Do you remember how much he lost?"

"Thousands. He was a terrible card player. And he never knew when to stop betting."

PASCAL JOINED the others on the main pier. He didn't stop to explain, just kept walking, waving them on. They walked quickly, in silence, to the parked car. Pascal put the top of the convertible up, and they were back on the road.

They bypassed the village where Arsène Delcroix had lived, staying on the main road and reaching Aix in time for dinner. They had booked rooms in the Bellemont hotel where Merle had stayed before but ate dinner at a Michelin-starred restaurant in Aix Pascal had read about. There were no complaints about the food. Guinea hen stuffed with morels, oh yes. Fresh trout with fennel and lemons, yum. Tristan tried steak tartare, chopped and mixed with eggs and herbs at the table. Everyone was happy.

They left Aix about ten-thirty. They'd gotten a late start at dinner because that's what you did on the Côte d'Azur. Pascal wasn't pleased with the rush, and no wine for him, but they had to go. They reached Bellemont finally around eleven-thirty and went immediately to bed in the stuffy rooms. Elise and Tristan shared a room with twin beds. Elise wasn't happy about it but since Pascal was paying, she didn't do more than pout.

MERLE WAS SITTING on the terrace the next morning, drinking *café crème*, when Stasia sent a text. They had arrived in Bordeaux late the night before and all was well at the townhouse.

"Thanks so much. We are off to explore."

Merle poised her fingers to respond when she saw Elise in the doorway to the hotel, squinting into the sunshine. She spotted Merle and joined her at the table.

"Sleep well?" Merle asked.

She shrugged. "Hot. And Tristan grunts in his sleep."

Merle smiled. "Do you have ear plugs?"

"Yeah. But my ears were so sweaty they kept falling out." She ordered a *café crème* from the waiter and looked around the terrace, already bustling with tourists. "This is a nice place. Much nicer than the farm." She glanced at Merle. "Are we going there today?"

"That's the plan. Did you call Conor?"

"I wasn't sure if I should. Did you want to surprise him?"

Merle frowned. "Why would we want to do that?"

"If you think he's a killer."

Merle blinked. "Well, I don't. Do you?"

Another shrug. "I don't know him. Not really."

"You know him better than Pascal or I do. Does he seem like a violent person? All you said was he's a good kisser."

A tiny smile crossed her face then was gone. She still had that subdued, tired-with-life air.

"Did Pascal finally tell you what the yacht guy said?" Elise asked.

"Yes but it's not going to help. He says Guy played cards, poker or something, with Ari regularly. And lost a lot of money to him."

"So that's why he had the IOU? Not for a loan but for losses at poker?"

Merle shrugged. "Maybe."

Elise sipped her coffee as her phone buzzed. She glanced at it and rolled her eyes. "Scott, telling me he is in Paris at Charles de Gaulle and he can't find his passport and can I help him."

"Tell him to go to the U.S. Embassy," Merle said.

Elise frowned. "He's on his own."

Pascal and Tristan joined them. Tristan announced he would stay in the village and poke around on his own. This was an idea Merle had given Pascal. Tristan didn't need to be involved in a homicide investigation.

"Get some of those little lavender sachets for your friends. Or at least the girls," Merle said. "You do have friends who are girls?"

"Sure, I do. Tons." He grinned. "Sachets. Got it. What's a sachet exactly?"

As they exited the hotel they fell directly into the throng at the weekly market, a hectic event filling the *place* with produce, cheese, nuts, dishes, tea towels, tablecloths, lavender oils, and all sorts of Provençal goods. Merle paused, momentarily dazed by a colorful display of peppers. "*Allons-y, chérie,*" Pascal said cheerfully, pulling her along. "No market for you."

"Buy me some cute plates," she called to her son as he vanished into the crowd.

CHAPTER THIRTY-THREE

LE REFUGE DE LA LAVANDE

*E*lise sat in the back seat of the Mercedes, slouching down so she could barely see out the side window. It was good that they were in a rental car. Maybe no one would recognize them. Maybe they could just slip away.

Merle was annoyed with her. Elise wouldn't go in, after Merle had said that Elise needed to be the one to talk to Vivianne. She couldn't. She didn't speak French well enough to comfort a stranger. If Vivianne wanted to talk to her she could come out to the car. She felt odd being back at the lavender farm. Maybe it would be just a quick visit.

Pascal and Merle stood on the front step and knocked on the big wooden door. No one answered. Merle turned back to the car and raised her hands in a 'what now?' gesture. Elise slid to the window and stuck her head out. "Check the shop," she called, pointing to the side door in the small barn with the sign overhead that read *'Huile de Lavande de Provence.'* Merle craned her neck, nodded, and touched Pascal's arm. They headed toward the shop.

The door was unlocked. They poked their heads inside then disappeared into the dark.

Elise slouched again, sighing. She was such an idiot. She hated that she didn't have the courage to go with them but she didn't. It made her so tired just thinking about it. Vivianne would be a mess, worried, crying, distraught. How would Elise be able to help? They weren't close friends or anything. The students were gone. They wouldn't help Guy anyway. He had been pretty harsh with some of the boys. And the girls, she thought, remembering her day pulling barbed wire. It felt like he had made a point of giving her crappy jobs.

But she hadn't come back to the farm for Monsieur Vernay, or for Vivianne. She was supposed to be helping Conor. But did he need help? Did he need an alibi? She couldn't give him one. It was better that she just hang out in the car and—

He rounded the barn, paused, and looked around. Conor wore his farming clothes which weren't attractive or well-fitting, but practical in brown and tan. He took off his straw hat and looked at the Mercedes as he slapped the hat against his thigh, sending dust flying. He was wearing sunglasses and looked like hadn't shaved in several days.

She slouched lower, peeking over the seat. He was coming this way. When it was obvious he had seen her, she straightened, trying to recover a little dignity. A difficult task these days. *What is wrong with you, Elise? Get it together.* Sometimes she wondered how she'd made it past age forty.

Her window was down. Conor looked inside the car. He took off his sunglasses and bent down with his blue eyes on her. She rallied.

"How you doin'?" She squinted up at him.

He reached for the door handle and swung the door wide. "Move over."

She slid across the seat and he climbed awkwardly into the back, leaving the door ajar.

"Hi," she said shyly.

"Your sister told me you were hiding out here." He stared at her then looked out the door. "Were you going to stay in the car? Not come inside—or find me?"

The unexpected pain in his voice made her cringe. It was her own hurt, her own heart, she had been protecting. "No, I'm sorry. I mean, I wanted to come find you. I just wasn't sure."

"About what?"

She rolled her eyes. "You know. You and me."

He was silent, staring at her so hard she thought she would melt.

"Plus Merle said you might be in some trouble. Something about an alibi the night of Ari's death. And how was I supposed to help you with that? I didn't see you that night."

"Why would I need an alibi?" he said finally.

She shrugged. "You seemed to dislike him."

"Hardly alone in that."

"You said to me 'Do you know what he's done?' Do you remember that?"

He nodded. "When you were going to dinner."

"What did you mean?"

"General debauchery, I guess. Picking up girls the way he did."

"That's it?"

Conor paused then said, "He's been here several times, trying to get Guy and Vivianne to sell. Making threats. Putting the squeeze on them. He was a snake."

"What would happen to your share, if they sold?"

"Gone. I wanted to buy them out, or at least buy in for half. I've been saving my winnings for the last few years. I've got fifty-thousand pounds saved but this property is worth millions."

"Pascal told you about the IOU they found in Ari's safe? It was for four hundred thousand euros. That wouldn't have covered the entire property, if it's worth millions, right? So Ari had to keep lending Guy money. I bet he cheated him at cards. We found this rich dude named Eduardo something, living on his yacht in Saint-Tropez. He says Guy played cards with him and Ari. He lost a lot of money, Eduardo said. Could that be the IOU—for losses at cards?"

Conor sighed, slumping back against the seat. "We tried to get him to stop gambling. Vivianne made me follow him one night when he went to Ari's. So, yeah, we knew."

"I saw Ari one night here at the farm, I think. Arguing with Guy then I found Vivianne crying."

He turned toward her. "Why did you go with him, to his house?"

"To get away from here. The students were awful to me, Conor. You weren't too nice either. I was a little sensitive, I admit it. But Guy kept giving me filthy chores. I loved Vivianne's food but I shouldn't have come here. It was a mistake."

Conor paused then turned to her, serious. "Did you and Ari—you know—do the *shelf-o?*"

Elise laughed. "The what?"

"Shag. Sexual relations."

"No! I told you. It wasn't like that. He was just rescuing me from my misery here."

He took her hand. She felt the rough texture of his palms and the warmth. He smelled like dirt and sunshine and sweat. "I could use a rescue from *my* misery." He pressed her palm to his lips.

"Are you miserable?" she whispered, touching his cheek.

"Terribly."

MERLE AND PASCAL stepped out of the shop into the morning sun. Where was Vivianne? Her daughter claimed she was out in the fields but the girl seemed frightened and maybe lying. It was more likely her mother was in the kitchen and didn't hear the knock or didn't want to hear it.

Hadn't Elise said something about a back door to the kitchen? Where was that? Merle started walking toward the Mercedes to ask her sister but stopped after three steps. The far door was open and sunlight poured into the back seat. Elise was not alone.

Merle gave a squeak and pumped her fist. She turned to Pascal. "Let's go around the back and look for her."

They walked around the corner of the manse and found the long rough tables set up for dinner under two large trees. Strings of lights hung over the tables, bare at mid-morning. Out in the fields they could see the tractor humming down the rows, and workers stacking bundles of lavender.

Merle paused, taking in the scent and the view of the fields with the blue mountains rising behind. Far off to the east was a huge wheat field, cut down to stubble. "So beautiful," she whispered.

They knocked on the back door but again, no answer. They pushed it open to find themselves in a dim hallway. Merle remembered this hallway and found the kitchen doorway. Vivianne stood in front of the large farmhouse sink piled with dishes. Before they could speak, she put her hands on the rim of the sink, lowered her head, and began to sob.

Merle frowned at Pascal. What now? They waited a minute and she seemed to run out of steam, or tears. Pascal rapped quietly on the kitchen door, making her startle.

"*Pardon, madame. Excusez nous.*" He stepped gingerly toward her, palms up. "Madame Vernay?" She nodded, wiping her face on her apron hem. "We are not police. You remember Elise Bennett's sister? She came here looking for Elise?"

Vivianne looked at Merle and nodded. She looked wary, and weary, with dark circles under her eyes and a sallow cast to her skin. Her hair was pushed up under a paisley scarf.

"*Madame,*" Merle said, smiling. "*Bonjour.*"

"She never came back," Vivianne said to both of them. "I don't know any more."

"We found her," Pascal said. "Did Conor tell you? She was at the Delcroix home when he was found dead."

Vivianne blinked hard, taking this in. Apparently, Conor hadn't told her much. "Did she—is she the one who killed him?" she asked sharply.

"No," Merle said. "We don't know who killed him. But we don't think it was Guy."

She met Merle's eye, questioning, then seemed to relax a little. "Please, sit. Can I offer you something? Coffee or tea?"

They declined, not wanting to make more work for the woman. She was apparently running the lavender farm herself, with Guy in custody. He told Vivianne about his connection with the wine fraud division, and how he was helping the police. "Although they are not exactly aware," he said, giving her a wink. "We want to help Guy, and Conor. We want to find out what happened."

"Guy knows nothing. He wasn't there that night. I told the detectives he was in bed with me, then helped capture the rat. But they don't believe me. The students have all gone home. They could help but—" She frowned. "Why do you want to help Conor?"

Pascal leaned on the table. "It is possible he has no alibi for that night. And is in love with Elise Bennett and so was jealous of Ari."

Vivianne scoffed. "Conor? In love? That is unlikely. And he won't even clean out the mousetraps, that's why he didn't help with the rat. After the bat in your sister's room he said he would never do that again." She lowered her voice conspiratorially. "I think he may be a Buddhist."

Pascal glanced at Merle. She asked gently, "My sister Elise, when she was staying here, she saw Guy and another man come out of the house, arguing. And she went into the kitchen and you were crying."

Vivianne shrugged and said nothing.

"Can you tell me what the trouble was?"

"I do not remember."

"Who was Guy arguing with?"

She shook her head, lips tight.

"There is a story we've heard," Pascal said, "that Guy owed money to Ari Delcroix, from gambling losses. A large amount of money. That is backed up by a document for the funds found in Ari's safe."

The blood drained from Vivianne's face. Her eyes darted between them. "*Oh, mon Dieu.*"

"Was Ari here, demanding money?"

She nodded, biting her lip.

"Did he threaten you or Guy?" Pascal asked.

"Maybe not in so many words but—" Her eyes filled and she couldn't speak.

Merle reached out to touch her arm. "Ari is dead. He can't hurt you now. And he can't collect on that loan."

Pascal added, "The police have the IOU in their possession."

Vivianne sat straighter, wiping her eyes. "But who did he tell? What about his family? His connections in Marseille? They are gangsters, thugs—drug dealers who kill people for much less or break their fingers or kidnap their children."

"Who told you this?" Pascal asked.

"Everyone. The village, everyone knows Ari Delcroix." Another tear leaked down her face. "He made himself known to everyone, in one way or another. He is an awful person."

"Was," Merle said quietly.

"He did not own his own place here? He stayed with someone?" Pascal asked.

Vivianne nodded. "At Château Grand Lac. Louise Gaillard is the owner. He stays with her in the summer, I'm told."

"Do you know Madame Gaillard?"

"Slightly. She comes to Bellemont sometimes, for the bistros and *fêtes*. She is hard to miss. Always a small crowd with her. All the restaurant owners speak of her. She is very wealthy. It is said she keeps—kept —Monsieur Delcroix around for her pleasure. I have seen them together, dining or at the market. Her husband is very old. And she is the kind of person who can buy anything or anyone."

"Is the château close by?"

"On the other side of the village, about ten miles north."

He asked her for directions and she found an old envelope and a pencil in the sideboard and drew him a crude map. They stood to go.

"You are running the farm alone?" Pascal asked.

"Conor is here. And my children. And the workers. The harvest is just days from finished."

"You have students again?"

"We cancelled them. It was too much."

Merle patted her shoulder. "Try not to worry."

Pascal added, "I will tell the *Brigade* that you are concerned about your safety. They will send someone around."

"*Merci*," she whispered, trembling. "*Merci*."

CHAPTER THIRTY-FOUR

$\mathcal{T}$hey found Tristan in the hotel lobby, looking hungry and bored. The market was winding down and he'd managed to avoid buying anything—no sachets, no pretty plates, *rien*. Merle sent Elise and Pascal to the café where they'd eaten before and took Tristan for one last pass through the market.

"Did you look for lavender stuff?" Merle could see a lot of vendors had sold out or closed up already. "It might be too late."

"This lady told me to try the shop over there so I didn't buy anything." He gestured to a souvenir shop across the plaza.

Merle walked quickly, scanning the market. She loved Provençal dishes, in their colorful shades of green, gold, and blue. She'd never found any she could afford in Paris or Bordeaux. But here, at the source, she had hopes. But after walking through the tables and wagons she gave up. "No pottery here at all. How disappointing."

A few minutes later they were seated with Pascal and her sister, ordering lunch. Merle couldn't keep her eyes off Elise. The change in her complexion was marked, no doubt due to Conor. She bit her tongue and didn't ask about him. Until Elise brought him up.

"Conor says they all knew about Guy's gambling," she said, sipping white wine. "Once Vivianne had him follow Guy, to see where he was going, and he went to Ari's."

Pascal asked, "Did they confront him?"

"He said they tried to get him to stop gambling. But I guess they couldn't."

"It's an illness," Tristan said. "Like alcoholism."

They all nodded soberly and set their wine glasses down. Merle said, "What now?"

"I think we go visit Madame Gaillard," Pascal said. "At the place where he stayed around here."

"It's a château," Merle added. "Do you want to come?" She asked Elise, then glanced at Tristan.

It was decided they would all go see this château and the rich lady after lunch. On the drive north out of Bellemont, winding through hamlets and fields of lavender, Pascal gave them duties. Tristan was to scout around outside, see if he could see anything or anyone suspicious or just interesting. Elise was to ask to use the toilet and wander around in the château as if she was lost. Pascal and Merle would see what they could find out from the lady of the house.

They could see the massive château nestled into the side of a hill, surrounded by olive groves and lemon trees. Lemons dotted the trees, and the olives, still green, made a fascinating contrast with the silvery leaves. The château itself was not ancient, definitely late 20th-Century, built of blocks of stone with one circular room that ended in a pointy turret. A blend of styles, some Renaissance, some Tuscan, some just country French—what it lacked in taste it made up in size.

They drove up the hill on a winding lane that ended outside an eight-foot-tall white stuccoed wall. Wrought iron gates arched even higher, keeping out the curious. They parked and stood by the gates, wondering if the trip would be futile. There was no intercom or buzzer.

There was however some surveillance as a security guard appeared from a small outbuilding inside the wall. He was a large man but not particularly threatening. His navy uniform stretched tightly across his belly as he wiped his brow with a handkerchief.

Pascal introduced himself and said they were hoping for a short audience with Madame. "Is she at home?"

"Does she know you?" The guard asked, eyeing them suspiciously. Pascal said no, they were not acquainted. It was a business matter. "Do you have a card?"

Pascal rummaged through his wallet and found one of his cards, proclaiming his status with the government. The guard examined it, checked the blank back, and asked for Pascal's identification. He compared the card and his government ID. Then he said he would see if Madame was available. They waited silently for ten minutes. The guard came lumbering back into the sun.

"She will see you. By the pool." He unlocked the large padlock and pushed open the gate. He gestured toward the right, around the side of the château. Merle stepped in to follow Pascal but the guard put out a hairy arm. "Just the one."

He locked the gates behind Pascal and scowled at the three of them left outside. "Well, that sucks," Tristan mused as they got back in the Mercedes to wait. "He gets all the fun."

MADAME GAILLARD WAS TOWELING off by the side of a large, sparkling blue pool in the back of the château. She wasn't alone. Another security guard, this one more fit and professional, lurked in the shade near the house. He moved a little closer to Madame when Pascal came into view. He wondered if she was always this well-protected, or perhaps paranoid.

The lady in question was a striking woman of fifty or so, with a slender figure, breasts certainly enhanced by procedures, and a face that no doubt benefited from doctors as well. Her honey blond hair was piled on her head. She wore large sunglasses as she stood in her black swimsuit, checking him out as he approached.

"Madame Gaillard. Bonjour. I am sorry for the intrusion on your privacy."

She smiled and waved a hand. "It is nothing. I am dying for company. Sit, please."

He sat under the umbrella at a bistro table. She sat on the other side, on a chaise under another umbrella, stretching out her shapely legs for his inspection. "Have you not been entertaining during this summer season?" he asked.

She pouted dramatically. She was quite beautiful or had been before the plastic surgery. "My husband forbids it. He is so unreasonable."

"Forbids entertaining? What a beast."

"And he hires all these men, these—I despise them."

"Is he worried about your safety?"

She sat forward, giving him her full attention. "What is this about? You want to see my wine cellar? Or perhaps some other private spaces?"

He gave her his secret smile, indicating he understood her meaning. "That would be delightful but I'm afraid I have friends waiting outside your gates. I just have a few questions about your friend, Arsène Delcroix."

She stood up suddenly and snapped her fingers at the guard. He rushed over and she ordered a pitcher of iced tea and two glasses. He disappeared into the house.

"They are good for some things," she said, smiling. She sat across the table from Pascal, taking off her sunglasses. He could see a large bruise on her right cheek, under the eye. She sat straighter, pushing forward her chest for viewing.

"Now, I see. You are here because of Ari."

He nodded and waited for her to speak. The guard returned with the drinks and backed away. She poured tea into both their glasses and topped them with slices of lemons. From her own trees, she said. "What do you want to know?"

"When was the last time you saw him?"

She sipped tea. "That's easy. It was the night he was killed. Or so I think. From the newspaper I think that is the date."

"What night was it?"

"July 27th. It was my birthday. I always have a party on my birthday. Why not?" She sighed. "We were a merry bunch. We had a feast out here, and cake. Very American, isn't it, birthday cake? So much sugar, just once a year. And candles, sparklers. I always love it. Ari came late; he had been down at his country house. You know it?" Pascal nodded.

"Some of my favorite people were here, and he was one of them. We had a special bond, Ari and me."

"I'm sorry," Pascal said quietly, letting his eyes drop slowly to her chest.

She took a deep breath, no doubt for his benefit. "It is good to talk to someone who is caring. You care about people, don't you?"

"*Bien sûr, madame.* It is a terrible blow to lose a friend."

She gave him her best pathetic smile. "That night is the reason my husband hires these men, these bodyguards. He is in Paris most of the time. He doesn't like the heat and doesn't care for my friends, even on my birthday. I'm not even sure he cares at all. Anyway he wasn't here. So, he couldn't protect me when the men came."

Pascal felt a jolt. "Men? *De quels hommes parlez-vous?*"

"Three of them, all in black, wearing masks. Ski masks, you know. Nobody knows who they were. They broke the lock on the gate and came in with guns."

"To rob you?"

"That's what we assumed. We all started taking off our necklaces and bracelets. Sadly, many of us have been robbed before. What is wrong with this country? They didn't tell us to stop but they weren't interested in jewelry."

She looked across the table at him directly. "They did this to me. I shouted for them to leave and they did this." She tapped the bruise lightly. Her hands were shaking with fury, or fear.

"What did they want, madame?"

"Ari. They wanted Ari."

IT WAS JUST AFTER MIDNIGHT, she told Pascal, when everyone was outside, music was playing, the guests were swimming, or eating and drinking. Ari had arrived an hour before, alone, although he had told Madame Gaillard that he might bring a girl. She was a little angry about that, she said, so he didn't bring anyone.

Then the three men appeared as if dropping from the sky. They ran through the house, holding the staff at gunpoint, pushing them outside onto the patio. They took everyone's cellphones. That angered some of her guests but the men had guns so everyone complied. Nobody wanted to be a hero. Madame—Louise—and Ari had been over in the shadows, making love noises, as she called it, when it all began.

She saw two of the men running toward the terrace, guns drawn. She left Ari in the shadows and rushed for the guests, bringing them to attention. A hush fell over the group. The third man held the staff at gunpoint. Then the women began to cry and scream. They took off their jewels. The men shouted. There are no neighbors here. No one to hear.

The men waved their guns, telling everyone to be quiet and moving them onto the terrace, guests next to the cowering staff. Ari came out and stood with Madame, holding her hand as she cried. Then the masked men lined them up, as if they were going to execute them all, one by one. This was frightening, to say the least, but they simply looked carefully at each person, especially the men.

Until they came to Ari. Then they stopped and demanded his wallet. After they looked inside it, they spun him around, put zip ties on his wrists and a cloth bag over his head.

"They led him around the house while we just stood there, shocked. We couldn't do a thing. We had no phones. They also cut the line to the house." Louise looked frightened and agitated, reliving that evening. Or maybe it was just a good show.

"What did the police say?"

She looked embarrassed, biting her lip. "We didn't report it. I thought of it, of course. Someone said we must. But some of my guests — they are men who don't like publicity. They thought it was a joke, a prank. The women hadn't lost their jewelry after all. Some said it was Ari's fault, because of who he did business with, the underworld, you know. I don't know who he did business with. They didn't want to get involved in something dirty—illegal. The possible retaliation, they said. All the men agreed. My husband was furious when I finally reached him. He demanded that I not involve the police."

"I see. What was Ari's business?" Pascal asked.

"Import-export is all he would ever say. I didn't ask too many questions. I liked him. He liked me. I didn't care." She sighed. "I suppose this is what I get for not asking questions."

Pascal thought of reassuring her, telling her the kidnapping was not her fault. But she hadn't even reported it to the police. She didn't really care about Ari or she would have done that at the least. She and her husband and guests were more concerned about their social reputations. Everyone would have to be questioned. It would be tedious and disagreeable. Pascal felt his bile rising.

"Did you try to reach Ari later?"

"All the next day. I had to go into Avignon and buy new phones for all my guests, and me of course. There was no answer on his phone. I suppose they took it away from him. I was so worried. But I gave up."

Pascal stood up and put his sunglasses back on. "It's time you told that story to the *Brigade* officers investigating Ari's death, Madame. Long past time."

She glanced up at him and put her own sunglasses back on. Her voice was carefree and airy. "My husband will be angry. But you're right. I suppose I owe it to Ari."

I suppose you do. He frowned at her *laissez-faire* attitude. What do you do with such people?

"You can reach them at the *gendarmerie* in Aix-en-Provence. *Bonne journée,* madame."

CHAPTER THIRTY-FIVE

*B*efore he left the château, Pascal had the *Brigade* detective on the phone, the man he'd spoken to at Delcroix's house. He sat behind the steering wheel in the Mercedes and waited for him to answer. Yount took his time and Pascal was readying his message when the detective picked up the call. Pascal told him about the concerns Madame Vernay had about her family's safety at the lavender farm. Then he brought up Madame Louise Gaillard.

"She's got quite a story for you, Yount," Pascal said. "I told her to call but I'm not sure she will."

"What is it? I don't have time to play games, d'Onscon."

"All right." He glanced at Merle, next to him in the car, and back at Tristan and Elise. "She says she had a birthday party at her château on the 27th of July. For herself. Big group of friends, including Delcroix. Three men in ski masks broke the lock on the gate and rounded up the house staff and all the guests. They picked out one person and took him away, handcuffed with a bag over his head."

"Delcroix?"

"*Oui.* Their mobiles were confiscated and the house line was cut. They had no way to call anyone. They were held at gunpoint. For what- ever reason they decided to hush it up. Madame Gaillard's husband is very rich, I believe. She says he was in Paris. But now he has ordered bodyguards for her."

The detective asked a few more questions about the location, names of guests— which Pascal did not know—and the certainty of the date in question. Then he rang off. Pascal put his phone in his shirt pocket.

Everyone was staring at Pascal in the car, waiting for more explanation. He turned on the ignition and backed away from the château. Merle put a hand on his arm as he shifted into a forward gear. "Wait." He stepped on the brake. "Three masked men broke in and kidnapped Ari Delcroix and nobody knew anything about it?"

"Well, obviously the party guests and the staff knew. And Madame Gaillard."

"But she never reported it?"

"The rich. What can I say? They don't want to be inconvenienced."

"The cops will talk to all the guests, right?" Tristan asked. "So boring for them."

"Exactly," Pascal said. "I told her to contact the Aix-en-Provence *gendarmerie* but I doubt she will. Her husband forbids it. Now however the *Brigade* is on it."

"Good." Merle sat back in the seat. "Do we tell anyone? Like Conor or Vivianne?"

"We should," Elise said from the back seat. "Shouldn't we?"

"It might make them more worried," Pascal noted. "These were professionals. Probably enemies of Delcroix from Marseille."

"But they should know," Elise demanded, her voice getting shrill. "They deserve to know so they can plan and be safe."

Merle turned back to Elise. "Call Conor and have him join us for dinner in the village. We'll tell him then. And ask him to make sure the *gendarmes* are watching the farm." She glanced at Pascal who nodded. "I don't think these masked men care about lavender but you can't be too careful."

As they wound their way off the hillside and back toward Belle-mont, two blue and white *gendarmerie* cruisers sped by them in the direction of the château. Pascal had a grim smile on his face. "There they go."

WHEN CONOR ALBION appeared in the doorway leading to the outside terrace at Bistro de Citron, Elise was flushed. They had placed her so she faced the doorway so he would see her first, at the table with the yellow Provençal tablecloths and red umbrellas. He was a little late, making Elise anxious. But then she broke into a wide smile, the likes of which Merle hadn't seen in her youngest sister in ages.

"Easy, girl," Merle muttered as Elise began to fidget, watching him approach. He cleaned up well, that was obvious. His khaki slacks and blue shirt, the color matching his eyes, didn't do him any insults. He reached his chair, kissed Elise on the cheek, and shook hands with everyone else.

They had ordered a carafe of house rosé. Elise poured him a glass as he settled in.

"Good to see you, Conor," Merle said, smiling and glancing at Elise. "How are things at the farm?"

"Carrying on," he said. "More work than usual without the vacationers to help." He winked at Elise.

"Not that I was much help," she said.

Conor pulled a small bottle from his shirt pocket. "This is for you. From Vivianne." He handed it to Elise. It was a bottle of lavender oil from the Refuge.

"It's lovely. Thank you." Elise looked at Merle. "I helped distill the lavender to make this."

"So, you did help," Merle said.

"She worked hard," Conor said, putting his arm around the back of Elise's chair. "It's nice to get out like this. I've never eaten here."

"Any word about Guy?" Pascal asked as the waiter brought menus and they looked over the choices.

"No. But a *gendarme* arrived an hour ago. He said he was assigned to give protection. I assume that is your doing?"

"Vivianne seemed anxious," Pascal said. "Did it make her feel a little better?"

Conor said it did, especially tonight when he was away from the farm. "I leave in two days anyway. She'll have to have someone to guard if Guy is not released."

"We have some news," Elise said.

"About Guy?"

Pascal sipped his wine. "Perhaps." He told Conor the tale of Madame Gaillard's birthday party and the kidnapping of Ari.

"I'm shocked," Conor said with a hint of sarcasm at the conclusion of the retelling. "I didn't think that sort of thing happened in paradise."

"That's what the police said about the murder, remember?" Elise said. "Nothing ever happens here."

"But it does," Merle added. "Sadly."

"So, who are these masked men?" Conor asked Pascal.

"Professionals, I'd say. Hired guns."

"Out of Marseille?"

Pascal nodded. "The *Brigade* will track down his business associates there."

"So, Guy is cleared?" Conor asked.

"Soon."

"We hope," Merle added. She lowered her voice. "I just wonder about this Louise Gaillard. Is it possible she made up this story out of some warped sense of drama? Is she really that callous that she wouldn't notify the police about a kidnapping at gunpoint at her home?"

Conor raised his eyebrows. "Vivianne says she is *une snob riche*. She called her *une crâneuse* which is a word I'd never heard her use before." He looked at Elise. "It means pretentious, a show-off."

"Despite her snobbishness I think she was telling the truth," Pascal said. "She showed me a bruise on her face where one of the men had hit her. And the bodyguards were in place."

"Oh. Will this tarnish her reputation as a *grande dame* of the Luberon?" Merle asked.

"She is not well-liked anyway," Conor said. "This might be the end of her association around here."

They ordered the *assiette anglaise*, a lavish spread of *charcuterie* and a *saucisson de Lyon aux pistaches,* then moved on to small but fabulous main dishes like warm lobster salad dressed with a truffled vinaigrette, grilled pork with wild mushrooms, a *foie gras* terrine with poached artichoke hearts, and guinea hen with lemon confit. There was much tasting across plates and sighs of delight.

Madame Gaillard was forgotten for the moment, as was fate of Guy Vernay.

Elise announced she was skipping dessert. This was frowned upon by all, especially when there was a special strawberry tart on the menu. But she rose and said she had to speak to Conor so they let them leave. Merle, Pascal, and Tristan had the intensely flavored tart and declared it the best ever.

"I wonder what they have to talk about," Tristan said, smiling knowingly.

"I doubt there will be talking," Pascal said. "No time."

Merle thought they were adorable together. The way he caught her hand as they made their way out of the restaurant. She couldn't wait to tell her sisters but she didn't want to say it aloud. Not yet. Things were still rather new.

They ordered three cheeses although they had no room for more food in their stomachs. But it would not be a proper French dinner, especially one of this quality, without a finish of *fromage*. They were sipping coffee and waiting for the cheese platter to arrive when Elise rushed up to the table.

"Merle. Where is your phone?"

She frowned. "In my purse, right here." She rummaged around for her mobile phone in the pocket of her purse. When she drew it out she saw it was off. "Dead. Is someone trying to call me?"

Elise walked around the table and handed Merle her cellphone. "It's Stasia. She says it's urgent. Wait, let me find the number." She took back the phone, scrolled, and tapped.

"Stasia?" Merle asked when her sister answered. "I'm sorry, my phone ran down and—"

"Is Pascal there?" Stasia said.

"Yes. You want to speak to him?"

"Please." Stasia sounded nervous, a little breathless. Was she in trouble?

"Where are you?" Merle continued.

"At your townhouse in Bordeaux. Put Pascal on."

Pascal took the phone from Merle. "I am here." He listened for a minute, glancing at each of them in turn, then back at his coffee cup. *"Oui, Monsieur."* He listened, then: *"Ah, je comprends. Merci. Bonsoir,"* he said finally and tapped the button to end the call.

"What's happening?" Elise asked.

He took a deep breath. "The police are at our townhouse. Another *Brigade criminelle*. That was a detective on the phone." He set a hand on Merle's. "No problems with the house. But when Stasia and Willow returned tonight they found several *policier* vehicles on the street and in the alley behind, lights flashing. All the neighbors stood out on the sidewalk, gawking. That is the word? Gawking?"

The cheese arrived. Pascal picked out a small square of *mimolette*, popping it in his mouth.

"Yeah?" Tristan prodded. "And?"

Pascal handed him the cheese platter. "A person living on the street behind the townhouse, a neighbor, saw two persons throw something into our back garden, from the alley. It was large, perhaps wrapped in a rug, and the two people struggled with the weight of it."

Merle put a hand over her mouth. Pascal set a hand on her shoulder.

"The object was our landlord, Henri St-Jean Delcroix. He is dead."

CHAPTER THIRTY-SIX

*A*fter the bill was settled, dinner completed, and the shock of Henri's demise had worn off, they gathered again on the sidewalk. Conor had returned to find Elise and they joined the small group, processing the news of the death, almost certainly another homicide. Merle borrowed Elise's phone again and called Stasia, filling her in on what the detective had told Pascal. Stasia was shaken and decided she and Willow would spend the night in a nearby hotel, as soon as they got their suitcases packed.

"That's wise," Merle said. "You'll sleep better there."

"We're leaving tomorrow. We already had train tickets to Paris. I'll see if I can get them changed to earlier." Her voice lowered to a near whisper. "Do you like Bordeaux? It seems—I don't know. Not entirely safe."

"Tonight, I'm sure it does. Pascal likes it. And that street is so pretty, I'm shocked. Unless—" The unspoken question between Merle and Pascal was the Delcroix connection. Was it a coincidence? It couldn't be. Two men named Delcroix murdered within weeks. They had to be connected. "Well, have a great trip. All our love to Willow."

She handed the phone back to Elise. She took it and glanced at

Conor. "I'm going to go back to the farm with Conor. That's okay, isn't it? Tristan can have some privacy to snore up a storm."

"Hey," Tristan protested.

"Of course, it's fine," Merle said, chuckling. "Kind of you to give him some space."

Conor squeezed Elise's hand. "Thanks for dinner. It was grand. *Bonsoir.*"

Pascal, Merle, and Tristan walked back to the hotel. Merle looked over her shoulder and saw Conor kissing Elise as they walked in the opposite direction.

Back at the hotel they said goodnight to Tristan and went to their separate rooms. "Elise seems so happy," Merle said.

"And Conor too," Pascal smirked. "Tonight's the night, as the song goes."

They undressed and climbed into bed. Merle rolled over to face Pascal. "What do you think is going on? Was our landlord, Henri, doing business with Ari? Were they related?"

"We will find out tomorrow, I am assured. I would be shocked if they weren't relatives, and in some type of import business together. As a provincial official, Henri was in a position to help with customs documents and such."

"Do you think drugs?"

"Perhaps."

"I wonder if some gang is wiping out its competition."

"A strong possibility."

"So, we can expect more deaths? Will they kill the entire family?"

He stroked her cheek. "Come here, blackbird, and speak no more of *la mort*. We must think of life, our wonderful lives."

They kissed then Merle pulled her head back. "How did you get Louise Gaillard to tell you about the kidnapping, Pascal? When she was told not to contact the police?"

"It was nothing, *chérie*." He smiled. "I looked at her breasts, that's all. Women enjoy that, I'm told."

"Oh, really."

"What? You don't like it when I look at your breasts?"

"Well, of course. But you look at every woman's breasts?"

"Strictly professionally, my darling. It is part of a Frenchman's training program, to make everyone think they are special and delectable and that you enjoy their assets." He lowered his head to kiss one of her assets. He whispered in her ear: "With you I do not act, *chérie*."

"Stop talking, Pascal."

CONOR WAVED at the *gendarme* stationed by the front door of the house when they returned to Le Refuge de la Lavande. Elise suddenly felt nervous. In the car, the adorable rusty Deux Chevaux, she'd already told Conor all the things she didn't have for the evening, like a toothbrush, hand lotion, a hairbrush. He smiled and told her not to worry about the little things. Instead she worried about the big things. Then he leaned over and kissed her mouth and she forgot about worrying.

Although she'd had plenty of boyfriends and lovers over the years, there had been longer and longer dry spells between them as she got older. She'd only slept with Scott once, months ago, when they were still getting to know each other. It hadn't gone well and neither of them initiated it again, then she broke up with him. Was there was something she was doing wrong, something men wanted that no one ever explained? She knew about all the, um, positions and all, but there must be something else. She really should ask her sisters, especially Francie since she'd had so many boyfriends. But it was an awkward subject. She could never find the words that wouldn't make her sound like an idiot.

Elise tried to clear her mind, to think about Conor. Beautiful, strong, kind, gentle Conor. The way he spoke, his accent which totally turned her on. She pictured his corgi boxers again. Everything would be fine.

Conor unlocked the front door with his key and relocked it behind them. Vivianne had left the light on in the stairwell. They climbed slowly up the squeaky steps to the second floor. He stepped over one stair and pointed to her to do the same, avoiding a loud creak apparently. Elise tried not to giggle. This tiptoeing made her feel like a teenager.

On the second floor, which Elise had never explored, the decor was decidedly fresher than on third. The hallway was painted a warm gold above a chair rail and striped green wallpaper below. Small, tasteful framed prints lined the walls. They passed one door, then another. Finally, at the very end of the hall, Conor stopped and unlocked a door.

"I have to go check in with Vivianne, tell her I'm back. Go in," he whispered. "Make yourself comfortable."

Elise stepped into his room and flicked on the light. Conor's room was plain, with grey walls, a pale blue chenille spread on the bed, a small wooden desk and chair, a colorful old rug along with the requisite coat rack and dresser. His farm clothes hung from the rack, still filthy. A stack of paperwork sat on the desk, anchored by a large rock. He'd made his bed. Maybe he expected her to join him, the cocky bastard. She smiled. It had been her own idea anyway.

She kicked off her sandals and sat on the bed, giving it a good bounce. It was a double bed, or as near to one as one found in France. The springs made a loud screech and she stopped bouncing, hoping no one had heard the noise. She turned on the bedside lamp and got up to turn off the overhead light for a better mood.

His window looked out over the front drive, to the right of the willow tree. The *gendarme's* police car was parked about a hundred feet down the lane, beyond the tree. As she watched, the policeman strolled to his car, glanced in every direction, removed his hat, and slipped into the passenger seat. Catching up with his girlfriend, or, more likely, his zzz's.

Did this window open? It was much bigger than her tiny third floor window, reaching nearly full wall height with fancy molding on the mullions. She felt for the lock on the sash, turned it, and pushed it open an inch. Just enough for some cool breezes but not enough for bats.

Wandering around Conor's room, she glanced at the pile of notes and receipts on the desk. Nothing she could understand. She put her ear up to the door. She could hear the murmuring of a conversation down the hall. Was Conor telling Vivianne about the kidnapping of Ari at the birthday party? And then the second murder, the old guy in Bordeaux? She hoped not. The woman would never sleep. But if it meant her husband would soon be cleared and come home, she deserved that hope.

Elise stretched out on the soft chenille spread. The pillows were quite nice. Maybe Conor was telling Vivianne about her, waiting in his room. How long would he be? She closed her eyes. The long day, the delicious food, the wine caught up with her. Without another thought, she fell asleep.

THE SCREAM WOKE her with a jolt. She opened her eyes and felt the weight across her waist and saw that it was Conor's arm. He lay beside her. The bedside lamp was off but she could see his eyelids were closed and veined with delicate blue. They were both still fully clothed. She reached out to touch his face. Then the second scream woke him. He jumped off the bed.

He was fully awake. "What was that?"

He went to the window and pulled up the sash. He stuck his head out and looked around. Another scream from somewhere. "Daniel? *Tu vas bien?*"

Elise blinked, trying to remember who Daniel was. A worker? The old man? The *gendarme*? A car door slammed and the sound of footsteps on the gravel came closer.

"*Qu'est-ce que c'est? Qu'est-ce que se passe?*" A man's voice from below.

"*Où est Daniel?*" Conor called out.

"*Qui?*"

"Daniel!" Conor pulled his head in. "I have to go down there. I think that was Daniel screaming."

"Who is he again?"

"The grand-dad. From the distillery." He was lacing up his shoes.

"Should I come?" she asked as he ran out of the room and down the hall. His pounding footsteps hit the stairs and faded away. Turning from the door she went back to the window and leaned out. Just in time to hear the *gendarme* squeal like a girl.

"*Les rats! Infernals! Démons!*"

Her eyes adjusted to the dark. Moonlight streaked across the drive. The *gendarme* had his jacket off and was batting the ground around his feet, cursing and shrieking.

She focused on the ground finally, her eyes wide. Large, furry, scurrying, squeaking rats crawled all over the yard.

Les rats. Everywhere.

CHAPTER THIRTY-SEVEN

*E*lise slipped back into her sandals and grabbed her sweater. She pushed her arms in the sleeves as she ran into the hall and pulled the door shut. She'd taken a moment to close the window. No point in bats *and* rats tonight.

She stepped quickly down the stairs, holding the railing. The prospect of dozens of live rats in the yard wasn't intimidating, she was relieved to realize. In fact she felt a shiver of adventure, adrenaline pumping, some new, wild, exotic thing to tell her friends about someday.

At the bottom of the staircase she found Vivianne in a pink night-gown and white crocheted shawl, standing by the front door. Next to the door stood Conor, his back against the wall, head back, eyes shut. Vivianne was haranguing him in French, waving her arms frantically as if trying to get him to do something. She poked him on the shoulder, cursing.

Elise frowned, confused. "Conor?" She touched his wrist but he didn't respond. Why wasn't he helping Daniel? Why wasn't he listening to Vivianne? She stepped up next to him.

"Conor! What's happening?"

He didn't open his eyes, his face drained of color, frozen in position against the wall. "Conor!" Elise repeated. She turned to Vivianne. "What's going on? Where did all those rats come from?"

Vivianne rattled off something in French. Elise put a hand on her arm. "Can you speak English? *Parlez Anglais?* What is happening?"

"*Les rats! Partout dans la ferme.* Everywhere! They eat the grain. *Toute notre récolte de blé!* Our whole harvest of wheat is here, waiting for the truck."

"Well, let's get out there and scare them off!" Elise said. She glanced at Conor who was still unresponsive, eyes shut. "What should we do? Do you have something? A broom or—what scares rats? Maybe a gun?" She mimed using a rifle and made a 'boom' sound.

Vivianne stared at her wide-eyed. She frowned at her cousin then turned and ran for the kitchen. After another nudge to Conor without a reply, Elise followed and the women almost collided in the back hallway. Vivianne was carrying a large shotgun and a box of shells. She looked pale, frightened, struggling under the weight of the heavy weapon under one arm. But she also looked a bit fierce as she headed toward the back door, throwing off her shawl. Elise reached around her to open the door.

The two women stepped gingerly outside, immediately on alert for vermin. Elise felt her skin prickle. She wasn't a fan of rats or mice but they didn't scare her. Vivianne on the other hand began to tremble all over, fumbling with the shells as she put them into the two barrels of the shotgun. She slid one into position and gave Elise a determined nod.

They tiptoed to the corner of the house and peeked into the side yard next to the barn. The sound of scuffling feet and small squeaks reached them. A muffled scream came from inside the barn. How was Daniel faring?

Elise squinted into the dark. In front of the distilling barn a teeming mass of animals squatted on a pile of some kind of grain. Where did that come from? Elise took Vivianne's elbow and pulled her around the corner, closer to the yard.

"There," she whispered to Vivianne, pointing at the rats. "*Là-bas.* Shoot there."

Vivianne nodded, handing Elise the box of shells as she struggled to balance the heavy shotgun in position against her shoulder. She should be closer, Elise thought as she backed away from Vivianne.

The gun shook wildly in the Frenchwoman's hands. She lowered her face to aim, closed her eyes, and squeezed the trigger. The blast rocked the night air. Elise felt the ringing in her ears and smelled the gunpowder. The recoil slammed Vivianne's shoulder, knocking her against the farmhouse. She smacked her head against the stone and dropped the shotgun with a clatter.

Elise looked back at the rats. They scattered for a minute then zeroed back in on the grain. She checked Vivianne. "Are you okay? *Tu vas bien?*" Vivianne nodded, rubbing the back of her head.

Elise picked up the shotgun. She had once shot clay pigeons in Connecticut at a law firm outing. She was a terrible shot but at least the weapon wasn't completely alien to her. She could at least attempt what Vivianne had done. Had any of the rats been killed by her shaky shot? Elise peered into the dark and saw it vibrating with life, like some creepy cartoon horror scene. But she didn't have time to be repelled by it.

She replaced the spent shell with a fresh one and slid it into position with a satisfying *cha-ching* the way Vivianne had. Then she turned on her heel toward her grisly task.

She'd taken two steps toward the mass of vermin when Conor suddenly appeared beside her, grabbing the shotgun from her hands and marching straight for the rats. He blasted them once, pointed, shot again. Elise ran up behind him and handed him two shells. He reloaded, walking toward a second pile of grain covered with rats. He pulled the trigger again, and again.

They repeated this, reloading six or seven times, until they ran out of shells, walking around the farmyard as the *gendarme* cowered behind his police car. The old man, Daniel, peeked out of the barn, watching. They didn't get all the rats but the remaining ones scattered. Daniel appeared with a bucket and began picking up carcasses.

The eastern sky brightened as they finished their horrible job. It would be dawn soon. Conor dropped his arms and let the shotgun point at the ground. He looked pale, sickened. The yard was a gruesome sight. Elise touched his arm and he startled, as if he'd been in a trance.

"It's done. Good work." She smiled at him but he had no expression. "It was awful but necessary." She tried to get his attention. "Conor?"

He looked at her then, pain in his eyes, and let the shotgun fall to the ground. She held him and felt a sob rise in his chest, release, and then it was gone.

CAREFULLY ELISE LED Conor back to the house. Inside the front door, in the tiled front hall, Natacha and Lucas huddled on the bottom stair, holding hands, with frightened looks on their faces. They stood up, looking at Conor. "*Sont-ils tous morts?* Are they all dead?" Lucas asked.

Conor didn't answer. Elise said, getting the gist of the French: "He got most of them. Maybe you could help Daniel and your mother out there? *Aidez Daniel et votre mère?*"

The teenagers slipped out the front door. Elise took Conor's arm and led him up the stairs to the second floor. She found the bathroom, much nicer than the third floor one, with a fancy rain shower head in the tub, and turned on the water.

Conor was like a zombie. She gave up trying to talk to him, just unbuttoned his shirt, unbuckled his pants, and stripped him naked. His socks and shoes were a struggle. Finally, she pushed him under the hot water of the shower, stripped down herself, and joined him.

"Turn around and I'll soap you," she told him. "Get clean of all that icky stuff." She had to push one shoulder but he turned, allowing her to soap up his muscular back, his fine buttocks, and strong neck. She put shampoo in his hair and scrubbed with her fingers, then angled the shower head to rinse him.

When he turned back to face her, he seemed more alert. His face had color and his eyes weren't so flat. He smiled at her, checking out her breasts. She raised his arms and soaped up his armpits, then his chest. She looked down finally and saw that he appeared to be himself again, in all his glory. She put the soap away.

"Are you okay?" she whispered, holding his face in her hands.

"I hate rats," he said.

"I'm not much of a fan either."

He blinked. "I really don't hate them. They are what they are. I hate killing things. My dad used to take me hunting and I couldn't do it. It drove Da nuts. Said I was soft. Target practice, sure. But killing animals? Sickening sport. No thanks."

"Even nasty rats?"

He smiled. "It appears I've conquered that hurdle."

She put her arms around his neck. "There's one hurdle to go. Are you ready?"

He wrapped his hands on the back of her neck and leaned closer and kissed her softly, then not so softly.

She pulled back, smiling. Water trickled down his neck and she couldn't resist licking it. In his ear she whispered: "Willing and able?"

He lowered his face against her neck and nuzzled her ear. "So it would seem, *chérie*."

THEY WOKE up in his bed with the sun streaming through the window. Elise checked her watch and saw it was nearly ten. She sighed and pulled the covers up again. What a night. If she ever saw another furry vermin it would be too soon.

Conor raised himself onto his elbows and stared down at her as if he'd never seen a woman in his bed before. As if the night before was a bad dream, or maybe a good one. She smiled, hoping what had come after the mayhem was what he remembered best.

"Hi," she whispered.

"Hullo."

They made love again, slower and even better than the one in the shower. She wondered, as they rolled apart, if every time would be better than the last. Maybe she hadn't been doing anything wrong in the past. Maybe it was just the wrong man.

"You said you were leaving soon," she said softly. "Is that true?"

"Mmmm. What about you?"

"I was supposed to fly home yesterday. I changed my ticket to next week. I wonder how many times I can change it. I never want to go home." She closed her eyes, thinking of that delicious possibility. Had she told anyone she'd quit her position at Webster, Lake & Osborne? She tried to remember if she'd ever mailed the letter. Maybe she hadn't. Maybe they would be wondering what happened to her in France. It wouldn't be the first time.

"Come to my tournament then," he said. "It's in Scotland."

Her mind cleared. She opened her eyes. "What?"

"My golf tournament. It's at the end of the week."

She sat up and looked him in the eye. He looked so sexy from this angle, his wavy hair, his reddish beard. She touched his chin. "When exactly?"

"Next week, on the weekend. I fly out of Marseille tomorrow." He pulled her down for another kiss. "Come with me."

CHAPTER THIRTY-EIGHT

*A*t noon that same day, Merle and Tristan walked out of the lobby of the hotel into the bright sunshine. They had packed their bags, checked out, and paid their bill. There was time for a quick lunch before the drive home. Pascal had already loaded their bags in the Mercedes and told them to meet him outside.

They found him pacing the sidewalk, his cellphone glued to his ear. They paused, waiting for him to finish. When he saw them, he put his hand over the phone and whispered, "Go ahead. I will meet you."

Their last day in beautiful Bellemont. The café with the terrace perched above the fields, looking out over the landscape of purple and green and gold, was Merle's choice again. This was where their Provence adventure had begun, hers and Elise's. She checked her phone as they sat down under a blue umbrella. She had called Elise once, to tell her they were checking out, but she hadn't heard anything from her. She would be enjoying herself with Conor. No point in breaking the spell.

They ordered drinks, a rosé for Merle and a Coke for Tris. The weather was hot, in the mid-90s, the August sun still baking Provence. It was 'Toasty AF,' as Tristan captioned his photos on Instagram. He'd taken some amazing shots in this easy-to-photograph place.

"We never got you that haircut," she said, reaching for his head to ruffle his scraggly locks. He backed away.

"No touching the merchandise." He smiled. "It's going to be hard to concentrate in class after all this." He waved a hand toward the fields and forests, the greens and golds and purples in a captivating array.

"At least you got to see Provence. It's as gorgeous as everyone says, isn't it? Sorry for all the extra excitement."

"Wouldn't have missed it for the world."

Five minutes later Merle's phone buzzed. It was Elise.

"Hey, little sister," Merle teased.

"Hey yourself. What's up?"

"Eating at that perfect café. What about you?"

"Well, it was an interesting night."

"I bet." Merle winked at Tristan.

"There was an incident," Elise said.

"I certainly hope so," her sister quipped.

"Merle. I'm serious. I'm standing outside at the farm. Conor and Vivianne are talking to the *gendarmes*. There was an incident, I don't know what to call it yet. Harassment? Vandalism? Intimidation? In the night."

Merle frowned. She could hear voices in the background. "What happened?"

"Someone dumped a bunch of corn around the yard, then let loose dozens of rats. They were everywhere. It was pretty gross."

"Ick. Did you—what did you do?"

"Conor shot a bunch of them. He just charged out there like a hero and blasted them with the shotgun."

"Good. I guess. Sounds awful."

"Yeah. A nasty crime scene. In fact, let's not talk about it again." She sighed. "So, I'm not going back to the Dordogne with you after all."

"You're not? What about your airline ticket?"

"I changed it, almost as soon as we left Malcouziac. I just had a feeling I'd need more time in Provence."

"Are you staying there?"

"No, Conor asked me to go to Scotland with him tomorrow. He has a golf tournament next week. Then I'll fly back to Paris and catch my flight. He's got it all arranged."

"Oh. I love Scotland. What did the firm say?"

"I haven't told them." She paused then said, "Merle, I hate the people at Webster. I hate the law. I'm going to quit my job when I go back."

Merle took a breath. "I wondered. Or rather Stasia did. She thought you were unhappy there."

"I'm going to debrief myself, Merle. I need a break from the law. Maybe I'll like it better somewhere else. Or maybe I'll just do something else."

"Elise. Honey. I am so glad you shared this with me. You don't need to be a lawyer just because the rest of us are. That's a crappy reason to choose a career."

"I know. I don't know what I was thinking!" She laughed then, a sparkly sound.

Merle smiled, suddenly feeling light, knowing that Elise was laughing and making decisions and, surely, making love with a fine half-French golfer. The glow she must be feeling at finally making choices she believed in, meeting people she liked, and having them adore her back, well, it traveled down the phone waves and warmed Merle.

"I'm so happy for you, Elise."

Tristan put his hand on his mother's arm as her eyes filled.

"I know, Merle. Tell the sisters for me, will you? It's a bit much. You're better at the sisterly communications than I am."

"Of course. We'll leave your suitcase at the front desk of the hotel. Love you, honey."

PASCAL ARRIVED as Merle was dabbing her eyes with a tissue. He looked concerned. "What is it, blackbird?"

"I'm just so happy for Elise. She's herself again."

He nodded, still frowning. "Did she tell you about the rats?" He proceeded to tell Tristan, who hadn't heard Elise's story, then fill in some new details. "The *gendarmes* found tire tracks on a side road, behind the farmhouse. Then a line of cracked corn, like breadcrumbs, that had spilled as the driver carried the sack to the farm. Another set of footprints following, possibly the culprit with the animals in a sack."

"Is this some sick French joke?" Tristan asked, disgusted.

"What could anyone possibly gain from that?" Merle asked.

"Vernay made some enemies in the area, as we were told. The *gendarmes* have information about a neighbor who wants to buy the farm. Everyone in the area heard they had money problems. The gambling problem was not a secret. The neighbors knew Vivianne would be there alone with only the golfer who hates mice to help her. They must have hoped to scare Vivianne off permanently, and Conor too."

"What jerks," Tristan said.

Pascal sat back in his chair. "Vernay is being released today. He is no longer a suspect in Delcroix's murder."

"Hallelujah." Merle said, raising a glass. "What happened?"

"It appears there is one more possible murder, in Marseille, of someone connected to the family. As you suspected, blackbird, a gang seems to be trying to wipe out their rivals. Henri had helped forge customs documents for the family and had been threatened with blackmail. Ari and his cousin ran the operation. The cousin is the one who is missing."

"Did Madame Gaillard cooperate with the police?"

"Eventually. It took some persuasion. The *Brigade* camped out at her château all night."

Merle squinted at her wine glass. "I was wondering something. How did whoever killed Ari get him and his car back in the garage with no one noticing, or even hearing it?"

Pascal gave her a coy smile. "He was killed elsewhere, of course."

"Yes."

"No one heard the shot, out in the middle of somewhere. They loaded him into their trunk and drove both cars back to his place. Transferred him to his car. We presume."

"But what about the garage door?" Merle asked. "It's metal, isn't it? That usually makes a racket."

"The detectives had the same question. But they tested it. There is a side door. They could get in that way or through the main door. Then from inside there was a way to open the big door without using the motor device. Just push it up, slowly, quietly."

"And push the car inside too," Tristan said.

"And no one was the wiser." Merle sighed.

"One other discovery—the housekeeper, Hannah, always goes to the market on Wednesday. She was gone most of the day. Elise went out as well, for a late breakfast. So, the house was empty. They could have brought him back then."

"Ah," Merle said. "I wondered if either of them left the house."

"I am curious about a few things too," Pascal mused, spinning his empty wine glass by the stem. Merle seemed to hear him but didn't ask what he was curious about.

Tristan looked at his mother, then at Pascal. They looked pensive, perhaps thinking about the deaths of the two Delcroix men, or drug gangs in Marseille, or using rats in harassment of your neighbors. Then Pascal reached for her hand, breaking the spell.

"How is your rosé, *chérie?* Shall I order one also?"

Merle smiled. "Always order rosé in Provence. It's the law."

CHAPTER THIRTY-NINE

$\mathcal{A}$fter lunch, Tristan and Merle waited for Pascal. Again. He seemed to be always on his phone, talking to someone—a policeman, a colleague, a witness. Merle wondered if he was missing work back in Bordeaux. She shouldn't complain. She had gotten a short Provence vacation out of this adventure.

The pieces had fallen into place. Guy Vernay did owe Ari Delcroix money from gambling losses but with his death they were wiped out. The Delcroix operation in Marseille was said to be a smuggling and money laundering enterprise. The cousin who was missing was presumed to be another victim. Henri, their landlord, murdered. He had told everyone he moved in with his brother, the local *gendarmes* explained. But he didn't have a brother and had moved in with an elderly sister who used her married name to avoid his blackmailers. But the threats continued. His move did not save him. He had been ambushed in broad daylight on the street as he exited a provincial government building. These gangs were vicious and bold.

Pascal appeared at last in the Bellemont *place*, walking to where they sat in the shade of an enormous plane tree. "*Pardon*. So many calls," he said, sitting next to Merle on the bench. He looked at her, his color up as if he was excited. "One last stop before we point toward the Dordogne and home."

"Does it involve ice cream?" Tristan asked.

"Back to the château."

"But you said you believed Louise Gaillard," Merle said. "You have an excellent bullshit detector, Pascal."

He smiled. "I did believe her. Then you put a little seed of doubt in my mind, blackbird, when you suggested she might have made up the story. I wondered about their very annoyed air about reporting the incident, as if the law was beneath them. The perfect way the operation was carried out. Why not report it?"

"I know. What sort of *citoyen* does that?"

"A rich snob citizen, I supposed at the time. But now, I dig a little." He smiled coyly. "Her husband has arrived at the château. He has been talking to the police."

"Will you interview him?" Tristan asked.

Pascal stood up. "If I can."

THE SAME FAT bodyguard was on duty at the front gate of Château Grand Lac. The name of the house was laughable. The only lake nearby was the swimming pool. Pascal parked in the shade of a tree this time, back from the stucco wall. There was a *gendarmerie* vehicle parked closer, next to the wall, as he had hoped. He rolled down all the windows and told Merle and Tristan to sit tight. He would not be long. As he climbed out of the Mercedes the *gendarme* also exited his car. They nodded at each other and stepped up to the gate.

"*Bonjour encore,*" Pascal said cheerfully. "We wish to talk to Monsieur and Madame Gaillard about a police matter."

The guard squinted at Pascal as if he didn't remember him, then looked at the serious expression on the uniformed officer. He shrugged and unlocked the gate. "Ring the bell. I don't know where they are."

In the shade of the veranda, the *gendarme* let Pascal take the lead. He pushed the doorbell and heard it chime inside. A maid came to the door, in a crisp grey and white uniform. They introduced themselves. The maid bit her lip and looked for guidance from someone.

"Who is it, Angelique?" A man's voice boomed across the tile entry. "*Deux policiers, monsieur,*" she answered.

"Well, let them in. I am not getting up for more lazy *policiers.*"

She led them into the vast parlor, where a wall of windows overlooked the terrace and pool, with flower gardens to one side. In one of eight seating arrangements, deep in a red velvet armchair, sat a wizened old man of indeterminate age. He had a full head of white hair that looked too stiff to be anything but *un postiche,* a hairpiece. He looked like a sour-faced tyrant, holding court. True to his word, he did not get up to greet them. Nor did he ask them to sit. The *gendarme* stood to the side, hands behind his back, feet apart, alert.

Pascal moved in front of the man. "Monsieur André Gaillard?" He nodded then made a 'get on with it' motion with a knobby hand. "I am Pascal d'Onscon with the *Police nationale.*"

"I have already spoken to them. I don't remember you."

"I am following up on a conversation I had with your wife. May I sit?"

"Suit yourself." The old man had a ruddy complexion and unnaturally tight skin on his forehead, above a sagging neck. He wore black dress slacks and a white shirt. His only concession to Provence was the lack of a necktie. His shiny brogues skimmed the thick carpet.

Before Pascal could begin, the tapping of heels on tile preceded the appearance of Madame Louise herself, dressed in a flowing orange sundress that accentuated her tan and other assets. Her hair was down, waving over her shoulders. She stopped at the sight of Pascal, who stood again to greet her. "Bonjour, Madame."

"What's going on? Why are you here again?"

"I have a few more questions. Would you care to join us?"

She straightened, nostrils flaring. "This is my house. I make the rules."

Pascal said nothing, glancing at the monsieur. The old man grunted. "Just sit down or leave, Louise."

Chastened, she perched uneasily on a chair near her husband. She tipped her chin up defiantly and glared at Pascal.

"I have come," Pascal began in a calm, easy tone that he knew often put listeners at ease, "to ask how much you had to pay the actors to perform for you at your wife's birthday party. What is the going rate to stage a kidnapping? Three of them, with possibly real guns? They must be professionals. It was quite convincing."

Louise stood up, furious, her face flushing. "What?! They struck me —the bruise is still there. Then they took my friend, my guest, away at gunpoint. You are saying they were fake? That somehow we staged it? How dare you?"

"Sit down, Louise," the old man commanded. To Pascal he said mildly, "I have no idea what you're talking about."

Their act was comical, how he played the rational one, allowing his wife her righteous indignation. But the time for that nonsense was over.

"No? Do you not own an import business on the Mediterranean, monsieur? An enterprise called Concepts Océaniques with fronts in Marseille, Cadiz, and Genoa?"

"What of it?"

Louise couldn't keep quiet. "It is a party rental business. We rent large tents for events and glassware and so on."

"Parties, is that right?" Pascal asked levelly. "No imports?" He took out his notebook. "Such items as huge vats of wine from South America, cheese from Russia—a very bad camembert, I'm told—as well as other banned and counterfeit items. Cocaine from Columbia perhaps? Were you not sanctioned by the French government for illegally importing grapes from Chile in 1996?"

"Ancient history," the old man growled.

"The Delcroix family was in direct competition, was it not? They even bought the warehouse you desired in Marseille, right on the docks. But you had a more personal bone to pick with Arsène Delcroix, isn't that so?" Pascal looked at Louise. "He was, after all, your wife's lover."

"That's a lie!" Louise yelled.

"Everyone in the area seems to know of your liaisons, madame," Pascal said mildly. "I spoke to two guests at your birthday party and one housekeeper who claim to have seen the two of you go into your bedroom together many times. Your husband doesn't like the heat, isn't that what you said? So, he never comes to Provence—until now.

How convenient for you. It was no secret, was it, Louise? You didn't even try to pretend."

"My personal affairs are none of your business," she growled.

"So, you admit it."

"And not illegal," her husband said cheerfully. His 'bored sophisticate' face was hideous. "This is France, after all. You are French, are you not? We are all adults here."

"A very gallant speech, monsieur. But it didn't work out that way, did it? The heart, they say, is not always cooperative," Pascal continued. "She must have been an embarrassment for some time, openly welcoming men to her bed. What a coup, to rid your home of the humiliation of your wife's lover and also a business rival. How delicious it must have been for you. What is that phrase of the Americans? Double bonus?"

The old man's jaw tightened and he glared at Pascal. "An entertaining tale but you are guessing."

"This is where it gets interesting. Even though the kidnapping was orchestrated the actors were very good; it went off smoothly. None of your guests was aware. Not even your wife knew. But killing the old man in Bordeaux was a little more complicated. Henri St-Jean Delcroix had gone into hiding but you found him. The *Brigade criminelle* in Bordeaux has the kidnapping on video from the security cameras. Choosing to nab him outside government offices was a mistake, I'd say. And your men weren't quite as discreet there. No masks."

"*Je n'ai aucune idée de quoi vous parlez,*" the old man said, sniffing. *No idea what you're talking about.*

"So you keep saying, monsieur. But you do know. *La Crim* has the men in custody in Bordeaux. They have confessed to the killing. The letter that Henri left with his sister in case of his death spelled out your threats. He even included the tape of the phone messages, and kept several menacing letters. The kidnappers say you paid them for the job but not particularly well. They may have been a little angry about the pittance you paid them. That's why I was wondering about the actors who kidnapped Ari Delcroix here at the house then shot him in the head. A message there, I see, bringing him home, dead in his own car, as if to say 'stay at your own home.' I hope you paid those men better or they too will confess. No hired killer wants to go to jail for a job. Especially when the man who hired them could obviously pay much more."

Louise was staring at her husband. She was now flushed bright red. "You—you killed Ari?"

The old man was mute. Pascal said, "Your Paris office tells me, monsieur, that you took the TGV south on the 28th, the day after your wife's party, as soon as she called to tell you about the kidnapping. Even though you claim to despise Provence. That bruise on your cheek, madame. That was a birthday gift from your husband, was it not?"

She sprang to her feet, her fists clenched in fury. "This is what I get for all the years I have thrown away on you, you...*sac d'os décrépit*. You abuse me, you murder my friends, you give me nothing in return for all I do for you—you ruin everything. I hate you!" She walked away, faced the wall, and put her hands over her face as she sobbed.

Pascal got to his feet. "Can you walk, monsieur, or must we carry you out?"

EPILOGUE

*T*he Thursday market in Malcouziac was in a frenzy. Shoppers, tourists and locals alike, sniffed melons, pinched peaches, poked strawberries, and acted as if today was the last day to stave off possible starvation. Market baskets overflowed with produce, sausages, goat cheese, and more produce. The leeks, in particular, were enormous.

Merle looked up through the crowd and saw Tristan at the far end, doing his own examination of local wares. The week or so since their return from Provence had been lazy, full of summer doldrums and little else. The quiet, this time, was most welcome.

Pascal had returned to Bordeaux on Monday morning but promised to return on Friday. Although all of France had August holidays, the men and women who serve and protect the citizenry—and their precious wines—still had to work. Not as much work, he promised. He and Tristan had some adventures planned, including a canoe trip down the Dordogne.

Merle bought three *crottins* of goat cheese and a new supply of *herbes de Provence* in a sweet little pot. She had been dreaming of lavender for the last few nights, having bought some pillow spray in Bellemont that took her back to those heavenly flowers. Was there anything like that scent? The French loved lavender so much they named 'to launder' after it, using it to scent all their sheets and undies.

Tristan met his mother halfway down the market. He was in charge of bread today and carried a baguette under his arm, along with a sack of croissants. He was mad for *pain au chocolat,* the chocolate croissant, as any schoolboy would be. He looked very French today. His heritage was showing.

They walked back through the cobblestone streets to *La Maison Chanceuse.* The stillness in the air, the heat rising off the cobbles, the air of drowsy contentment, all combined to give Merle the idea of a nap today. After that last day in Provence, when Pascal helped arrest the old man at the château, none of them complained of rest and relaxation. The five police vehicles that had surrounded the Mercedes, blue lights flashing off the white wall, the high-pitched screeching of Louise from the veranda, the dragging of the old fellow out the gate, cursing and writhing: Merle wouldn't forget that scene for a while.

And yet, France in August worked its wonders. The sunshine washed clear the bad memories, the scents beguiled the mind with thoughts of better days, although there were no more perfect ones than today. *Right here, right now*, as the wise Annie always said. Days to cherish, nights to dream.

Merle had written to Annie, as well as to Stasia and Francie, about Elise's new adventure, her new tractor guy/golfer. She glossed over the mess with Scott; that could wait for a dark winter night. She had to mention the death of Ari Delcroix but promised details later. It had all worked out for Elise, as mucked up as it had been along the way.

Elise had written to Merle twice since they'd parted in Provence. The first one was from the airport in Marseille as they waited to board the flight to Edinburgh. She sounded giddy with excitement and confessed to possibly—maybe—falling in love. "For the first time, Merle, so I can't be sure."

The second text had come from Scotland, with a photo attached of a hotel room overlooking endless fairways at a golf resort. Elise announced she was getting a pedicure and a manicure and a massage that day. She didn't see enough of Conor as he had to practice nonstop, to make up for all the time he'd spent sitting on a tractor. But that things were still mad good between them and she herself was 'quite chuffed.'

Stasia had also written with news. Willow had filed for an annulment with the local registrar. She'd been told because it was a French religious ceremony and not a civil one at a town hall, it wasn't valid. There was no license, or any of the documents the French require. Foreigners, in particular, had to submit lots of things, including a form that says you are not already married to someone else. So, there was no official marriage at all. Just two kids trying to run away from their responsibilities, as Stasia put it. "Is it any wonder the French don't bother with marriage? Too much paperwork!"

The Hoovers pulled Teague out of the university and away from all his friends including his so-called fiancée, Amber. It seemed house arrest was in order. "Poor Teague," Stasia wrote with a googly-eyed emoji. No one had heard from Scott. He might still be wandering around the Charles de Gaulle airport, a man without a country.

As Merle and Tristan approached the cottage, Madame Suchet—Paulette—opened the door to her house. *"Une livraison pour toi!"* She pointed to a large box on her stoop. Tristan ran over to get it.

"Merci, Paulette," Merle called. "Later I will be making a peach *galette.* I will bring you some."

The sharing of food, the favors back and forth paid by delicious dishes, was a joy to Merle, even on a hot day when she would rather not turn on her oven. But who was this box from? Tristan brought it into the house and set it on the dining table.

"It says it's from Le Refuge de la Lavande," he said. "I hope it's not dead rats."

Merle set down her market baskets in the kitchen and began to put away the cheese and sausages. "If it is, I have the worst judgment in people."

"Yeah, probably not. Maybe Elise forgot her head or something."

He slit the tape, opening the box. Merle took out crumpled newspaper and peered inside. An envelope sat on top of something in bubble wrap. She opened the flap and pulled out a card decorated with dried lavender. It was written in purple ink in (yes) a flowery hand.

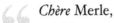

Chère Merle,

Conor and Elise left these for me to send to you. I hope they are something you will enjoy. These days have been hectic, trying to finish the harvest, clean up after all the troubles, and get our nerves back on an even keel. Guy is recovering and feeling better after his ordeal. He has promised to stop gambling and is seeing a therapist recommended by the doctors at la *Caisse nationale de l'assurance maladie*— the national health insurance. It gives me much hope.

He asks me to extend special thanks to M. d'Onscon. We are informed he was especially helpful in the search for truth. M. Gaillard has been transferred to Paris where he will no doubt get special treatment. Still we have hopes that he will pay for his crimes. Louise has fled to Italy, we are told, where she has friends on the Cinque Terre. I'm sure it will all be marvelous for her there.

And lastly, our sentiments to your sister Elise. She appears to be making my cousin very happy. He is a morose soul until now, but I see him smile like he's never smiled. It warms the heart.

Please stop in at Le Refuge if you are ever in the area again.

Vivianne Vernay.

MERLE TOUCHED the pressed lavender on the card and put it to her nose. The delicate scent was still detectable. She reread the part of the note about Elise and Conor and felt the same sense of possibility that Vivianne expressed. Time would tell if their romance could survive across the ocean, and what exactly Elise would do with the rest of her life. But there was hope for happiness, and that is never a bad thing.

Tristan was lifting something out of the box. He took off the bubble wrap to reveal a blue plate with a shimmering Provençal glaze.

"It's beautiful," Merle said, running her fingers over the surface.

She turned it over to reveal it had no markings. Handmade: the best kind.

"There's more." Tristan unwrapped plate after plate. There were four large ones, four smaller ones, and a set of espresso cups. Each set was in four colors: the red of Provence dirt, the gold of sunflowers, the green of forests, and the blue of the Mediterranean.

"They're so cheerful."

"Too much color?" Tris asked.

"There is no such thing. They're perfect for this dark old cottage."

"Wait, there's more at the bottom." Tristan pulled out two large round dishes, one with scalloped edges, in green. The other was gold and had holes like a colander. Merle immediately set them up on the shelves of the big cupboard near the dining table, face out.

"This is exactly what I was looking for in that market in Bellemont. Elise must have been paying attention."

Tristan smiled. "I might have dropped a hint."

Merle grabbed her son and held him in a bear hug. "And now it's time for your haircut, *garçon!*"

He wiggled out of her grasp, protesting, and ran into the garden. She chased him, just for the sheer craziness of it. He yelped, skidding on the gravel path. With a leap he vaulted the garden gate, shimmied under the wisteria, and sped away down the alley, laughing at life and the tangible joy of summertime.

ACKNOWLEDGMENTS

A special thanks—*encore*—to Micheline Brodeur for her French copy-editing and more. What would I do without someone to correct my French?

Thanks too to Helen Mulroney who tramped around Provence with me, flagged down the postal service van when I broke my ankle, plied me with wine, and is generally a most agreeable travel pal in every way.

A special merci to readers who continue to enjoy the Bennett Sisters. So many stories to go! Stay tuned, *mes amies*.

ABOUT THE AUTHOR

LISE MCCLENDON is the author of numerous novels of crime and suspense. Her bestselling Bennett Sisters Mysteries is now in its thirteenth installment. When not writing about foreign lands and delicious food and dastardly criminals, Lise lives in Montana with her husband. She enjoys fly fishing, hiking, picking raspberries in the summer, and cross-country skiing in the winter. She has served on the national boards of Mystery Writers of America and the International Association of Crime Writers/North America, as well as the faculty of the Jackson Hole Writers Conference. She loves to hear from readers.

For more information visit
lisemcclendon.com

Join the newsletter to keep up with new releases, giveaways, reading recommendations, and bonus material
copy this link: http://eepurl.com/A6bsD

facebook.com/LiseMcClendon
twitter.com/LiseMcClendon
instagram.com/LiseMcClendon
bookbub.com/authors/lise-mcclendon

THE BENNETT SISTERS MYSTERIES

Blackbird Fly

The Girl in the Empty Dress

Give Him the Ooh-la-la

The Things We Said Today

The Frenchman

Odette and the Great Fear

Blame it on Paris

A Bolt from the Blue

DEAD FLAT

1: Bottle of Lies

2: Outside the Bubble

3: Uncorked

Lost in Lavender

plus

The Bennett Sisters French Cookbook

featuring recipes from the books

ALSO BY LISE MCCLENDON

Alix Thorssen Mysteries
by Grier Lake
The Bluejay Shaman
Painted Truth
Nordic Nights
Blue Wolf

The Dorie Lennox Mysteries
One O'clock Jump
Sweet and Lowdown
Snow Train

Thrillers by Rory Tate
Jump Cut
PLAN X

All Your Pretty Dreams: a New Adult Romance

BEAT SLAY LOVE by Thalia Filbert
STOP THE WORLD: Snapshots from a Pandemic

Lightning Source UK Ltd.
Milton Keynes UK
UKHW020918010223
416291UK00013B/1700

9 780578 764924